PAUL E. HORSMAN

THE BOKKANERS OF THE NORTH

BOOK 3

WYRMS OF PASANDIR

I0567433

Editor: Kira Tregoning
Book cover and map designed by Deranged Doctor Design
For more info: paulhorsman-author.com

There is a list of names at the back of the book.

Paul E. Horsman's books:

Zilverspoor Uitgeverij (Dutch Editions):
Rhidauna – Schaduw van de Revenaunt #1
Zihaen – Schaduw van de Revenaunt #2
Ordelanden – Schaduw van de Revenaunt #3

Red Rune Books (Dutch Edition)
De Shardheld Sage

Red Rune Books (English Editions):
The Lioness of Kell
The Road to Kalbakar – Wyrms of Pasandir #1
The Pirates of Brisa – Wyrms of Pasandir #2
The Bokkaners of the North – Wyrms of Pasandir #3
The Jinn of Ozzoon - Wyrms of Pasandir #4 (upcoming)
Building a Trade Empire (upcoming)

Shardfall – The Shardheld Saga #1
Runemaster – The Shardheld Saga #2
Shardheld – The Shardheld Saga #3
The Shardheld Saga, trilogy

Rhidauna –The Shadow of the Revenaunt #1
Zihaen – The Shadow of the Revenaunt #2
Ordelanden – The Shadow of the Revenaunt #3
Vavaun – The Shadows of the Revenaunt

THE NATIONS

The Weal of Four Nations is the political union of Kell, Vanhaar, Unwaar and the Chorwaynie Archipelago

Kells: The tall, bronze-brown people of the Radhaijan Plains in Kell; famed for the fighting prowess of their warriors and the quality of their ordnance.
Vanhaari (the second tribe): The magician people of Vanhaar, warlocks and mages. They are of small stature and a slate-gray complexion.
Chorwaynies: The coppery-brown coastal people of the Chorwaynie Archipelago. A nation of sharp merchants and sea traders.
Jentakan: The golden-brown inland people of the Chorwaynie Archipelago. Fishers and sailors, their painted fabrics are priceless works of art.
Unwaari (the first tribe): The Singers of Aera; mage-priests, living in Unwaar. They are Vanhaar's brother people.

Other Nations

Ma'aweshi (the third tribe): The people of the Pasandir Peaks; brothers to Vanhaari and Unwaari, distinguishable through a faint reddish sheen to their gray complexions. Followers of Bodrus the Sleeping God.
Qoori: The people of the far northern empire of Qoor; distantly related to the three tribes, but of greenish complexions.
Hizmyrani: The olive brown people of the kingdom of Hizmyr. A rich nation to the north of Nanstalgarod.
Nanstalgarodians: The late people of Nanstalgarod (now the Hellesands desert). The only living Nanstalgarodian is Princess Jem.

The nations of Malgarth, the small continent to the west:

Thali: The dark-brown people of the frozen south; inventors and technicians, who develop wonders like steam engines, airships and other contraptions.
Garthans (the High Kingdom of Malgarth): A rural people of pale complexions.
The Five Tradeports (Brisa, Reveul, Lismer, Dibloon and Veurdel): Hotbeds of piracy and crime on the northwestern coast. Populated by Garthans and renegades of all the peoples in the region.

Both Kells and Vanhaari have settlements on Malgarth: the cave city of Tar Kell, and New Winsproke.

CONTENT

FOREWORD

The Wyrms of Pasandir tells the adventures of Eskandar, a Vanhaari ship's boy who serves in the Weal navy sloop *Tipred.*

It is a sequel to the standalone book *Lioness of Kell*, in which the lioness Maud with the warlock Basil, his brother Jurgis, and his lover Captain Yarwan manage to defeat an ancient enemy.

At the finish of *Lioness*, Maud becomes the ruler of Kell and Basil is the new Lord Spellstor in Vanhaar.

The first **Wyrms** book *The Road to Kalbakar* takes up the story twenty-five years later. Maud and Jurgis are married, and so are Basil and his Yarwan.

Eskandar meets Kellani and Naudin, the next generation of young heroes, who help him in his endeavors. He finds out he is grandson to the late Kambish, and heir to his position as wyrmcaller of Kalbakar Keep and Defender of Bodrus the Sleeping God.

In the second book, *The Pirates of Brisa,* Eskandar finds a bunch of pirates are kidnapping street kids from the orphanage he once lived in. He and his friends free the orphans, capture the pirates' ship and sail for the Chorwaynie Archipelago. Here Darquine, one of Maud's friends from *Lioness* and now ruler of the islands, lends them a hidden fort and her training schooner to teach the kids how to sail their captured ship. Together, Eskandar and his crew manage to teach the pirates of Brisa a hard lesson.

In this book, *The Bokkaners of the North*, third of **The Wyrms of Pasandir**, the story of Wyrmcaller Eskandar and his friends continues.

6

But Eskandar's tale is not the only one worth writing down. For Shaw, the quiet little daughter from a long line of ship chandlers, finally comes into her own alongside him.

Her adventures are only hinted at in this book, and will be told in full in her own book: *Birth of a Trade Empire (Traders of Pasandir).*

Eskandar's story will continue in the fourth book, *The Jinn of Ozzoon.*

MAP OF THE WEAL

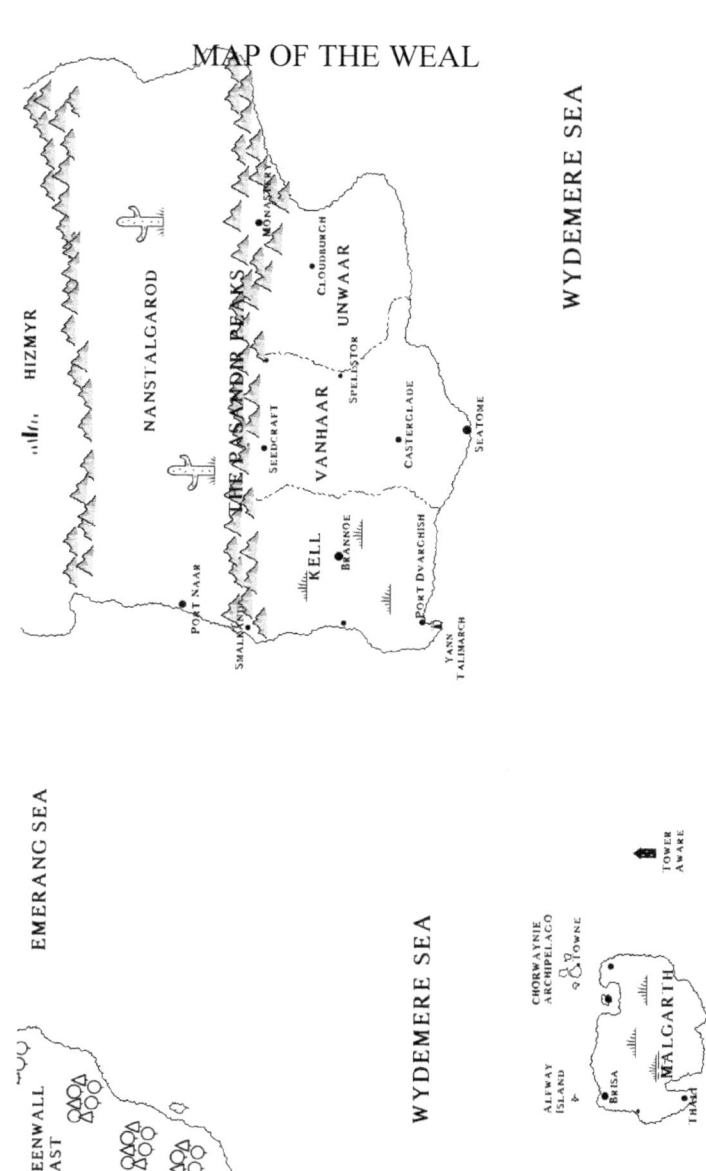

CHAPTER 1 – WE MUST GO NORTH

Six days after our victory at Brisa, I sat on Fort Jamril's upper balcony, my chair tilted back, my feet upon the railing and my homemade straw hat deep over my eye, thinking of nothing much.

Lothi-Mo lay curled up in my lap, snoozing. Not long ago my wyrmling girl used to fit snugly inside my tunic, or perched on my shoulder with her tail wrapped around my neck. By now I realized that she grew a lot faster than me, for she was the size of a twenty-pound tabby cat. I rubbed her neck absently; another few weeks and she'd have to sleep on the floor.

I closed my eyes and let the sun play over my bare chest. I wasn't afraid of sunburn; my slate-gray skin wasn't sensitive, as I basked in the sun, with the smells of sea and jungle, and the laughter of my friends coming up from the small beach beside the fort. The former street kids were happy, and with good reason.

Last week's attack on the pirate town of Brisa had been a wild success. We'd captured the big ship now riding at anchor in the bay below, we had freed her imprisoned crew of sailor trainees and used the ship's cannons to shoot up the pirates' harbor. It had been great fun.

I sipped my cold lemonade and sighed.

'Eskandar, you blidiot! Stop wasting time!' an angry voice exploded in my head. *'Get off your lazy butt and move!'*

I nearly spat lemonade over Lothi-Mo.

'Teodar? What's wrong?'

'Everything!' my holy friend snapped. *'While pirates and madmen rampage through my monastery, you are basking in the sun like a lazy bum, frittering away invaluable time. Get up, gather your precious kids army and go north.'*

'What's the sudden hurry?' I said, trying to sit up and put my lemonade down without dislodging Lothi-Mo. *'It's only a week since our big victory at Brisa.'*

'*Big victory!*' His voice rose to a shout. '*You only got the little ones at Brisa. Those never were more than a diversion. The dangerous ones are out in force, trying to destabilize the kingdoms, ruining sea trade, and making life hell for everyone. My dreams are filled with their wickedness. They're hunting kids!*'

'*Why would they do that?*' I said as reasonably as I could.

'*How should I know?*' he said, not reasonable at all. '*To make you fail?*'

'*Make me fail? Do I need more kids, then?*'

'*Yes! Many more, from all over the continent. Don't ask all those stupid questions! Go north to Hizmyr and kill them Bokkaners right out of the prophecy.*'

'*I'd rather take my forces to your monastery directly,*' I said. '*I would kill that lich and his minions and end the whole thing then and there.*' Yeah, I knew he'd blow his top, but I was so fed up with it all.

'*No!*' he cried furiously, and I hid a grin. '*I told you before! You-Can't-Do-That-Yet. You must follow the prophecy, or we'll lose everything.*'

'*All right, keep your cool, brother!*' I said soothingly. '*I want to go north.*' I really did. We had discussed it, Kellani, Naudin, and I. We agreed we were going, only not today. Not this week. '*There's one teeny problem; it is four thousand miles. We can't sail back and forth over that distance; we need a base up there somewhere.*'

'*Is that all?*' he screamed. '*Mountain's Holy Spittle, why didn't you ask? You idiot! You...*'

'*Hush,*' Lothi-Mo said lazily, lifting her head a little. '*Boys shouldn't quarrel.*'

I goggled at the curled up wyrmling in my lap. Teodar and I had been mindshouting at each other on a very private level and she had never shown she could follow us.

'*Yes. You are right,*' Teodar said. '*Apologies, Lady Lothi-Mo. He sometimes infuriates me.*'

'Wyrm boys aren't very clever,' she said, with only a hint of her familiar chirp in her voice. *'But he tries, so you be nice to him.'*

'When you two are finished, shall we go on?' I said.

Teodar grunted. *'Had you asked me, I'd have told you before. I have the place you want. A secure cave system with lots of rooms, fully furnished; a beautiful bay for your fine vessels, free treasures and no rent.'*

'It sounds too good to be true,' I said. I wondered why he had never thought to tell me when we discussed the subject of bases in the north before. *'Do we have to steal it from some nasty guys first?'*

'Of course not,' he said, sounding peeved. *'It is a deserted property. Ask that bottle-girl about Smalkand Keep.'*

Bottle-girl? That was Jem, our spellbound ghost princess. *'It's in Nanstalgarod then?'* I said. *'A desert ruin?'*

'No and no.' He sighed in exasperation. *'I'll show you.'*

I sat back, stroking Lothi-Mo, and waited until an image appeared in my mind of the western coastline as I'd seen it so many times from the old *Tipred*'s quarterdeck. There were the sheer cliffs of the Kell highland plateau, passing by with a speed not even a steamship could match, let alone my old sloop-of-war. Then I saw the craggy mountains of the Pasandir Peaks; endless snow-topped peaks scratching the clouds, with their sunward sides sparkling. It was so familiar I could feel the crunch of snow under my bare feet as I trudged across the high passes and I shivered in spite of the heat on my balcony.

'The mountains of home,' Lothi-Mo said wistfully. *'Wanna go there.'*

'I've seen that stuff before,' I said.

'But you never looked,' Teodar said. *'Watch for a big red rock.'*

Scowling, I peered at the image. *'I don't...'* There! A tall, red-stained rock protruded from the mountainside, clearly visible if you knew what to look for. *'That bleeding stone, you mean?'*

'Yeah. Now look well.'

It was as if we sailed straight at the mountains, with our sails full of wind. Involuntarily I braced myself against an impact that didn't come.

Teodar snorted. *'Tricked you there, didn't I? Watch.'*

Darn, the red rock had concealed a crevice in the mountains!

'Is that a passage?' I asked, but already we shot into the opening, with looming cliffs on both sides. The sunlight disappeared, and I shivered. For several seconds we sailed on in near darkness before we emerged in a wide bay, sparkling in the sun.

'Phew,' I said. *'You have a realistic imagination, bud.'*

'The caves are to the left, behind those tall firs,' Teodar said primly. *'Glad you like it.'*

'Ni-ice place,' Lothi-Mo said. *'It has a wyrm ledge. I really wanna go home.'*

'It's Peak territory?' I said. *'That makes it ours. Great; I'd better get going.'*

'Yes, you'd better,' Teodar said. *'Go there; settle in. Not too long, mind you! Then go out. Collect all the kids the prophecy needs, and kill those idiot pirates before they come knocking on my door. Remember you're the big, hulking Defender of Bodrus, little brother.'* With that, he was gone.

I lowered my skinny five feet back in my chair and closed my eyes. *North,* I thought, calling up the images of the bay again.

'North big place,' Lothi-Mo said drowsily. *'Many many pirates; good battles coming. Let's go there.'*

'We will,' I promised. *'We'll go looking for that pirate fleet and for their secret base, Angsthafn.'*

'We'll find,' she said. *'Then we'll fight.'* Then she opened one eye at me. *'The kids?'*

The kids Teodar had mentioned; the remainder of the Clam Street orphans. I had enlisted a double handful of them, but there were many more waiting for a chance at a better life. *'Let's see those caves first,'* I said. *'Then we'll go and hire the others.'*

I drained my lemonade. 'Off my lap, you lazy girl. If we're leaving soon, I'm going for a swim while I can.'

Lothi-Mo uncoiled and sprang into the air. 'Like that,' she said. 'The water is a good place.'

Before we came here, I hadn't known wyrms could swim, but she moved through the sea as if she'd been born in it. She could hold her breath a lot longer than our kids, and she swam like an eel, slithering at great speed.

I picked up my broomstick from underneath my chair. 'Race you down.' I dove over the balustrade for the two hundred feet drop to the little inlet beside the fort.

Lothi-Mo won, of course; she always did. She's too darned fast, that girl.

CHAPTER 2 – RECRUITING

The next morning after breakfast, I took Kellani aside. 'What about a nice trip to Seatome?'

'Now?' Kellani said, eying me with suspicion. Somehow she always knew I was planning something.

'Why not?' I said nonchalantly. 'Just you and me. We're still several ship's officers short.'

'You and me.' I saw a slow red creep in her face as she looked at me and for a moment I wondered why that would make her blush. Then she grunted and prodded my chest with a strong reddish-brown finger. 'What aren't you telling me?'

I grinned. 'Teodar called; he wants us to go north soon. He knew of a place to stay, too, right at the feet of the Peaks. I'm thinking we go ahead with a small group to look it over. If it's suitable, the others can follow in the ships. Only we must have more officers first. We can't expect Xailin and Chagan to sail across three thousand miles without other watchkeepers.'

'Of course not.' Kellani patted my shoulder. She was so much taller than me she couldn't help acting the big sister now and then. 'I approve. If Xailin is right, north is where the action is. After Brisa, there won't be much of interest going on here.' She stretched and moved her big muscles. 'North. Yes, we can use a change of scenery.'

'Right; I'll tell the others we're going away for a while. *Lothi-Mo, Kellani and I must go to Seatome. Would you help guard the fort for me?'*

My wyrmling didn't like it. *'You be in danger,'* she grumbled. *'Me not there to save you. Well, go, go! Wyrms watch good, so me watch kids.'*

'Seatome is dull,' I said, suddenly feeling guilty. *'You'll have the fun part.'*

Lothi-Mo made a little sound almost of scorn. *'Sure, me have fun with the kids. Now go.'*

I felt a heel as I turned to Kellani in time to catch her hide a smile.

I sighed. *Girls!*

It rained in Seatome. It always rained in Seatome. The place had a grand harbor; sheltered, spacious, and secure, but the mountains around it stopped the rain clouds coming in over the sea and held them captured over the town until they were squeezed dry.

The water cascaded off my straw hat and soaked my tunic. 'Should've taken cloaks,' I said. 'Miserable place, this is.'

Kellani ran a hand through her rain-plastered hair. Little things like the weather rarely bothered her. 'Now where do we go first?'

I shrugged. 'Port Captain's office, I suppose.'

'That silly lieutenant who kicked us out the last time?' Kellani said contemptuously. She had taken that slight very personal.

'They won't try the same stunt again,' I said. 'I won't stand for it; diplomacy be darned.'

Upstairs in the dusty outer office, the clerks rose as we entered and bowed. 'Good morning, Wyrmcaller,' they said almost with one voice. 'Good morning, Broomrider.'

This time, the port captain received us himself, smiling and corpulent in his fine uniform, and there was a different lieutenant hovering behind him. Apparently my complaint to Proprietor Darquine had reached the navy and someone had done something about it.

'Lord Wyrmcaller!' the port captain said affably. 'And Lady Kellani. Your visit honors me. I heard of your success at Brisa. Congratulations; a most welcome action.'

News travels fast, I thought. 'Thank you. These villains had kidnapped my friends, attacked my base, and threatened my homeland. The Peaks don't take kindly to that, so I returned the favor. Now I find myself in need of some small assistance, Captain.' *Darn, do I sound pompous, or what?* I thought, but the port captain bowed, smiling broadly.

'Anything within my power,' he said. 'We are here to serve.'

Things have *changed,* I thought. 'Thank you. At Brisa, we captured the pirates' biggest vessel. Our navy is yet small, and we are short of certified officers.' I smiled. 'We need a full captain and two watch-keeping officers. There is one stipulation – they shouldn't be too much older than us.'

The port captain cleared his throat. 'You won't find a licensed ship's master below thirty years,' he said. Then he turned to the window, opaque with rain. 'Perhaps... Bumboat Abia.'

The name didn't ring a bell and that must've shown in my face.

'She's the girl running the harbor bumboat,' the lieutenant whispered.

The port captain turned back to us. 'Abia used to be second mate of the *Irobas,* an independent trader vessel. She wasn't well off; her widower father peddled supplies to the navy ships. She had a brother, Sylas, who was five years younger. Five years ago, there was a nasty accident; the lad lost his legs while visiting his sister on board her ship.

'A few months later, their father died. Abia wanted her captain to take her brother on as a supernumerary, because she couldn't leave him alone in the house. The captain refused. She then tore up her contract and left.

'Since then she runs the bumboat service, but whatever she makes will barely sustain the two of them. Sylas is quite educated, I believe, though totally helpless. He must be seventeen and she twenty-two or three. She kept up her studies, in her spare time. Passed her deep sea master's examination not long ago.'

I remember seeing a girl poling a flat-bottomed boat from ship to ship. She never came to the *Tipred;* my first lieutenant would see to that. A bumboat peddling strong drinks and such would be irregular, and he hated anything out of the ordinary. I glanced at Kellani and she nodded.

'This Abia sounds exactly the one we want,' she said.

'We'll have a word with her,' I said. 'Where can we find her and her brother?'

'They have a shack beside the main dock. Ask around, anyone can point you.' The port captain walked away from the window. 'As to the others you seek... Check the *Downed Anchors* tavern. There are two brothers, late off a collier. Both are licensed mates. Their skipper was a drunken fool who ran them aground just outside Port Dvarghish. The whole crew survived, but they lost the ship. The lads worked their way back to Towne, and now they're looking for another berth. With little success, alas; sailors are superstitious, and a shipwrecked officer is said to bring bad luck. A pity, for they are young, sober fellows. I suppose they'll ship out before the mast when their money runs out.'

Before the mast, that would mean as common sailors. What a pity if you were a licensed mate.

I regarded the harbor commander with unfeigned respect. 'Those are excellent suggestions. Do you know everybody in the harbor quarter?'

He smiled. 'I try to. Every solid citizen that is; not all the crooks.' His eyes twinkled. 'Though I know many of those as well.'

Seatome Naval Port was large. After the war, and with more of the trade going through places like Dvarghish in Kell instead of here, the navy had taken over all of the harbor past Blasted Pier, and rebuilt it into a bustling home base for the ever-growing Weal Navy.

Here were the ropeyards, the sail makers, a large meat preservation factory, and all other industries that kept the navy afloat.

'Eyes left!' some blue-clad subofficer shouted as he trotted past with his little group of sailors on their ship's business.

He saluted us punctually without losing speed, barely giving us time to reply.

I grunted. 'Foolishness; spending time answering salutes.'

'Well, you *are* a highly placed foreign official,' Kellani said. 'They honor you.'

I snorted but swallowed my retort, as we had to jump aside for a rattling cart loaded high with provisions, blackpowder and other stores.

'Naudin is right,' I said. 'His dad's navy *is* darned dangerous, especially ashore.'

We wound our way past the long piers where the frigates and dreadnoughts lay until we came to a bit of dead-end water beyond the dock's slipway. There was the little bumboat jetty and at its head, a wooden shed.

As a home, it wasn't much; a sagging hut built of greenish, weathered boards, surrounded by the clamor of the builders working in the nearby dockyard.

'I've seen this place,' I said. 'Always thought it was a tool shed, not something where people lived.'

We walked to the rickety door and knocked.

'Door's open,' a boy's voice called.

We stepped into a single room, scrupulously neat, where everything seemed to have its own spot. On the floor sat a Vanhaari of my age, with short hair and a strong face. His upper body was bare and muscled, but below the knees, his trouser pants were empty.

'You are Sylas?' I said loudly over the dockyard din.

The boy put his book aside. 'I am. Do you come for my sister? She'll be home any moment. Sit on the ground if you want to, we have no chairs to offer.'

We sat on the hard-packed floor.

'We come for both of you, actually.' I scratched my cheek with my hook as an act of kinship and I saw him look at it. 'We have at least the loss of a limb in common,' I said. 'Though you beat me with two legs.'

'Did you come to tell me that?' he said coolly.

'Not really. I was told you are an educated fellow?'

'I study; what else is there to do?'

'You could teach.'

He snorted and waved a hand at the dockyard. 'With that racket outside? I've had a few kids coming for their letters, but I haven't seen them for some time. What is your business with us?'

I grinned at his directness. 'We are looking for someone who can captain our ship, who isn't too much older than me and my friends, and who has an adventurous spirit. Someone mentioned your sister. And why she quit her last ship.'

He looked at me steadily, but didn't say anything.

'Besides a captain, we can use a lettered fellow,' I said bluntly. 'To teach a bunch of kids, keep records, and act as secretary. Pay starts at four pennies a day, with room and board, plus a share in the loot.'

'You're not serious,' he said, flabbergasted.

'We're very serious,' Kellani said. 'On the honor of the Kell, we are perfectly serious.'

At that moment, the door burst open and a girl lurched in, carrying a crate of goods.

'Syl, I've...' Then she saw us and frowned in surprise. 'Visitors?'

'Either bringing golden opportunities or selling gilded shit,' the boy said.

The girl set the crate down with care. 'I'm Abia. Who are you and what is it you're selling?'

I told them of the Peaks and the ships, the Bokkaners and everything. After a few moments, Abia sat on the crate without taking her eyes off me.

When I was done, she sighed. 'So you're the ones that kicked Brisa where it hurt. That was a great thing. Now what do you want from me? Advice?'

I grinned. 'We captured a ship. A fourmaster steamship. We need a captain. Interested?'

She stared at me. 'A captain? For a fourmaster? And you're asking *me*?'

'The port captain gave me your name. He thinks you can do it,' I said. 'We're a young folks' navy and we want a young captain. Someone who can enter into our spirits and still stay in command. We offer regular pay for licensed officers, same rates as the Weal Navy uses.'

'I have a master's ticket,' she said slowly. 'Never been more than second mate, though. *Port captain* told you?' There was a world of surprise in her voice. 'I didn't know he remembered me.' She looked at her brother. 'But...'

'Now you're not going to be silly again,' Sylas said. 'Think of yourself for once and take these guys' offer before they ask someone else. I'm all right.'

She shook her head. 'I...'

'We offered him a job as well,' I said quickly. 'We've got a bunch of kids who need an education, so I want to hire you both. Or your brother alone, should you refuse.'

'Without legs?' she said, staring at me.

'It's a shore job.' I tapped my hook hand against my knee. 'We have a wisewoman healer. I'll ask her and see what we can do to provide him with prosthetics.'

'We can't pay,' the boy said, sounding almost angry.

'We'll find a way to share the costs,' I said.

He relaxed. 'It would be something to be able to move about again.' He looked at his sister. 'Well?'

She snorted. 'Divine Chottapan would sink me if I'd refuse a deal like this. When do you want us? I must arrange something for the business.'

'Soon,' I said. 'Actually, tomorrow. I'll come back to pick you up. After that I'll be going north. The ship lies at Fort Jamril, in the Chorwaynies. When you've taken command I'll probably want you to follow me north, to the Pasandir coast. Do you need an advance?'

'We'll manage, thanks,' she said. 'I... am grateful.'

'So are we,' I said, and I meant it. 'I think we're fortunate to get both of you.'

Once outside, I looked at Kellani. 'We struck lucky here.'

'Shame on that captain for not helping them out,' she said angrily. 'Especially if it was his men's fault.'

I shrugged; my trust in the adult world wasn't overlarge. 'Let's see if those two mates are in the same class.' I took Kellani's hand and ported us back to the Liberator, the big statue in the center of the harbor quarter.

From there we crossed the cobblestoned square to the *Downed Anchors*, a decent-looking inn on a nearby side street. Over the door a sign bore two anchors resting on a bottle-strewn seabed.

Here we found the Longash brothers, Vence and Perre. They were tough, capable guys of twenty and seventeen years, who would command respect from our kids, and we hired them on the spot.

Vence of Longash was the eldest; tall and wiry, with a ponytail of red hair, which was rare among Vanhaari.

'Could you use a third hand?' he said once we were done.

'As bos'n or quartermaster perhaps?' his younger brother added. Perre was shorter, with a complexion nearly as dark gray as mine; only his hair was a white stubble on his head.

'Depends,' I said. 'Qualifications?'

Vence looked at me as if gauging me. 'She was master's mate of a Brisan merchant,' he said slowly. 'Jumped ship because she didn't hold with her captain's criminal plans.'

'She's a Brisan herself,' his brother said. 'A good one.'

'*Marigold* needs a first officer,' Kellani said in my ear.

'True,' I said. 'Where would we find her?'

Vence smiled. 'Right here.' He lifted a fist toward the bar and beckoned. A tall, squarely built girl came to her feet and walked over.

'This is Miyra,' Vence said.

I looked up at the girl. She was a Garthan, with the strangely pale coloring of her folk and blonde hair in two thick braids over her ears.

'Before we discuss anything, two days ago we shot up the port of Brisa,' I said bluntly. 'Let's get that out of the way first.'

'I heard and rejoiced,' she said coolly. Her voice was remarkably melodious. 'If that was you, bravo for a job well done. Brisa's a rotten pool of crooks, criminals, and slavers. The world's well rid of it. You are seeking a master's mate?'

'We have a steam cutter in need of a first officer,' I said. 'Her captain doubles as our airship pilot, so you should be able to take command now and then. Interested?'

'I can do a cutter,' she said. 'First officer; that sounds very formal.'

'It's an acting-lieutenancy for starters,' I said. 'Officially we're the Pasandir Navy.' I thought of Naudin's dislike of gold-braided nincompoopery. 'But without most of the naval trimmings.'

'We are hunting pirates,' Kellani said. 'If you want a quiet life, we don't promise that. On the other hand, we offer a chance to rid the sea of the Bokkaners and to earn a nice bit of booty at the same time. *Marigold* was a Brisan pirate ship before we took her.'

This shook her. 'I know the ship. Hadn't heard she was captured, though. *Marigold* was bewitched. Her crew members were the usual lowlife drags, but their bos'n was a very bad man.'

'He was a jinni,' I said bluntly.

Miyra stared at me. 'That ugly toad?'

'Yes.' I smiled. 'He's dead.'

'I didn't know jinn could be killed,' she said slowly. 'Not by a mortal.'

'This isn't the place to speak of things like that,' I said. 'Later. For now, you're hired, if you care to.'

'I do,' she said, and her eyes glittered. 'I want to hunt pirates too.'

I waved at their tankards. 'One thing; we're a navy of kids, so we're strictly no booze.'

The brothers looked at each other and nodded.

'So are we,' Vence said. 'We've seen one captain drown his senses in rum and lose his ship; that's enough.' He lifted his mug. 'The barkeep here serves a mean *tzaih*, that's an herbal drink with a kick that suits us fine.'

Miyra shrugged. 'I like a beer now and then, but I can do without fine. Sweet tea will do as well for me.'

'Then that's settled,' I said, well content. 'I'll be back tomorrow to pick up you three.'

'We'll be ready,' Vence said.

CHAPTER 3 – ORPHANAGE

With our business finished, we walked to the market square to do some shopping before going back to the fort. As we crossed the busy main street, something small shot out of the shadows between the houses and crashed into me.

'It is you, it is you!' a hysterical voice whispered. 'Cat thought he'd seen you, an' he had! Come! Come quickly, soldiers arresting everyone. Come to the Clam!'

It was Brat, the little boy from the Clam Street Orphanage, his face screwed up and wet with tears and rain as he clutched Cat, his kitten, with one grubby hand and my clean tunic with his other.

'Soldiers?' I said. 'Seatome soldiers?'

'Yes, yes!' he said, tugging at me. 'Come, we must hurry.'

'We'll port,' I said. 'Brat, give me a hand and take a deep breath. Cat will be all right, kittens handle porting easily.' Before he could protest, I sent us away to that dingy street, with its crooked houses and starved looking trees I remembered so well. The times I'd been in Seatome as a ship's boy I had wandered everywhere, but I'd avoided Clam Street.

There was the orphanage; a tall, badly kept building standing in the rain in a small paved garden. This area of Seatome had suffered hardly any damage during the war, and as a result saw little or no renovation afterwards. The effect was depressing.

Soldiers in the green-and-red uniforms of Seatome stood in a large half-circle, watching the front of the building, with halberds and swords ready to strike. Their faces were determined; radiating a strange, empty resolve that gave me the creeps. I touched their minds and found their fear adrift in a familiar fog which made them see not the orphans, but hideously deformed shapes capering and jeering at them, making obscene gestures.

'They seem under that same compulsion,' I whispered to Kellani. 'You stay outside with Brat. Gather any kids who escape. I'm going in.'

Kellani began to protest, but I shook my head. 'I can do it. Please keep the orphans from running off,' I said. 'We don't want to chase all over town for them.'

'You're an idiot,' she said exasperated. 'But go alone if you must. I'll be right outside the front door.'

The soldiers looked through me when I passed them, and I hurried inside, into that awful memory smelling of turnip stew and unwashed youth. Nothing seemed changed since I'd left this place. The walls, papered in dreary patterns dirty with the imprints of thousands of smudgy hands and the dim light of the cheap oil lamps, all was as I remembered.

Only there shouldn't be soldiers in the hall.

In the corridor, the sounds of crying and shouting children assaulted me. Then I had to jump aside as a crowd of kids ran for the door and the waiting soldiers outside.

'Arrest them all!' a high, hysterical voice yelled. I saw a small Vanhaari army captain waving his sword and kicking out at the howling kids trying to get away.

Beside him stood a fat man in a stained robe, whispering and smiling. It was Llynsing, the creep from the pawnshop, who had tried to swindle Tangrid. The gods know what he was doing here, but his malignant expression promised little good.

'Outside!' the captain screamed. 'Take them outside and we'll drag them to the castle. They'll be locked up and in the morning Master Llynsing will take the beasts away. Then, finally, Seatome will be safe again.'

A stout girl in a faded surcoat over her tunic said something, and the captain cuffed her.

'Silence!' he yelled. 'You'll shut up, you lying bit of dogspittle.'

I saw blood drip down her face as a soldier kicked her toward the door.

'Wait!' I cried, as I ran toward the little captain. 'Stop this!' Automatically I checked his mind—it wasn't there. My breathing nearly stopped – a jinni!

The captain wheeled around, his face twisted and his eyes mad. 'Another little monster!' he said. 'You'll join the others, ratface, and tomorrow you will get your deserts!'

Now that I knew him, my heart ran faster. Should I call Kellani? No time, I must fight him alone. 'You are mistaken,' I said, feigning an assurance I didn't feel. 'I come for you, jinni. I'm the one who killed Ozoezd, and Yathub of the *Marigold.*'

The captain stopped his arm waving and stared at me.

'So I was right,' he said, speaking perfectly rational. 'I *knew* you would come here to fulfill the prophecy. Thus I went to collect those mongrels before you could. You have failed, little human; failed like your foolish grandfather Kambish before you. And like him, alone and unaided you will die!'

He swelled, bursting out of his captain's skin and uniform like some loathsome insect emerging from its cocoon. His real shape was a mass of flesh, a blobbish sathee like the *Marigold* jinn had been, but a lot bigger and brandishing a sword in each hand. A mockery of a face smiled at me from the region of his tummy, with the late captain's eyes and a hungry, sharp-toothed mouth. 'Lie down, you are defeated, puny wyrmcaller boy!' he said. 'I am Izzour and those little beasts are mine to feast upon.'

'Run!' I shouted over the screaming of terrified kids. 'Get out, go to my friends!'

The jinni glared at me. A quick look over my shoulder told me his soldiers had forgotten the kids and all pointed their long halberds my way.

'You're a fool to defy me, sathee,' I said, trying to hide my desperation. 'You are nothing but a lowborn underling and way out of your depth.'

The drip-candle face turned purple with fury and his octopus-like arms waved his two swords in agitation, but the sathee jinni waited until all kids were out of the way and he had me *alone and unaided.*

Without new orders, the bewitched soldiers paid no attention to the Clammers as they ran into the street, and in moments, the corridor was empty of orphans.

Now! I whirled around and sent a wave of air down the corridor, bowling the soldiers over like ninepins without killing them. Only the fat pawnbroker remained standing, pressed against the wall, his eyes big with both rage and fear.

Then Izzour attacked, his two swords cutting the air with a swishing sound that made my blood run cold.

I jumped back, out of reach of those long arms. With a single word, I turned my broom into a glittering spear and ran forward again. I twisted my weapon around and danced like mad, stabbing and prodding, trying desperately to avoid his swords as I went.

The jinni squealed every time I cut a hole in his lardy body and with each squeal his blades flashed faster. Back and forth we went, until suddenly my foot hit a warped floorboard. For a moment my steps wavered and Izzour sprang, whirling his blades at my head. I ducked, stumbled and fell. The jinni kicked me in the ribs and I gasped. His swords went up, ready to strike.

'Hold on!' A tall shape jumped over me and Kellani swung her big sword at the jinni, pressing Izzour back and back until he stood inside the keepers' dining room. Behind him, I saw the table laid for the evening meal, with meats and sauces no orphan would ever taste here. I shook my head and sat up, clutching my side as the pain lanced through me.

Down the corridor, the soldiers had regained their feet and came running to aid their "captain". Like Lord Thaar's men in Mazuun's camp, they were unable to see their officer had been taken over by a jinni. Gathering the tatters of my magic, I sent another wave of air and blew soldiers, doors, and part of the wall out into the street. Then I went back to watching Kellani. With one hand she swung her sword, whistling contemptuously, while her other hand drew the long hunting knife from her belt. Then she yelled something in Kell, slashed Izzour diagonally across his body with her knife and rammed her sword deep into his lumpish body. The jinni gave a high-pitched screech, shattering all windows in the building, and raised his arms to the ceiling. He cried out and dissolved into a mass of flames. Tongues of fire leaped onto the keepers' dining table, jumped at the curtains and the upholstery of the chairs, then all of a sudden, smoke billowed out into the corridor.

'We gotta move,' Kellani said, and without as much as a by your leave, plucked me from the floor and ran for the front door.

Outside in the rain, she put me down on my feet. 'You all right?' she asked anxiously.

I felt my ribs. Nothing broken; I could handle the pain, so I nodded.

'Darn,' she said. 'That jinni had one heck of a suicide spell!'

'Where's the fat guy?' I asked, looking around. He was nowhere to be seen. Leaning on Kellani's arm, I limped out of the little garden to where the orphans waited.

'Where's fatso?' I asked urgently. One of the kids pointed wordlessly and I saw Llynsing in an impossible heap on the ground, with at least fifteen Clammers standing round the body, some crying and others staring blankly.

'Well done!' I said. Then I took a deep breath and turned to the soldiers, standing around, looking dazed. The jinni's death had broken the compulsion and left them adrift, without orders, yet unable to think for themselves.

'Corporal,' I snapped to a guy with a gold stripe on his sleeve. 'Wake up, man! There's a fire in the town, do your duty.'

The man looked at me and his eyes cleared. He nodded. A fire—that was something he could understand. He shouted an order, and a soldier ran to the late captain's horse and galloped off, I assumed to get help.

I looked at the huddled groups of kids, shocked and forlorn in the rain, staring at the smoke coming from the open door and windows.

'Gild bosses, to me,' I said as authoritatively as I could manage.

They hurried over; five lost but outwardly calm youngsters. The girl in the surcoat held a dirty kerchief to her split lip, but above it her eyes were watchful.

'Are all your people out?' I asked, clenching my fingers around my hook hand to stop them from shaking.

Four of the bosses nodded, but the fifth, a pigtailed girl, hesitated.

'Has anyone seen Brat?'

I looked around and saw him standing with Kellani, cradling Cat in his arms. 'He came with us,' I said. 'Brat and I met before. Somehow, he knew I was in town and he came to warn me about what was going on here. That guy is a triple hero!'

'What the heck was that monster?' a sharp-faced boy in a fancy cloak asked. 'I thought the captain had gone mad, but then he changed and...' He swallowed hard, looking ill.

'What's your name?' I asked.

'Rawe, of the Rocks.'

'Mage quarter gild.' I forced a smile. 'What we killed was a jinni. A minor one. Those fellows are shapechangers.'

With screaming sirens, a large steam car arrived, carrying a water tank in the back and pulling a pump on a trailer behind it. Aided by the soldiers, four men in leather suits rolled out hoses, while a fifth connected the pump to the tank.

'I don't think they'll save the building,' I said, watching them for a moment.

'Where shall we sleep?' the girl in the surcoat said vehemently. 'That's our home burning.'

'You're Hella of the Harbangers?'

It was a guess, but she nodded.

'How do you know our names?' she asked, scowling.

'Willow told me about you all,' I said. 'We rescued them, you know.'

'Was that you?' the pigtailed girl said excitedly. 'I'm Dadine; filling in for Willow. I know Brat came home the day our boss and her girls disappeared and said that wyrmcaller guy Willow had met before was going to bring them back. The others...' She looked at the rest of the bosses. 'They didn't believe him, but I did. He's a strange kid, but I've never known him bein' wrong. You have Willow? Aya and Keena too? Are they all right?'

'We've saved all twenty-three missing kids and they are fine,' I said. 'I'll tell you later. We need to decide some things first. Where are the keepers? I haven't seen them around.'

'Them!' a guy with dark curls said in a voice high with disgust. 'Those cowardly rats high-tailed it, leaving us to fend for ourselves. Out the back door they went, the rotten lowlifes.'

Somehow, the keepers deserting the kids didn't surprise me.

'I'm Nate,' the boy added, biting his lip. 'Those stupid, useless scumbags. Keepers!'

'They made it easier for me,' I said. 'Me, I am Eskandar, the wyrmcaller of Kalbakar.'

'What's that?' a heavily built guy said and he scowled at me. 'You can't call wyrms, they're stupid.'

I gave him a steady glance until he looked away.

'You must be Bamson.'

He started guiltily. 'Yeah, why?'

'Thought so,' I said, giving him a vague smile. No need to tell him the unflattering description Jornyll had given of him. 'Friends, I'm both wyrmcaller and mage. When Willow and the others disappeared, they were taken by pirates and another jinni.'

'Pirates!' Rawe said explosively. 'So they really were that?'

'They sure were,' I said. 'They kidnapped all those kids, then they took Willow and her two seconds, and sailed. Young Brat saw what happened. He braved Hella's fury and came to the Broomrider guesthouse to warn us. We went after the pirate vessel, killed the jinni and his men, and took their ship. Then we hired the kids on board and sailed to the Chorwaynie Archipelago.'

'*Hired?*' Nate of the market gild said cautiously. 'Like paying them money?'

'That's what the word means, isn't it?' Kellani said. 'We signed them on for our ships; two pence a day and a share in the loot.'

'Loot?' Rawe said. 'What loot?'

'What we get from capturing things,' Kellani said.

Bamson spat in a puddle. 'You wanna hire us too?'

'Patience,' I said. 'I'll come to that. For the moment, we stay in a big fort in the tropics but soon we'll go north, to the Borderlands. We have two ships and a big war dirigible, and a score to settle with those pirates. To go after them, I need more hands. That's where you all come in. I offer all older kids, fourteen-up, say, a place on one of our vessels. We need all kinds; sailors, warriors, cooks, technical people, the lot. You will be trained in ship handling, fighting, letters and numbers, anything you need to know.'

I paused a moment, studying their faces. Excitement, greed, and hope, it was all there.

'The younger kids will stay at our place and go to school. In between we'll teach them some sailing and weapon handling, too, but they won't go to war with us until they're ready.'

'So you wanna hire us?' Bamson said with dogged single-mindedness.

'That was the idea,' I said.

Bamson nodded. 'Good. I'm in.'

'Us too,' Hella said. 'It's time my kids had a chance.'

'You have Shaw?' Nate said, unable to hide his anxiety. 'Is she all right?'

'Girl's doing fine,' I said. 'She's our purser, getting all that gold into our pockets.'

He suddenly grinned. 'That doesn't surprise me. She's brilliant; always dreamt of running her own business.'

'Now you go and tell your gilds,' I said. 'Kellani and I will answer any questions.'

They ran off, and all at once I felt dizzy. That jinni had a hard kick, and my self-healing was a slow process.

'Come here,' Kellani said and she put her large hands on my chest. A sense of wellbeing spread through my body and the pain in my ribs lessened.

'Thanks,' I said and looked up at her. Then I hugged her and for a moment we stood there, all nice and cozy.

Until a polite voice interrupted us. 'A thousand excuses.'

I turned to find a man in dark clothes watching us. His face was hidden under a big, floppy hat dripping rain down a long riding-cloak. 'Lord Wyrmcaller?'

'Yes?' I said. I didn't have the foggiest notion who he was, but there hung an indefinable aura of magic and stealth over him.

He bowed. 'I am one of my Lord Spellstor's agents. Our paths weren't supposed to cross, but under the circumstances I have no choice.'

'Were you watching me?' I said quietly, not relishing the idea at all.

'Oh no, no; certainly not. I was here because of that,' he said with a nod to the soldiers and the burning orphanage.

'After the prior disappearance of several orphans, the Spellstor placed the orphanage on our watch list. The moment our own soldiers arrived to arrest the children, I came to see what was going on. While I was contemplating a path of action, you intervened. I thought it wise to wait a while. You did a remarkable job, I may say. That creature seemed dangerous. He was real, too; not an illusion.'

'He was certainly not an illusion,' I said. 'A jinni shapechanger, one of the lower classes.'

'Another jinni?' the agent said. 'You are sure about that?'

'I am quite sure,' I said. 'We fought two of them in Seatome, and several major ones up north in the Pasandir Peaks. They are very real and very dangerous. This chap was in the slave trade; he was about to sell the whole orphanage to Llynsing, the pawnbroker near the market. That one didn't escape the wrath of the orphans, I fear.'

'And the keepers?' the agent said.

'The children told me the keepers deserted their post the moment the attack started. It would perhaps be worth the trouble to investigate whether they had a part in this matter.'

'Your suggestion has merit,' the agent said. 'Well, I will not keep you. I must report what occurred here to the Lord Spellstor. That distraught captain, would he...?'

'He's dead. When a jinni impersonates you, he uses the original body in the process.' I suppressed a shudder at the horror, but the agent merely bowed again.

'Most ingenious,' he said. 'What will you do with the orphans?'

'I shall relieve Seatome of their presence,' I said grimly. 'They never were welcome here, and I can offer them both jobs and schooling.'

'I will inform my lord,' the agent said. He turned to look at the soldiers helping the firemen. 'Those men will need some counseling, I suppose. I will state so in my report. My apologies, Lord Wyrmcaller; I must take my leave now.'

I answered his final bow and went back to the orphans.

Kellani stood waiting, arms crossed and a curious expression on her face.

'Uncle Basil's spy?' she said. 'I always wondered. So he *was* keeping an eye on things.'

I snorted. 'Don't think his eye would have helped the kids much. Are they finished discussing yet?'

'They all want to come,' Kellani said. She lowered her voice. 'It's not much of a choice, is it, coming with us or living on the streets?' Her voice sounded bitter.

'I know,' I said. 'But it's the only choice we have.' I turned and faced the kids. 'You decided to join us; we are happy to have you. We'll discuss the details later, when we're out of the rain. Listen well; I'm going to port us all to Fort Jamril. You're the largest crowd I ever did, so I want to point out a few things. Keep as close together as you can. When I port, we'll be going through another world. It is a place of instant death; no air and freezing cold. Before we go, take a deep breath, or you'll be dead on arrival.' This got their attention and their faces became anxious.

'What about the babies?' a girl asked.

'They will be all right,' I said. 'Like Brat's kitten, small children know instinctively what to do.

'We'll come out in a large room with tables and chairs. Wait a few seconds before running around; else you'll break your neck, or a leg. Or even worse, some furniture. Any more questions?'

'We won't get stuck inside a wall or something, would we?' an anxious boy's voice asked.

'Are they still saying that?' I said. 'No, you won't. You can't; the wall doesn't want you. No two things can be at the same place, so you'd end up next to it.' I looked at them. 'Let's go. Gather round, guys.'

Immediately I was the center of a crushing group of kids.

'No pushing!' I called. 'Just stand, please. If I start suffocating halfway, you're in trouble.' Immediately they all froze.

'Breathe in now,' I called, and off we went.

It took longer than usual. Not minutes, but still noticeably longer, and several kids gasped for air when we came into the second floor common room.

'There we are,' I said. 'Welcome to Fort Jamril. For the moment, this floor will be yours. The others have the floor above, but they'll be outside, swimming. We fought a battle last week, so they have some days off.'

'I'll go tell them you're all here,' Kellani said. She pulled her broom from its sheath and flew off.

'She really is a broomrider!' a kid exclaimed. 'I wasn't sure, but she is! Oh boy, I'd love to ride a broom!'

I winked at him. 'You'll get your chance.' I waved around the room. 'Walk with me, please.' I showed them the bunkrooms, the washing rooms, and finally the balcony.

Here, several gasped as they took in the blueness of sea and sky, the jungle surrounding the bay, the smells and the sounds.

'It's beautiful,' a boy said, with a look on his face as if he could barely believe it. A toddler tugged at his sleeve, and the boy picked him up. 'See the pretty boats?' he said.

'Whose ships are they?' a girl asked, leaning dangerously far over the balustrade.

'Ours,' I said. 'We captured the big one last week and the white cutter is the former pirate ship that took Willow and the others.'

'You captured that big one?' Bamson demanded. 'Where are your soldiers?'

I stared at him. 'The kids are our soldiers; Jornyll, Aya, and the rest. They captured the ship and the pirates.'

'That punk Jornyll?' he said, incredulously.

'He's quite handy with a sword,' I said. 'Let's go down and join them. Stairs are to the right.'

I shooed them all down to the little beach, where they were received with cheers by a sun-darkened and dripping-wet bunch of kids.

Before long, they all were in the water, naked as the day the gods kicked them screaming into the world. Only Brat, still carrying his kitten, stayed apart.

'You're not a swimmer?' I asked.

He shook his head mutely.

'That's all right, you don't have to,' I said. Then I saw Cenn watching us from a distance and I beckoned him over.

'Cenn, meet Brat,' I said. 'And Cat, of course.'

'Will he be a ship's boy, too?' Cenn said carefully.

I smiled at him. 'He won't; Brat ain't a sailor. I think he would be a great help in the purser's department. Will you show him around the place?'

The two boys eyed each other.

Then Cenn nodded. 'I'll put on my trousers.'

'Excellent,' I said and left them to it.

I walked to the edge of the small quay beside the wall and sat down. I felt suddenly tired. That fight with the jinn and then porting over a hundred and fifty kids, it took a lot of energy. I leaned back and watched the kids. There were several babies and toddlers, and some older kids taking care of them as they played at the shallowest end of the inlet.

'I must check with Willow how that's arranged,' I thought. *'If they have a day's work caring for the small ones, that's a job as much as being a sailor or a cook. They should be paid for it, and go to school as well. Better make a list of all the jobs we need and...'* I sighed and went back to the office.

CHAPTER 4 – SHAW

Shaw sat in the shade while the others swam. She was small, even for a Vanhaari, with knobby limbs, a middling-gray complexion, and a squint in her left eye. She didn't care about swimming; her mind was focused on trade. Her parents had owned a chandlery store in Seatome until a fire destroyed all. In the orphanage, she had clung to her dream of becoming a big and respected merchant. That's why she sat apart from the others, filling her cherished notebook with everything she one day hoped to need. *Materials to clothe one child...* Blue and red cloth, thread, buttons; reeds to plaid a hat. Underwear and socks. Shoes or boots they couldn't make, so she'd need a cobbler for those. Everything she learned she wrote down. Food for one; lemonade, tea, cookies and things. Plate, mug, and forks.

She looked up as the door opened and a lot of kids poured through. *Clammers!* she thought, sitting up straight. *Has Eskandar brought...? Nate!*

Then he was with her. 'Darn, girl,' he said, gripping her hands.

'Nate...'

'You all right?'

'Sure,' she said. 'Nate, I've been to the MCTC headquarters! Gods, that's big!'

Nate grinned and they both sat down. 'Tell me,' he said. 'Everything.'

So she told him of Darquine, the warehouse, and all she had learned. She spoke of the *Marigold*'s cargo, of the ship, Eskandar and the jinni.

'Curse it all,' she said angrily. 'I miss the market. What are the prices doing?'

'They were slightly up, the last time,' Nate said. 'Now after the fire they'll be even higher.'

'Fire!' she said, stricken, remembering the flames, the heat on her face and the hands of the smith's wife holding her back.

Nate looked at her. 'The Clam,' he said. 'We're all right, all of us. Truly! We had our own jinni. Eskandar and Kellani killed the beast.' Then he told her and she looked at him as she listened.

When he was done, he picked up her notes.

'Working?' he said, skimming the pages.

'Of course,' she said. 'We've been making our own uniforms. I want a list of needs per person.'

'Good,' he said. 'Dash it, gal. I've missed you.'

She looked at him, surprised at the admission. She'd missed him, but he her?

'The water looks good,' he said. 'I'm feeling all grimy from that fire. Let's swim.'

He slipped out of his clothes, and together they joined the others.

CHAPTER 5 – MEETING

That evening we dined on a thick stew with fresh greens and rice, and plenty sweet narangos and bananas. To the newcomers, brought up on boiled greenstuffs and beans, this was enchantingly strange and a huge success.

After the washing-up, we held a meeting in the third floor cafeteria. Over two hundred faces; it was an impressive number.

First, for the benefit of the newcomers, I explained about Teodar the Kavid Jar and Bodrus the Sleeping God. I told them what my part was as Wings of the Mountains and that we were fighting pirates to protect our god and the Peaks.

'Teodar wants us to go north,' I said. 'It seems the pirates are stirring up trouble in the local kingdoms and he wants us to stop them.'

'Us?' a girl said. 'Your invisible friend wants *us* to stop the gods know how many pirates? You're mad, begging your pardon.'

I smiled. 'We stopped other pirates before.'

'Well, I'm not a fighter,' she said in a tight voice. 'I won't do it.'

'If you think you can't fight, then you won't,' I said. 'There are plenty of other jobs we need filled, like cooking, cleaning, and taking care of the little ones.'

'I'm not a coward,' she said defiantly. 'I just can't.'

'All right,' I said mildly. 'I'm not mad at you.'

'It's a long way north by ship,' Naudin said. 'We'd be cut off from everything; help, provisions, all those things we have here at the fort.'

'True,' I said. 'Teodar spoke of a base on the Peaks' west coast. He said Jem would know.'

'Me?' The ghostly princess started and promptly drifted up from her chair. She cursed and screwed up her face as she concentrated. Slowly she sank back in her chair and put her hands on the table. I'd seen her do it before, but it always got me how strong her will was to appear a normal, solid girl.

'What place might that be?' she asked, as if she hadn't seen the awed faces of the new kids.

'Smalkand Keep.'

She frowned. 'The *hushavran!* How would you call it in Vulgar? The traders' place? Does it still exist? It's been there for centuries; headquarters of the Smalkandar family, a big trading house from what you call Port Naar.' She pulled a face. 'The Smalkandar were distantly related to the royal family, and they always had the king's favor; even Grandfather's. They operated camel caravans all over the Peaks. It was big business, as they had a monopoly trading the products of Nanstalgarod to the locals.' She looked at our purser further down the table. 'They got very, very rich.'

'I must see that place,' Shaw said and her eyes narrowed. 'Where does one buy camels?'

'Hizmyr,' Jem said absently. For a few seconds she stared at a point past the purser. I guessed the memory of Smalkand had taken her back to her own time, five centuries ago, and her next words confirmed it.

'At my birth, the kingdom celebrated,' Jem said in a distant voice. 'My parents, my brother, Grandfather and the kingdom; happy and thriving. When I turned fourteen, all was gone. The sand covered the lands from the Eastern Marches to the walls of Atnortod and Grandfather had murdered my family. With their cities in ruins, the Smalkandar lords had nothing left to trade. They will have stayed at their keep, for there at least they had enough to eat.' She looked at me across the table. 'Perhaps they even survived to the end, when Grandfather ordered all his remaining countrymen to kill themselves.'

I knew what she meant. When I was in ruined Atnortod I had experienced the floating bits of memory of that last day; horror-filled reminders that had been too strong to die with their owners. 'They won't have survived,' I said. 'Not after five centuries.'

'Not a chance,' Jem said. 'Grandfather's command was irresistible. My people are dead. I am the last Nanstalgarodian.'

Some of the new kids gasped at that and Jem gave a tired shrug. 'That's how it went. My country is now a desert. The Hellesands, your people call it.'

She looked at me. 'The keep and all their possessions were inside caves, so perhaps something can be salvaged.'

'Teodar mentioned it was fully furnished,' I said. 'I propose we go and see for ourselves.' I looked at Wylmer and Tangrid. 'Are you guys and the airship up to it?'

'Of course,' Wylmer said, and Tangrid nodded. 'We have the maps.'

'Could we leave in three days time?'

Wylmer looked at the engineers. 'What do you say?'

Ulaataq and Imooga exchanged glances.

'He will go,' Imooga said, and she smiled. 'Ulaa knows the *Pewbara* better than me.'

'We have enough fuel to sail around the world,' the young Thali engineer said. 'All her crystals are nearly new and we have a spare set.'

'All right,' I said. 'It will be a little over three thousand miles. How long will it take? A week? More?'

'Twenty-four hours,' Wylmer said.

'At most,' Tangrid agreed.

I blinked at them. 'You're kidding.'

'Not at all,' Wylmer said. '*Pewbara*'s a war dirigible; she's fast. Those Qoori make excellent stuff.' He grinned at Xailin across from him.

The Qoori third officer gave him an inscrutable look. 'Yes.'

'Twenty-four hours is better than I had thought,' I said. Then I glanced at our purser. 'You'll get your wish pretty quickly.'

'Who else will go?' Kellani asked. 'Apart from you and Shaw?'

'You,' I said. 'Naudin and Lothi-Mo. Jem and Amaj, Willow, and to give us strong-arm backup, Jornyll and Aya.'

Bamson sprang to his feet, his face dark. 'If *he* goes, then I go too!'

I noticed his anger and Jornyll's scornful glance. Somehow, Bamson saw Jornyll as a threat to his position. It hadn't occurred to him yet that both the Clammers' organization and his position as boss had died in the flames of the orphanage, and Jornyll's obvious contempt for his former leader didn't help either.

'Let him come along,' Kellani said. *'Those two will settle the matter soon enough, with their heads or their fists.'*

'Jornyll uses his brains now and then,' I answered. *'That guy Bamson is solid bone.'*

'Amaj can handle them,' she said.

'We'll take you,' I said. 'You will have a chance to prove yourself. Both of you report to Amaj.'

Bamson's mouth sagged.

'That's me,' Amaj said grimfaced. 'I told Jornyll and now I tell you. I am a warrior, you are not. If you want to survive, follow my orders. Got it?'

I didn't think Bamson had counted on that, but he could only swallow and nod.

'Good,' Amaj said. He turned to me. 'I want Zaotinq as well. You said he could be a soldier. He's shaping up nicely, but he needs to do army things.'

'You're right,' I said. 'I promised he could.'

Amaj wasn't done yet. 'Aya has more experience than any of those boys; she'll be corporal.'

The big girl smiled. 'I can show them a trick or two.'

'Done and done,' I said. 'Now we have the Pasandir army.'

'Anyone else?' My glance caught Brat sitting near the door and staring hard at me. 'You and Cenn come with us,' I said, remembering the child's hatred of the sea. I saw him relax and exchange some secret message with Cenn across from him.

'Sylas, you too,' I said to our legless teacher. He was tough, but a week at sea wouldn't be fun if you couldn't move about.

I put my hand and hook on the table. 'That's it. Fifteen of us and the *Pewbara*'s crew makes twenty.' I looked at Abia. While the kids amused themselves, she had gathered the Longash brothers and Xailin, and taken command of the *Drakon*. Following her example, Miya had arranged for Chagan to show her around *Marigold*, and now all of them sat together.

'Captain Abia is in charge here while we're gone,' I said. 'Keena, you'll be mindspeak officer here. As soon as we have seen Smalkand, I'll call you. If the place proves a ruin, we'll return. If it is suitable, I'll signal you to sail.' I grinned. 'You guys will have to make your own way north. I probably could teleport the *Marigold* but I'd rather not try it with a big beast like *Drakon*.'

'If you thought to try, I'd knock you out first,' Kellani said, planting a big fist under my chin. 'No way will you risk your life just to save them a week's sea travel.'

'Actually, that week would be good for the ships,' Abia said. 'It will shake down the crews and give us time to get to know each other.'

CHAPTER 6 – SMALKAND KEEP

Three days later, the Smalkand expedition boarded the *Pewbara*. I watched the departure procedure in surprise. It was the first time, but Wylmer's crew handled it as if they'd done it a hundred times.

Averson stepped outside to disconnect the mooring line from the tower. She waited until the pilot had pulled the whole length of the line back into the nose of the ship before steering her broom after the slowly rising dirigible. Once inside, she locked the door behind her, reported to the pilot and took up her place behind his chair.

Meanwhile Byroon, the ballast and floatgas handler, watched his dials and adjusted the gas pressure to keep the ship steady. Only yesterday I'd seen him playing with the others on the little beach, doing what all kids do. I knew Tangrid as co-pilot had a second set of controls and kept an eye on things, but it was good to see how serious and concentrated Byroon worked when he had to. I hid a grin. The boy had been a pickpocket and got this job because he had quick fingers and steady nerves.

'Anchors aweigh,' Wylmer said with satisfaction. 'Smooth take-off, kids.' He shoved the chart under my nose. 'We'll go to Port Dvarghish first. That means for the next sixteen hours we'll be over sea. From Dvarghish we'll follow the overland route to the foot of the Peaks. Then we'll go the last stretch over sea again. Those mountains of yours are a mighty obstacle for dirigibles.'

'Why?'

He grinned. 'They're too tall. We can't fly over them; up there the air is too thin to carry our weight. We can pass through them, but that's dangerous; too many treacherous winds peering around mountaintops for a chance to pound on us. So making it easier on all of us, we'll sail around them.'

I gave a wise nod and left them to it.

Pewbara was a big ship as dirigibles go. Beside the crew, she could carry a hundred souls with ease. There was a messroom, two twenty-five bed bunkrooms, a kitchen, armory, and several other rooms.

The whole interior was an echo of the Qoori taste, just like *Drakon*. The walls and floors were of a lightweight green wood, decorated with strange, many-colored signs and the stylized golden wyrms that symbolized the northern empire. It was too florid for me, but Lothi-Mo liked it. She liked everything with a wyrm on it.

Still, even in an airship this size it proved a long journey for a bunch of kids unused to sitting still.

'Sea!' Amaj said to me, staring into the large windows lining the mess. 'You said the sea was a lot of water, but I never thought it would be this much.' He shook his head. Before he joined us, the most water the young lord had seen were the small mountain rivers of the Peaks.

'Somehow, on a ship traveling is different,' he added. 'There is always something to do on board. This flying thing is, well, dull.'

We filled an hour with silly guessing games. When that flagged, Jem and Lothi-Mo led us into songs, while Kellani and I told of our adventures in Nanstalgarod. Naudin had come prepared, and brought the book he used for the kids' reading lessons, and we spent time reading aloud some of the naughty adventures of the story's rich heroine.

After that, the kids dozed. Only Jem and Shaw played a board game with beautifully carved pieces. Amaj understood as little of it as me, but he moved Jem's red pieces where she told him to.

I watched them for a moment, and noticed that Shaw often stared at the board with a hand over her squinting eye.

'Why do you do that?' I asked suddenly.

'What?' She looked up, her mind still with her next move.

'Put your hand over your eye,' I said.

'Because I see blurry with two eyes,' she said. 'Stupid left eye never did what it should do.'

'Have you asked Na'a?'

She shrugged. 'Why? I always had it.' She sounded defensive now. 'I'm used to it.'

'Still, Na'a can regrow muscle and bones, perhaps she can help you too. Ask her.'

She sighed. 'All right.'

Then the ship's voicepipe crackled and Wylmer's cheerful voice boomed us all awake.

'Wakey wakey; it's an hour past sunup of a brand new day and we're nearing the beautiful Kell coast.'

With yells of relief, the kids all rushed to the windows, pushing and shoving to get the best view of the distant haze. As we came closer, the horizon solidified into a rocky plain rising from the sea, covered with purplish bushes and coarse grass.

To the left, a large promontory protruded a distance into the sea.

'Yann Talimarch,' Kellani said. 'Cape Return. From the sea that is the first you see of Kell. The bay city beyond it is Port Dvarghish, the biggest harbor of Kell.'

Aya stood alone in a circle of kids, watching the home city of the mother who had disavowed her. After a few minutes, she turned away. Willow gripped her arm, without saying anything. Then the big girl shrugged. 'It's just a place.'

As we came close to the city, with the sun low on the horizon, the ship slowed down.

'Wyrmcaller to the Bridge, please,' the voicepipe said.

'Trouble.' Lothi-Mo had been napping, but now her whole being showed her both alert and wary as she joined me.

As I came to the bridge, Wylmer pointed ahead. 'Wyrms,' he said. 'Don't know what they're doing, but those soldiers below don't seem to like it.'

There were two wyrms circling lazily over a large field. The largest, a massive bronze-green, had smoke trickling from its mouth.

Below, a regiment of leopard archers was eying them, bows at the ready.

'Mustn't fight!' Lothi-Mo snapped. 'Many will die then.'

I wheeled around. 'Someone open the door for me.' While Averson hurried to unlock the entrance port, I readied my broom. Lothi-Mo shot outside first, and then I dropped toward the archers.

'Hold your fire!' I shouted; my amplified voice loud enough for all to hear. 'I'm coming in.'

I'd spied a trio of Kell officers to the front and I landed beside them.

'Wyrmcaller Eskandar of Kalbakar,' I said. 'Can I be of assistance?'

The officer in charge was a hard-faced senior leopard archer. She eyed my face and my uniform, and then she saluted.

'Wyrmcaller! The queen informed us you are an ally, sir.' She eyed Lothi-Mo, who had appeared at my shoulder. 'Another wyrm? Is it tame?'

'No, Lothi-Mo not tame,' my wyrmling said. 'Me fighting wyrm of high degree, not tame at all, archer woman.'

The leopardess unexpectedly smiled. 'Your pardon,' she said. 'No offense intended, just caution.'

'Is all sad,' Lothi-Mo said. 'Must settle this with no fighting. Honorable elders are confused, they mean no harm.'

'Maybe not, but they did,' a younger officer said. 'Those two beasts have been playing merry devil for two hours at least, damaging fields, scaring people. They're out of reach of our arrows, but we're expecting the Rapid Riders any moment.'

'They are not beasts, leopardess,' I said. 'Or would you call the seniors of your clan so, when their minds begin to wander? They once were intelligent and friends of our peoples.'

The younger Kell bowed, abashed. 'I will contemplate on your words, Wyrmcaller.' My rebuke had touched her honor and like a true Kell, she would evaluate it.

'Good,' Lothi-Mo chirped. 'Let your wisdom grow. Meanwhile, I will address elders; they must listen.'

'I wish you luck,' the leading leopardess said.

We would need it, I knew. Those wyrms might be old and confused, but they were powerful enough to cripple a naval dreadnought, let alone a small guy on a broomstick.

Up we flew, boldly towards the biggest one.

'I, Eskandar, Wyrmcaller of Kalbakar, would bid to speak with you, wise wyrm,' I said.

The wyrm turned her head to me, eyes rolling, but she didn't answer.

'Hold god,' Lothi-Mo whispered. *'Let god-power flow into you and to me. I must be big, big girl now.'*

I had no idea what she wanted to do, but obediently I gripped the little statue of the roadside guy in my pocket. As before, when Bodrus had spoken to the singers in Fort Jamril, I felt power flow into me. I put my hook-arm around Lothi-Mo and steered the power toward her. Slowly, around us a giant wyrm grew, intangible, but of immense majesty. Soon, the vague wyrm shape was larger, much larger than the others.

Then Lothi-Mo spoke. Her voice was deep, vibrant, and her words alien. She addressed the wyrms and I felt their minds clear. They answered, and after a few moments, turned and flew away from the town.

The wyrm-form enveloping Lothi-Mo wavered and dissolved.

'Done,' she said. 'Sent them to Kalbakar. Will nestle, hunt vole; forget again...'

'You were fantastic,' I said. 'What did you do?'

'Became adult. Just for a little while.' She sounded so tragic it shocked me.

'Can't...' she wailed. 'So wanted to heal them! Can't! They'll forget again.' She sank down on my lap and keened.

With her so troubled, I thought it better to go back to the ship, so I sent the senior leopardess a thought. *'It is done. You can dismiss your archers; the wyrms won't come back. I must return to my airship; this very much upset Lothi-Mo.'*

'Our thanks to both of you,' the woman said, relieved. *'You and the lady wyrm spared us a lot of grief, Wyrmcaller.'*

Back on board, Lothi-Mo disappeared, not to her spot in the mess, but retired into the captain's cabin and refused to speak.

'We saw her grow,' Kellani said when I rejoined the others. 'Was that what you did with Ozoezd?'

'It was an illusion,' I said. 'She made herself appear an adult wyrm. Then she managed to clear those other wyrms' minds long enough to give them orders.' I sighed. 'She is very upset.'

'Why? It was a great feat for a young wyrm.'

I thought I understood. 'It wasn't enough. She wanted to *stay* an adult. She wanted to heal them permanently, but she couldn't. So to her mind, she failed.'

'She was very big, wasn't she?' Naudin said.

'I won't carry her around when she's older. She was easily twice as large as the bigger of the two wyrms.' *And very beautiful*, I thought.

The *Pewbara* passed over Dvarghish and followed the rocky line of the Kell coast. Another few hours would see us at our destination.

Amaj yawned. 'I'd better check my gear.'

Jornyll and Zaotinq took the hint and soon they were assiduously going over their swords and axes. The arms were still the old ones they'd taken from the *Marigold* pirates; worn but serviceable and looking a lot less rusty.

Aya snorted as she glanced at the three boys. 'I'm always prepared. You!' she said, and laid a big hand on Bamson's shoulder. 'Come.' She pushed him toward the armory with its small stock of spare weapons.

I smiled; our former Basher was about to be introduced to some real fighting.

All of a sudden the sunlight dimmed, and the messroom became dusky. A boy yelled and pointed at the windows. On both sides, immense mountainsides blocked the daylight. We had entered the high ranges of the Pasandir Peaks; the route Wylmer had said was too dangerous for airships.

We all stared at the rocky faces passing by close enough to distinguish the patches of moss growing in the cracks.

'We're inside the Peaks,' I said, trying to sound cheerful. 'Don't worry; this is Bodrus's country and he won't let anything bad happen to us, ' I said. *Mountains' Breath, make it so,*

With a false smile and squared shoulders I made my way to the bridge. Both pilots were at their posts now, with Averson standing behind them and Byroon the ballast handler at his controls. Tangrid had the con; with one hand at the helm and the other on the elevator wheel, he weaved us past the snow-capped peaks. Beside him, Wylmer looked relaxed, but his eyes were watchful and his hands rested close to his own controls.

'I mentioned we'd go the coastal way,' he said without turning his eyes away from the looming mountainsides. 'But the aerodrome tower at Dvarghish warned of thunderstorms thataway, so we're giving you the scenic route after all.'

'This seems like nervous work,' I said.

'It is. We're mountain-dodging. It will cost time, but we will get there. Tangrid is the best dodger in the world. Why don't you relax and enjoy the view?'

'Wyrms like this,' Lothi-Mo said. With a flurry of wings, she appeared beside me and managed to hang almost motionless. 'Gliding, wind under your wings, skimming the mountainsides, soaring high, swooping low—such fun. But not alone...' She sounded wistful.

'I know, dear,' I said. 'When I have time, I'll get my broom and we'll do it together.'

'Brooms don't fly,' she said. 'Wyrms fly. Big wyrms.'

She had said it before, and still I didn't know what she expected me to do. Grow wings, perhaps.

For over an hour I watched my homeland pass around me. I saw the snowy ridges, the high passes and the long, wooded valleys, and I remembered my days as a toddler. I had walked these mountains with my family, fleeing an unknown enemy. I'd trudged those frozen trails, kept alive by Teodar's wisdom and, perhaps, by Bodrus's hand.

There were ruins; the many broken towers of the strangers who had lived here before us. Then I saw buildings pass underneath. A village? I sent out a trickle of thought. People, a keep, and a few farms. All were my folks, Ma'aweshi, with the same red sheen to their gray skins. I added it to the map in my mind—village, name unknown.

We would have to start up that camel caravan business again, I thought. That would be the fastest way to get into contact with our people. I'd have to talk with Shaw. If anyone could do it, it was her.

'Look!' Wylmer said suddenly. I rose from my thoughts and stared out the window. We'd come onto a mile-wide bay with a sloping sandy beach, circled by snow-hatted mountains. Beyond the sand was a sizable copse of trees and then I saw a large, dark hole leading into the mountains.

'That's it,' I said. It matched the images in my head. 'That's Smalkand.'

'Woot!' Wylmer shouted and they all shook hands. 'We did it!' He sighed. 'My instructors taught me the Borderlands couldn't be crossed. Too many dangerous winds, not enough room to maneuver, the air too thin to carry the ship... Hogwash! It was nervous work, but not impossible at all.'

I stared at the bay, the beach, and the sheer wall of a high plateau leading into the mountains.

'Wyrm Ridge but no wyrms,' Lothi-Mo said. 'All empty.'

I let my mind roam the place. No wyrms, no people, no large animals.

'They will come, dear heart,' I said. 'People and wyrms will come back.'

'When?' She sighed. 'Lothi-Mo so wants other wyrms to talk to.'

I had no answer, nor did she expect one.

The *Pewbara* drifted down low enough for us to jump the last few feet, and soon we were all out, leaving it to third pilot Averson and Byroon, to secure the vessel.

We ran towards the cave mouth. I stopped, but Jornyll ran past me. He looked over his shoulder to say something and crashed into an invisible barrier. The shock sent him sprawling, and Amaj could only just prevent himself from following the boy's example.

'A shield?' Kellani said, dumbfounded, stretching out her hands. 'A good one, too. But how?'

I thought how the mad monks had protected Kalbakar Keep with a mechanical forcefield and the trouble we'd had turning it off.

'Another dratted generator?' I glanced at Jornyll scrambling to his feet looking sheepish. 'As a demonstration how not to enter a strange place, it was quite effective.'

Bamson guffawed, but Jornyll only turned his back to him.

'You all right?' I asked. 'Then go and ask Ulaataq to hop over.'

Without a word or nod, Jornyll ran back to the ship.

'It's not one shield,' Naudin said with his eyes closed. 'They're a linked series.'

I sat down and let my mind slide along the outside of the shield. It made a good-sized dome, easily as large as Proprietor Darquine's main storeroom at the Malgarth &

Continental Trading Company headquarters. Beyond it was another one, and another, and after a while I'd counted twelve shields, some smaller, others bigger and all strong.

Then Jornyll returned with Ulaataq, both panting and disheveled.

'What's this about a shield?' the engineer said belligerently. 'That's impossible. Five centuries ago there weren't any...'

I put my good hand on the invisible barrier. Ulaataq followed suit and cursed. 'It is a shield.'

'Not one,' I said. 'At least a dozen.'

'No,' the boy said, taut-faced. 'That can't be. Where do they get the power?'

'I counted twelve,' I said, 'and there are even more behind them.'

'Found a generator,' Naudin said. 'Now that I know what to look for it ain't difficult. This one is different from the one at Kalbakar. More... crude. There's a symbol on it; a Qoori symbol.'

'Qoor!' Ulaataq said in a flat voice.

'It may be crude,' I said softly. 'But that machine has been working without breaking down for five centuries.'

'Five centuries...' Ulaataq's face worked. 'The Qoori built mana generators when our people were still hunting walros? So it *was* bull! All that talk about how unique our stuff is, and how brilliant we Thali are—it's just puff snow. Those darned Qoori built machines centuries ago we can't even design *right now*!' He stood there, head back and fists balled, filled with a boundless anger.

'Welcome to the adult world,' I said. 'It's all humbug.'

'That Thali talk sold machines and protected engineers,' Kellani said. 'It may seem piffle, but it is piffle with a purpose. Now keep your minds on the job, boys. How do we get in?'

'There must be a way,' Naudin said. 'An emergency entrance.'

'Lothi-Mo says go look.' My wyrmling slapped my face with her tail. 'Up, up; answers above your head.' With a few wing beats, she was on the ledge. Over the entrance was a small ledge leading to a second hole large enough for the *Pewbara* to enter.

'Here be door,' Lothi-Mo said.

I drew my broom from its sheath on my back and moments later I joined her.

'No go in big hole,' Lothi-Mo chirped. *'Is shielded. Use little door.'* She dove forward and disappeared into another opening, about large enough for a big cat. Or a wyrmling. Or even a too small guy with one hand.

'I see it,' I said. 'A cat flap. I wonder where it leads to.'

'Come,' Lothi-Mo called.

I turned to the others watching me below. 'You're all way too large.' I waved and crept through the opening.

'Into the wyrm hole,' Lothi-Mo said, cackling.

I didn't find it funny. Even though I knew I could port out any time, even though I *knew* I was safe, it was scary as heck. It was narrow, dark, and airless, and I hated it. I couldn't even make a mage light. Those things were hot, and I didn't fancy burning myself.

Using all my senses, I kept a grip on myself and propelled myself forward on my elbows.

'Come,' Lothi-Mo said again. *'It's a nice hole,'*

I didn't answer but clenched my teeth and crept on through the dark.

After a while, the tunnel made a sharp turn, and I had to force myself on my side to wriggle past it. That was not at all funny.

Lothi-Mo began to hum, and in the darkness her song was comforting.

The narrow tunnel took an unexpected dive and it was like falling head first down a narrow staircase. I know I cried out and, using hands and feet against the walls to slow my speed, hit the ground without breaking anything. I lay still, waiting for my breath and my heart return to normal.

The next segment went just as steeply upwards, and I had to push myself forward with my feet. It was tiring, and I was panting like a steam engine when I reached the highest point.

I wiped the tears from my eyes and looked down. *'Darn,'* I shouted. *'This tunnel has no floor! I am crawling like a cockroach over the shield itself. I'm over a common room now. There's some sort of bluish light coming from the walls, so it's not pitch dark. I can see tables, seats, a counter, all looking like the owners had only just stepped out.'*

'Would the forcefield preserve it all?' Kellani said.

I caught a vague comment from Ulaataq, but his mind responded badly to telepathic speech, so I couldn't hear what it was.

'Could be,' Naudin said. *'Ulaa doesn't pooh-pooh it. He's getting more 'n more unhappy.'*

'Tell him I'm willing to change places,' I snapped, suddenly livid. *'I'm not exactly bubbling with joy either.'*

That anger spurred me on and the slide down the second dome was almost a nosedive. I managed to halt myself in time, and made my way up, down, and up again over what was a series of large dormitories, followed by a smaller dome with bedrooms. Real classy rooms, with four-poster beds and handsome furniture.

Beyond them it was dark again. As I began the next slide down, I heard Lothi-Mo call out. *'Wait! Wait!'* Then the tunnel walls were gone, and I dropped down into the darkness, and crash-landed on a stone floor.

I came to my senses spread-eagled on the ground, with Lothi-Mo on my chest, crooning in my face.

'Wah?' I said

'You fell,' she cackled, caressing my face with her tail.

'Yeah.' I lay still, checking my body. 'No damage. Nothing. Not even a sore spot.'

'*Eskandar!*' Kellani said, and she sounded worried. '*Are you there?*'

'*Seems so,*' I said. '*Missed the steps.*'

'*Otha! You all right?*'

'*Sure,*' I said absently. I was far too all right. Somehow, my body must have healed itself without my doing anything.

I sat up. There was a faint humming in the air, and a tickling smell. I called a mage light and looked around. We were in a machine room, somewhat like the *Marigold*'s engine room—incomprehensible.

'That's Ulaataq's job,' I muttered. 'Lothi-Mo, we're going. Must get our engineer.'

She jumped into my arms and I ported back to the entrance.

Kellani wordlessly embraced us both. 'You frightened me, you idiot,' she said. 'You didn't answer, and Lothi-Mo said you were unconscious.'

'I fell off the forcefield,' I said, feeling very stupid. 'That whole tunnel thing was open underneath; it wasn't made for humans. Flying wyrmlings perhaps. There's a machine at the end; a big one. So I came to fetch our brilliant Thali.'

'Let me see it,' Ulaataq said impatiently.

'Can you do another port?' Kellani said as she let go of me.

'Yes,' I said. 'I'm not tired or anything. The others have to stay here though; it's not all that roomy over there.'

Kellani didn't like it, but she stepped back. I grabbed our engineer's thin shoulder and with Lothi-Mo still in my arms ported to the other side of the domes. Then I made another light and smiled as I heard Ulaataq's gasp.

'Dancing penguins on an ice floe,' he whispered. He peered at the control panel. 'It's locked,' he said. 'Of course it is. Now what?' His hand slid over a row of copper buttons, each marked with a letter. 'These are wheels,' he said, touching one of them. He looked at me. 'A coded lock. Ten letters.'

'You mean...?'

'I mean I need to turn each wheel until the display reads a certain ten-letter word,' he said. 'We use that system on bank safes and padlocks. It will be something simple, especially if it's for emergencies.'

'Smalkander,' I said. What is simpler to remember than your own name?

Ulaataq turned each wheel to the right letter, but nothing happened.

'Darn!' I said. *'Guys, a simple ten-letter word that has to do with this place?'*

'You're doing puzzles?' Kellani asked, surprised.

'Smalkandar,' Naudin said.

'We did that one... Wait, what? Repeat, please.' I said.

'Smalkandar,' he said again.

I slapped my forehead. '-Dar, not -der,' I said to Ulaataq.

The engineer turned a wheel and the control panel buzzed, with lights blinking all over it.

'That did it!' I said. *'Don't run away now.'*

I heard Ulaataq groan and turned around. He had buried his face in his hands and shook his head until I thought it would fall off his shoulders.

'No,' he said. 'Gor'dashit no! Those darned Qoori did it. So many of our people have been working on it and here it is.'

'Here is what?' I said.

He straightened. 'Remember that generator you used to kill Ozoezd? I told you that thing got its mana from its surroundings, didn't I? Well, there ain't enough wild mana anywhere to power all those screens. That means only one thing, you know. This... this supergenerator gets the stuff directly from the Intermedium. Our top people knew it was possible; they built a mombadillion prototypes, but none worked. This one does. How?' He turned to me, his eyes glittering. 'You wanted Thali engineers? For this you will get as many bigwigs as you want.'

'I don't want bigwigs,' I protested. 'I have you and Imooga. A third engineer would be handy, but certainly not hordes of greedy high-ups.'

'You mean that?' he said incredulously. 'You would leave this to my cousin and me? I could get you a few other kids and we'd make a study group. All of us here would get rich and famous!'

'Let's talk about that later. For now, I want those shields down. Can you do that?'

Ulaataq squinted. He pointed at the uppermost dial, whose needle crept to the right. 'It's a strange language; I have no idea what they're saying.' He tapped a label. 'Gibberish.'

'M/V Mana Suction,' Lothi-Mo said suddenly, and she cackled. 'That's the words, what do they mean?'

'It will be the pump sucking the mana out of the multiverse into our world,' Ulaataq said. Then he whirled around. 'You can read this?'

'Sure can,' the wyrmling said. 'Qoori, Nanstalgarodian, common Vulgar and more; read, speak—not yet write, but shall.'

'Read me those labels, will you?' Ulaataq said urgently.

Lothi-Mo flew up to the machine and started to translate the words. When she had named them all, the engineer touched a lever with his fingers. 'This was Shield Override, wasn't it?'

'Yes, yes, override.'

'Great-Grandmother aid me,' he muttered and flipped the switch.

I heard a soft *whoosh* and turned around. The shield was gone and before us was a plain, unpainted door. With three steps, I was there and had thrown it open. Mage lights went on in a narrow corridor dividing the posh bedrooms. There was a faint humming of machines in the air, and a smell of beeswax and clean linen.

'You did it,' I said, awe-struck.

'Of course.' Ulaataq breathed on his fingernails and polished them on his tunic. 'You don't need an engineer for that!' Then he laughed delightedly, and so did I, while we slapped each other's shoulders.

Then I turned and ran to the next door. Another hallway lit up, with dormitories on both sides. Past those, in the common room, I ran into Kellani's arms and we hugged and crowed our elation.

'It's big!' she said as she put me back on my feet. 'And you were right; it's just like they stepped out for a minute.'

'It's so grand,' Jornyll said in a low voice. 'From Clam Street to this is... I almost can't believe it!'

'We've found a home,' I said. 'A place all our own.'

CHAPTER 7 – HOME DANGERS

Entering the caves from the bay valley, we came into a half-round hallway with three doorways. The double central doors opened on the large common room. To the right was a guardroom and to the left another closed door.

Curious to know what was behind it, I looked inside. It was a storeroom, much like the ground floor of Darquine's headquarters. There were rows upon rows of high racks packed with goods I couldn't immediately identify.

Then I heard the sound of wings, many wings, beating the air and coming closer.

'Danger!' Lothi-Mo said. 'Many many danger!'

'I'll have a look.' I shielded up and turned to the door.

'*Wait!*' Lothi-Mo called, but I was confident in the strength of my force field as I walked into the first cave.

'*Come back,*' Lothi-Mo urged. '*Danger!*'

Before I could react, a mass of winged creatures the size of rabbits dove at me.

'*Bats!*' I thought and the next moment they all crashed into my shield. Being bumped by a rabbit-sized bat or two wouldn't be dangerous, but five dozen all at once was like being hit by a rockfall and I went down beneath them. My shield held, so they couldn't get at me with their pointy teeth and taloned claws. Inside, I was protected... and helpless. No spell worked through the field around me; I couldn't fight back, so the monsters kicked me criss-cross over the floor while I bounced around inside my big ball.

It wasn't funny at all and it wasn't painless either. It was curst scary, and I couldn't do a thing inside the shield but scream. So guess what I did? Yes – well, am I supposed to be a hero? I rolled over that big storeroom, bumping into storage racks, with a mass of biting, drooling little monsters all trying to get at me.

Then I saw Kellani move into the room, unshielded, her hands outstretched, and Amaj with his troop right behind her, their swords at the ready.

Seconds later, a violent blast of energy splattered off my shield. Instant death, had the spell failed, but it didn't. Only the glare blinded me with a universe of suns and I screamed a bit more. Around me, the buffeting stopped as the monsters charred and smoked all over me. *Calm down*, my magic lower mind said. *Calm down, idiot!* Slowly, my body obeyed and my muscles relaxed. I saw Naudin's bees fighting the last bats and Lothi-Mo among them, all in a soundless scene, for inside my shield nothing worked but my vision.

Kellani came running, straight at me. She dropped to her knees beside me.

'All clear,' she mouthed. 'Open up.'

I dissolved my shield and clung to her arms. I cried and she held me close. Funny that nobody laughed.

Then I cursed, wiped the snot from my face, and stumbled to my feet.

'Warned you,' Lothi-Mo scolded me, wrapping her tail tightly round my neck. 'Should have waited, silly boy. Would have told more.'

'Next time,' I promised, hugging her. 'What the heck where those monsters?'

'Make-belief bats,' Naudin said, patting my shoulder awkwardly. 'Some illusion spell – when the last one died, the bodies all disappeared. It's probably a burglar defense.'

'Burglars!' I exploded. 'It flippin' worked, too!' I blew my blood-clotted nose empty. 'Darn, I've never been so helpless in my life.'

'It would make a handy spell,' he said, deep in thought. 'I wonder, if I made my bees bigger...'

I took a deep breath. 'Well, the place isn't undefended. Sorry, all, I was overconfident.'

'You looked like a hare among a pack of wolves,' Amaj said. 'Y'all right?'

I grunted. Now the shock had passed, I even felt ashamed. That was no way for the Defender of Bodrus to behave! 'Yeah, in a day's work and all that.'

Amaj frowned. 'I suggest we stay alert, keep together and check everything funny.'

Jornyll walked up to him and looked the lordling over.

'What's that?' Amaj said distrustfully.

'Check everything funny, you said.' Jornyll jumped out of the way before Amaj's fist could hit his nose.

That bit of silliness broke the strain, and we laughed as we went on, weapons at the ready.

At the entrance to the next hall, Lothi-Mo chirped a warning. 'Wait! Danger hiding. Ulaa-danger.'

I froze first of them all.

The young engineer joined her at the door. 'What is it?'

'Look at door post,' Lothi-Mo said. 'Me feel energy, but don't understand. Not wyrm things.'

Ulaataq stopped a few paces from the door. We all waited while he studied everything. 'Gimme a blade,' he said finally.

Without a word, Jornyll handed him his sword.

Ulaataq walked forward and drew the weapon along the doorpost. Lightning flashed and a pungent smell assaulted our nostrils.

'If I'm right...' he muttered, and walked through the door. Nothing happened.

'Of course I was right,' he said, satisfied. 'Look closer, all of you.'

He pointed with the sword at a small hole in the doorpost, about a foot above the ground. 'See that? On the opposite side is another one. They're eyes – mechanical ones, not real or magical. When you walk past them, they see you. Then they make a deadly beam between them. I used the sword to break the beam and the eyes died.'

'Fine,' Amaj said. He looked at his little army. 'Seen it, guys? We'll go first and check every door we pass. You find any eyes, call out. Can we go in now, engineer?'

We walked on, through a second enormous storeroom.

'Poor Shaw,' Naudin said, gazing at the stocked shelves. 'She won't get all this stuff counted in a hurry.'

I shrugged. 'We'll all help.'

We found several more of those eyes and Amaj's troop made a sport of blowing every one of them. In total there were five halls filled with goods we might be able to trade and the sixth was a large workroom.

'Well,' Ulaataq said dreamily, staring at gadgets I didn't even recognize. 'Well, well, well. If you need me, I'll be here.'

'Not now you won't,' I said. 'All seems safe, but there will be more places to search.'

We went back to the entry hall and opened the door to the right.

'That's my department,' Amaj said. 'Guardroom. I wondered if they would have had any guards for this place.'

'Be wary,' Lothi-Mo said suddenly.

I looked around at the desk, the benches, the empty weapon racks. 'Do you feel anything?'

'Do, know not what,' she chirped. 'Walk small steps. Something lurks.'

Amaj stiffened. 'Best be careful, mates,' he said to his troop. 'You ain't got no shields.'

The next room was an armory, with racks full of old-fashioned swords, axes, and halberds lining an indoor training ground.

From the ceiling hung two enormous, whitish sacks, fastened to the walls with arm-thick ropes.

'What would those be?' Jornyll said. 'Storage bags?'

'It moved,' Amaj said. 'I saw it twitch.'

'It *does* move,' Aya said. 'Let's pull back a bit and see what happens.'

'Gods!' Bamson yelled, pointing. One of the sacks had torn, and a mass of writhing legs ripped it further and further open. Then, with a hideous sucking noise, a giant larva dropped down before us.

Kellani threw a beam of fire at the monster, but it splattered harmlessly off its hairy body.

'Another one!' Jornyll yelled, as the second sack expelled another monstrosity.

I stared at them, at the same time disgusted and fascinated. They were big, with sucking jaws, a thousand feet, and bright green hair all over their segmented bodies.

'At them!' Amaj shouted, and his little troop attacked the monsters. Kellani sprang forward to help them, but after only a few fruitless swings she turned to me. 'Our blades don't hurt them either!'

'Think of the fishbeasts,' Teodar's voice said unexpectedly. Now I knew he had been watching me making a fool of myself.

Fishbeast... Those parasite monsters I'd fought on the *Tipred*–they'd been some kind of undead. I made a trident out of thin air and whirled around to the first monster.

The larva towered over me, each hair on its body twisting as some loathsome snake. I ran up to it and struck, aiming at its head. It reared up, and my spear entered its body, causing green goo to gush from its patchy skin. Its many feet made a trampling sound that trembled through the floor, as it twisted its body around and with its hind end swept Amaj and Jornyll off their feet like bowling pins.

'Take cover!' I screamed, without looking at them – like that day on the *Tipred*, I entered a world of my own, in which I danced and swung at the two undulating bodies, getting splattered with their bright green blood.

The larvae pursed their disgusting mouths and tried to grab me with their two pincher-like horns, but I outran the monsters two feet to a hundred, and the more I damaged them, the slower they became. I struck, and struck, without sense of time or body.

Jumping, I felt my spear cut open a swathe of skin, and one of the monsters twitched wildly, curled up, and exploded in a stinking mess of slime. Faraway, I heard someone cheering, but I was dancing and stabbing in a dream. Hours? Days? An eternity – then the second one reared up and exploded all over me.

I let my trident dissolve and turned to the others. Gods, they all stared at me as if I were some hero, not a guy who screamed at a few bats.

'Darnation,' Jornyll said, wiping his face with a dirty hand. 'I never saw a thing like that! How you fought those big monsters! I won't match that in a million years.'

Amaj slapped his shoulder. 'You'd need to be a god's defender for that, mate.'

'They weren't a spell,' Naudin said, looking troubled. 'I would have noticed.'

'Are you sure?' I said. 'A summoning spell wouldn't leave a trace. They were undead.' I shivered and gave a shaky laugh. 'Like that octicalvo I told you about. Those fishbeasts couldn't dance either.'

With the larvae and a few more eyes in the doorposts gone, we had exhausted the keep's defenses, and we could examine its treasures at our leisure.

And there were treasures in abundance. We didn't find a trace of the previous owners, but wherever they'd gone to, they had left a fully stocked establishment behind. Grain, beans, and peas, small cheeses, fruits, and even fish were as fresh as the day the shields had gone up.

The armory was filled with heavy, old-fashioned weaponry and armor, there was a small library stocked with leather-bound books – great had we been able to read the lingo – and we even found a cave full of carts, with everything in stock but the draft animals.

To the side of the central common room was a small four-room apartment, furnished in the same style as the cafeteria and the dorms – making me remember what I'd seen in the ancient ruins of Atnortod. The walls were lined with blindingly white marble, inlaid with mosaic murals of places long gone. Most of the furniture was brass, except for the wooden desk and some comfortable chairs. It was a promise of privacy and I wanted it very much for my own. I glanced at Kellani.

'There's no tower here,' she said. 'Will these rooms do for you?'

'They'll have to,' I said with a great show of nonchalance that didn't fool her for a moment.

All the apartment doors were unlocked but one. It rang solid as Jornyll knocked on it.

'Metal door,' he muttered and went straight to the nightstand beside the bed to check the drawers. 'Gotcha! People are all the same.' He returned with a big key in his hands.

'Have you been a burglar?' I asked, surprised.

He shook his head. 'Not me, I'm too impatient. But there were one or two Clammers walking that road and I listened to their tales.' He smiled. 'They left two years ago; none of the present crowd was that soph... What's the word?'

'Sophisticated?' Naudin guessed.

Jornyll grinned. 'Yeah. I knew it was something with fish.' At his touch, the door opened to a dark room. Quickly he inspected the doorposts for those treacherous eyes, but there weren't any.

'It's all yours,' he said.

I stepped over the threshold, and froze as the lights flashed on.

'Mountain's Breath...' There was enough gold stacked away here to buy a small kingdom. Barrels filled with solid, fat coins, all bearing the same head of Wrachazd, Jem's grandfather the lich king, and there were stacks of bullion in gold and silver.

Naudin whistled. 'There's Nanstalgarod for you; those guys were awash in gold.'

Kellani snorted. 'They dug up their whole country, plundered its riches and thought to coax three harvests a year from what remained. That's why the sand came.'

'We didn't dig for gold,' Jem said. She'd been studying the backs of the fat volumes lining the shelves on the wall behind the desk. 'Gold wasn't anything special; it was the cheapest metal in the land and there was plenty of it. Iron, *that* was precious, and we never found enough, however deep we dug.'

'To us gold is precious,' I said. 'This will be our national treasury.'

'No eight-eighth?' Kellani said, grinning.

'That wouldn't be a good idea,' I said. 'There will be a nice bonus for every one of us, but this gold and the whole keep are the property of the Pasandir Peaks.'

'Sure,' she said. 'I was only joking.'

'It's far too much money to share out,' Naudin said. 'You would ruin those kids.'

'That's what you say,' Jornyll retorted. 'You were born rich.'

'Not that I noticed,' Naudin said. 'No tripping over servants, had to clean my own room, just plain three course meals, some silver for pocket money, that's all. Ask Wylmer; *he* knows. He's happier with the bit of prize money he earned with us than with the fat allowance his father would have given him.'

'Darn, it would be fun to be rich.' Jornyll shrugged. 'I suppose you're right. A *nice* bonus?'

Shaw was shaking when she came back from inspecting the storerooms.

'What's wrong?' I said as she grabbed my arms.

'Nothing,' she said, her voice thick with emotion. 'It's... it's all so *big*. So beautifully big. Those stores... All the carts are there, we only need camels and drivers.' She looked at me, her face taut. 'Can we do it? Go trading like those people who were here before?'

'I think we should,' I said. 'It is the best way for the country to stay in contact with all villages and castles.'

She stood motionless, staring at a point behind me. 'I knew it,' she whispered. 'I knew I was doing the right thing, choosing you instead of Darquine. We will make it!' She looked at me. 'I must have Nate here. He has to help me; this is too big for one girl.'

'He'll come with the others,' I said. 'For now, young Brat will assist you; I need a place for him and he's quick and clever.'

Shaw suddenly grinned. 'He's strange. But I guess we all are.'

That evening after our first meal in our new stronghold, we came together in the keep office.

I must have looked very strange in my cheap tunic behind that big boss desk, with my iron hand resting on the fine desktop, for I saw Shaw glancing at me and trying to hide a smile.

'Well?' I said, looking around at their faces. 'What do you think?'

'Great,' Naudin said immediately. 'Jem's people had a lot of faults, but they didn't think small. I wonder what happened to them.'

'The whole place is empty of memories,' I said. 'Those ruins in Atnortod were full of them, but here I sense nothing. Still, they were careful people who kept records, so we know more or less what happened.' I opened the fat, leather-bound book before me on the table. 'Perhaps Jem will read the last page to you.'

'The day we feared has come. The king has summoned us home. We are to destroy the merchandise and stocks, blow up the entire stronghold, then sail for Atnortod and the Ritual of Ending,' Jem's voice was rock-steady and her eyes were full of remembered hatred as she read.

'Our hearts are heavy; we had so much success here. This must be a mistake. His Majesty's advisors must have misunderstood. To end it now, while we could feed all of Atnortod for years to come would be a waste. We will convince His Majesty to reverse his decision. The glory of Nanstalgarod will not die thus!

'Today we sail for the King's palace. We cannot in all consciousness destroy what we built here. In case the locals think to rob us, we will put the keep on lock-down, to await our return with His Majesty's blessing. May the Gods grant us his favor as they have done in the past.'

Jem drifted slowly up as if she wanted to distance herself from the open book.

'They were fools,' she said in a hard voice. 'Grandfather wasn't interested in their food. He didn't care to keep his people alive. Not he! Grandfather wanted everybody to die, so he could go on with his plans.' She gave a dry sob. 'I don't know what happened to the Smalkandars. I suppose Grandfather had them killed and their gifts of food burned.'

She looked at us. 'Don't say it, I know; he was mad.'

'At least it explains why we found no bodies here.' I closed the book and put it back on the shelf behind the trade lord's desk. There was a whole row of them, describing centuries of merchantry.

I saw Shaw staring at the shelf.

'Darn, I would love to read them,' she said.

'They weren't the only treasures Jem and I had found in the office,' I went on. 'There's a map with all settlements in the Peaks, though the data is five centuries old at least. Shelves full of ledgers with notes on every item they ever bought and sold, so you won't have to count everything anew.'

Shaw was almost jumping up and down with excitement. I knew how much trade meant to her, and this place must feel like a dream come true.

'It is enormous,' Kellani said. 'The most perfect base for pirate hunters imaginable.'

'With this, do we need Zanadur Keep?' I asked.

'I do,' Amaj said firmly. 'This is all very grand, but it's not Ma'aweshi. I want a keep of my people.'

'I agree with him,' Jem said. 'This would never be his place.'

I understood; Smalkand was very much a Nanstalgarod affair. Amaj wanted a keep of his own. His half-brother had Kalbakar, and Amaj wasn't going to be left behind. He knew Smalkand would never be his; it was too rich, too important for the Peaks to give it to a lord.

I held out a hand. 'I promised Zanadur, and I'll not go back on that. We'll go for all of them. We'll open Zanadur when we have kicked the lich out. For the moment, I need you here, Amaj.'

'I know,' he said, accepting my hand. 'I'll not run out on you either.'

'Now to the big questions. Do we get the others here from Fort Jamril?'

'Yes!' Shaw snapped. 'I need Nate here.'

The others laughed at her, but she lifted her chin. 'Well, I do need him,' she said defiantly.

'You'll get him,' Kellani said. 'I agree with Shaw; this place is perfect. It's not the tropics, but as a home this is much better.'

'You can always port groups of kids back to the fort for holidays,' Naudin said.

'Sure, let's start a travel service,' I said. 'If we all agree, I'll call the fort. You can all listen in.' I leaned back in my chair. *'Keena?'*

She answered immediately. *'Eskandar! We were getting worried.'*

'We had some trouble getting inside, but we're all set now. This place is useful. Were you kids doing anything tomorrow?'

'Nah, we had a big party planned, with wine and musicians from Towne, nothing special.'

I grinned. 'A pity, for tomorrow you will sail to join us here in the wilderness.'

'Oh joy!' she said coolly. 'All right, we'll postpone the party. We weren't really, of course. I'll tell Abia it's on. We packed most of our stuff, so we can leave at sunup. How's the weather with you?'

'Fine. No tropics, but far better than Seatome. Tell the others we long to see them; we've got a lot of work to do here.'

'Oops,' Keena said. 'Is it that much of a mess?'

'Well, it's been deserted for five hundred years,' I said.

'Oh, gods. Well, we had it nice while it lasted...'

'You beast, Eskandar!' I caught Shaw whispering. 'Making those kids think we're living in some hole here.' I winked at her and she blushed darkly.

'Go have a final swim, Keena,' he said. 'The only ones swimming here are the penguins. See you in a week's time.'

'You were kidding her, the water ain't that cold,' Aya said. 'Actually it's rather warm.'

'I remember something about hot springs keeping the bay free of ice even in winter,' Jem said.

'I hadn't thought of that,' I said, startled. 'Excellent! We wouldn't want our ships having to spend those months in Port Naar.'

CHAPTER 8 – SPIES?

'Watch out what you're doing, dimwit!' Jornyll said sharply, when Bamson narrowly missed his legs, swinging a heavy bench around. They were tidying up the common room and this was the third time his former boss had pulled the same stunt.

'Shut up, *kid*!' Bamson shouted, flushing darkly in sudden anger. 'I'm boss, not you.' He put the bench down and turned to Jornyll, shoulders hunched and fists balled.

'Don't you *kid* me, fathead,' Jornyll said, and his heart sped up in anticipation. 'I could've taken that boss-title away from you any moment these last years.'

'Yeah,' Bamson sneered, sticking his nose almost into Jornyll's face. 'You wish you could, kid. I can beat you anytime.'

'Your mouth always was the biggest part of you.' Jornyll gave the other boy a mocking grin. 'You're a lazy, slow no-good slug. A pig would've been a better boss 'n you.'

Bamson swung a fist, and Jornyll ducked.

Amaj interfered. 'No fighting inside.'

Bamson jerked his head. 'Outside, punk.'

Jornyll laughed. For three years he'd let that nitwit play at leader. He'd turned his back, shrugged off the sneers and taunts, and now there was going to be a reckoning. 'Come, then.' He was sure he could take the looby. Bamson was a tad bigger and heavier, but he was out of condition. Even now Jornyll heard him breathing as they ran. The lazybones had been boss too long, letting the younger kids do the work. Well, Jornyll thought, *he* had been exercising. And fighting several battles to boot.

'Here,' he said, as they came to a grassy stretch inside the copse. 'No one will see you fail, slob.'

Bamson's color heightened. He yanked off his shirt and flexed his muscles.

'I'll slob you, kid,' he said darkly. 'Slob you all over the place.'

Jornyll threw his uniform tunic aside. 'Don't blab so much, fatso,' he said. He slapped his hands together. 'Come on; show me you're not all talk.'

Bamson stepped forward and threw a fist. Jornyll chuckled as he evaded the blow and answered with a few quick feints. Then they grappled, hands around each other's necks. They swayed, moving over the grass as they sought to unbalance each other. Suddenly Bamson kicked Jornyll's shin. Painfully.

Jornyll cursed. 'Is that how it's gonna be?' he said softly. 'All right.' He moved like Amaj had shown him, gripping Bamson's right arm and twisting. The bigger boy cried out and tried to pull back. Jornyll's other hand went to his opponent's throat, his foot blocked the boy's legs, and Bamson crashed down.

Jornyll dove on top of him, and for a few minutes they wrestled. Then Jornyll got an arm around Bamson's neck and squeezed. Bamson gargled and his gray skin slowly turned dark as he fought for air. Desperate hands tugged at Jornyll's shoulders, but the boy gritted his teeth and kept the pressure on.

Then, suddenly, a nearby movement caught his eyes. Someone was watching them. Strangers. Two strange guys, hiding in the shrubbery.

He lowered his head to Bamson's ear. 'I won,' he whispered. He relaxed his grip a little, so the other could breathe again. 'Don't speak. There's two kids spying on us; strange kids, right ahead. I'm goin' to let you go and try to catch one. If you're really a tough guy, go after the other. Got it?'

Bamson coughed and nodded.

Jornyll tensed his muscles. Then he roared and sprang toward the bushes.

A cry rent the air; he grabbed a wiry arm and had to fight for his life. The kid was a darned tiger! Twisting and biting, using every muscle in his body, the strange boy fought like a maniac.

'Bamson, help me,' Jornyll gasped, trying to keep the stranger from strangling him.

The former boss hurried up and drew his arms around the unknown boy's torso.

Then, like a flash, a second boy joined the battle, fighting with the same fierce determination. For a while it looked like they'd be ignominiously beaten.

Jornyll relaxed and as his opponent thought to press his advance, he caught the first boy's torso between his legs in a scissor-like lock and squeezed. For a moment longer, the stranger tried to break out, but then he cried, 'Stop!'

'You give up?' Jornyll panted, without letting go. 'And the other guy too?'

'Yes! Yes! Howy, stop.'

The other boy grunted and let go of Bamson. The former boss had a nosebleed and a puffy eye, and he breathed like a steamcart as he came to his knees.

Jornyll relaxed his grip. 'Shall we talk this over?' he said. 'Who the heck are you guys?'

His opponent rolled away and sat up. He rattled, spat and wiped his running nose with a bare arm.

'We live up there,' he said in an accent that was strangely familiar to Jornyll's ears. He was of their age, thin and wiry, with fiery red hair to his shoulders. He looked terribly filthy, clad in an old, overlarge jack without sleeves and pants cut off at the knees. 'Bout five miles away.'

Then Jornyll recognized the accent, it was a rougher version of how Amaj spoke. Must be a Peak thing, he thought.

'Where?' he said. 'What's there then? A village? A farm?'

'A keep,' the boy said. 'Pashwend; and the village of Pash.'

'Why were you spying on us?' Bamson said, scowling.

'We weren't spying!' the second boy said angrily. He was taller, and muscled where the other was sinewy, with a skin the color of a copper penny and a nose like a gull's beak. His scalp was a mass of wavy hair and a scar on his cheek gave him a mean look.

'We really weren't.' The first boy bit his lip. Then he nodded once. 'I'll tell ya.'

The second boy gripped his friend's arm. 'You sure?'

'That's wot the plan was, weren't it?' the first retorted. 'We need help.' He blew his nose on his fingers. 'Our keep – them bullies stole it.'

'What bullies?' Jornyll said.

'Robbers,' the second boy said.

'Yeah.' The first boy nodded. 'For as long as I lived they've been lording it over us. Having our village feed them, having our women bed them.' He grinned suddenly. 'Giving me a brother like Howy.'

Jornyll looked the taller boy over. 'You a robber's son?'

The boy snorted. 'One of them; don't know who though.' He stuck out his chin. 'Problem with it?'

Jornyll shrugged. 'Not if you don't side with them, no. Only those robbers bother me.'

'He doesn't,' the first boy said. 'We hate the bloowits. Course I don't know life without them spoiling the place. But our mother told us how it was when me father still lived; how happy she was and not afraid.' He pulled a face. '*I'm* not afraid, but not happy either. We talked, Howy and me, an' we decided we had to get rid of those robbers.'

Jornyll found nothing strange in that thought. 'How?'

The first boy turned his eyes on Jornyll. They were hard and black, like Amaj's looked when he was angry.

'We need help,' he said. 'That's why we were watching you. I needed to know if you are friends or more foes.'

'And if you're not foes, we wanted to warn you. Them robbers sent out a raiding party,' the second boy said. 'We dunno whereto, but your folks should know.'

'We'll warn them,' Jornyll said.

The first boy grinned. 'You don' seem enemies, so who are you? This beach's been deserted for ages. You got no ship; did you drop from the sky?'

Jornyll glanced at Bamson, but the slob's face told him he was way out of his depth; no help there. 'I can't say much,' he said. 'It's for the wyrmcaller to decide what to tell you. If we call someone else to join us, would you run or stay?'

The first boy scowled. 'If they come unarmed, we'd stay.'

Jornyll looked at Bamson. 'Hurry back and tell Amaj.'

Bamson swallowed and nodded. He came to his feet and ran a bit unsteadily to the cave, pulling on his shirt as he went.

'Those caves are closed,' the first boy said noncommittally.

'No longer,' Jornyll said. 'That much I can tell you.'

'Why were you guys fighting?' the second boy said.

Jornyll grinned. 'He needed things explained to him.'

'You have some nasty tricks,' the first boy said.

'I'm training to be a fighter,' Jornyll said, and he picked up his uniform tunic. 'Sword, spear, and hand-to-hand. You two nearly won though.'

'Nearly ain't enough,' the first boy said. He held out his hand. 'Me name's Razoon. My brother is Howy.'

'I'm Jornyll, and the other guy is Bamson.'

Soon, the former boss came trotting back, his face wet with sweat.

'He's gone!' he managed to say. 'Enemies sighted; all the fighters just left.'

Jornyll cursed. 'Without me!' he cried. 'Darn, I'm missing a battle!'

'They must've seen the raider party. Your people gonna fight them?' Razoon said unbelievingly. 'Why?'

'Because that's what we do with robbers and such,' Jornyll said. 'We're the Pasandir Peak Armed Forces.'

Razoon closed his mouth with a snap. 'Yer whot?'

Jornyll shook his head. 'Later. You two come to our keep. My boss will shoot me if I let you walk away now.' He grinned. 'Don't worry, we're friends. You came to the best place in the world for help, guys.'

CHAPTER 9 – TEACHING A BROOMRIDER

'Barbarians,' Naudin said disdainfully as we saw Jornyll and his former boss storm away. 'Why don't we stop them and discuss it?'

I shrugged. Bamson didn't strike me as a talk-it-over type. I was fairly certain Jornyll could take him, and to lose a fight would help Bamson settle in. 'This once, let them fight it out the Clammer way. They won't murder each other.'

We walked into the entry hall, basking in the light of the sun. Here we found Sylas in his riding chair, staring after the two running boys. He hadn't seen us, and the wishful look on his face was painful to watch.

I turned to Naudin. 'Go get me another broom, will ya.'

Naudin looked from me to Sylas. 'Sure, great idea!' He got his broomstick from his back and shot away.

'Hi,' I said, walking out.

'What's with those guys?' Sylas said. 'Are they finally going to have their boss fight?'

'Yeah, finally is the word.' I drew my own broom from its sheath. 'Ever tried one of these?'

'Don't think I can,' Sylas said. 'Na'a is working on my upper leg muscles, but I can't use them yet.'

'You don't need them,' I said. 'I should have thought of this sooner. The broom keeps you upright. Its spell was designed for war, and wounded soldiers had to use it too.'

I shoved my broom between the legs of his riding chair.

'Move forward and sit in the middle of the handle. Don't worry, you'll not fall.'

'I'm not scared of falling,' he said grimly.

'I know,' I said. 'Just do it.'

Sylas lifted himself up on his arms and slid off the seat of his chair. As the broom's invisible harness caught him, he gasped.

'I can sit!' he exclaimed.

I grinned at his surprise. 'It's a good spell. Now listen. There are only a few commands, but you won't want to mix them up. The first one is "forward"; that will move you along. You can specify what you want—forward slow, forward fast. Now choose "forward slow".'

'Forward slow,' Sylas said softly and obediently, the broom moved away from the entrance.

'Second command is "stop",' I added as I hurried to keep up with him.

'Stop,' he said. His face was strained, but not from fear.

'Next is "up",' I said. 'Try it.'

He rose and when he was at shoulder-height to me, he said, 'Stop.'

'Very good!' I said as he hung motionless. 'Now "Down".'

He repeated the command and sank until his stumps touched the ground.

Then Naudin returned, waving another broom like a spear.

'You've done it!' he said as he came to a halt beside Sylas. 'Welcome to the Pasandir broomriders.' He handed me the broomstick.

Quickly I spoke the spell and joined them. *'Lothi-Mo,'* I said. *'Wanna fly a bit, dear heart?'*

'Wyrms fly,' she tweeted.

I gave Sylas the next commands and let him try them.

As he flew in circles with Naudin, I called Kellani. *'Naudin and I will be out a while,'* I said. *'We're teaching Sylas to ride a broomstick.'*

'You're what? Hey! He can do that! Right, good luck.'

I hurried after the other two, watching Sylas' face surreptitiously. He looked caught in silent ecstasy as he zigzagged over the field, narrowly clearing an ancient stone wall and leap-frogging over some low flowering bushes.

'How does it feel?' I said. I saw him start, so I knew he had heard me. He had no magic, but I could mindspeak him more or less over short distances. *'I'm doing the talking, you just think your answers; all right?'*

'*Crazy this,*' Sylas said. '*I'm flying!*'

'*You're brooming,*' Lothi-Mo said. '*Wyrms fly. Sylas brooms very well, too. Good, good!*' She flashed down from whatever she'd been doing on Wyrm Ridge, and took up position beside the boy.

'*Let's have a look around,*' I said. I rose up to a hundred feet over the lake and the others followed. I skirted around the bay, noting in passing how clear the water was. Then I led them over the trees of the copse to the mountains beyond. That was new territory; none of us had had time to scout around yet.

'*Is that a path?*' Naudin said, pointing ahead.

Without a word, Sylas spurted forward, racing toward the towering wall of rock that was the foot of the Peaks.

Darn, I thought. *He's got it already.*

'*First flight euphoria,*' Naudin said with a chuckle in his mental voice. '*He's quick.*'

'*Lothi-Mo, stay with him, dear,*' I said.

'Whoopee!' she cried and winged away after Sylas. I knew she'd overtake him; no broom was fast enough to leave her behind.

When we came closer, there was indeed a stony trail leading from the bay valley to a forested plateau some ninety feet higher. Here the path turned both left and right, wandering out of sight between the trees. We saw Sylas hesitate for a moment before he turned left and disappeared into the forest.

We followed him and soon found him hovering in the shadowy crown of a large oak, with Lothi-Mo perched on a branch over his head.

Sylas held a finger to his lips as we joined him, and nodded toward the forest floor. Through the trees we looked upon an open spot with a small lake, and there a group of men lounged.

'*Wastrels!*' Naudin said, his thoughts dripping with disgust.

CHAPTER 10 – RESCUE OPERATION

I stiffened at his mindspoken words. Wastrels, the murderous robbers of the Hellesands desert, who had attacked Lyster's reclaimer camp when we were there. Wastrels, who had killed my parents when I was a little child. I felt a shiver of hatred run down my spine.

'Careful!' Sylas whispered. 'They've got prisoners.' He pointed and then I saw two small figures sitting, with their hands tied to their backs and their mouths gagged.

'Kellani!' I called on the thin line she and I used for our private mindspeach. *'Trouble.'*

She answered immediately. *'What's wrong?'*

'Wastrels. Eight of them, with two prisoners. Get our fighters and wait for me. I'm porting in.' I turned to Lothi-Mo, Naudin, and Sylas. *'Stay here; don't do anything. I'll go get the others. Be right back.'* Then I ported, broom and all. I'd never done that while flying, but it was nothing; I came out where I aimed for, only at an oak-height above the ground.

As I rushed into the keep, Kellani met me with Amaj, Aya, Zaotinq, and to my surprise, Averson. The trainee pilot carried a ten-pound sledgehammer, swinging it round like it weighed nothing. Then I remembered she'd been a miner, used to heavy equipment.

'Jornyll and Bamson aren't back yet,' Amaj said.

'Darn!' I said, for a moment forgetting I'd let them go off myself. 'I'll roast those fools when we're done. No time to fetch them; we'll go without.'

I explained what was going on. 'We'll destroy them,' I added harshly. 'Wastrels get no mercy. They're worse than pirates.'

I drew my spell around the group and ported back to the forest. We landed on the narrow trail, a row of tall shrubs away from the lake and the sounds of yelling voices and metal meeting metal.

'They're fighting,' Kellani said. 'At them!'

Followed by the others, she rushed down the path. I steered my broom to the open spot and saw Lothi-Mo diving round, snapping and clawing at the Wastrels. Naudin's illusionary bees swarmed among them, stinging where they could.

A big man in long, flowing robes waved a scimitar at Sylas. He had the strange eyes of his people, deeply sunk in the face, with remarkably long eyelashes, possibly as protection against their desert sun. His long hair and beard were curly, and interwoven with colorful beads, not unlike the costly jewels the men of Nanstalgarod wore in their murals.

Sylas had picked up a branch somewhere and tried to hit the man while circling over his head.

Kellani's broomrider battle cry caused a shock, and several Wastrels rushed to intercept her. Amaj darted past and buried his sword between an opponent's ribs, oblivious to the blood spattering over his armor. Beside him, Zaotinq shouted something in Qoori as he jumped over Amaj's fallen victim and planted his sword in a yelling face. A Wastrel ran at me, swinging his blade. My fist of air stopped him in his tracks, and my hook slashed his face open. Screaming, he ran until my second wind slammed him over the edge of the ledge into the bay valley ninety feet below. On the other side of the road, Averson swung her sledgehammer and broke a fat man's collarbone. I heard her curse, and she whirled the heavy maul again. This time, the man went down. One bandit hitched up his desert robe to his waist and ran. But Sylas cut off his escape route and Aya's well-sharpened twohander sword removed the Wastrel's legs as if it were a scythe cutting down wheat.

Sylas laughed a little hysterical. 'Poetic vengeance,' he shouted.

Aya shrugged. 'He'll be dead in seconds.'

Kellani plucked the last Wastrel off the ground, swung him round by the ankles and bashed him against a tree. A rain of branches, leaves and some bird's nest rattled down on the Wastrel's body as she dropped him.

'Done,' the broomer said, and so we were.

I landed beside the prisoners, who'd been watching the fight with scared eyes, unable to run or even to scream.

I smiled at them and removed their gags. The boy gasped and took a deep breath, while the girl stared at me in silence, as if she couldn't believe we were real.

Then I drew my knife and started on the ropes that bound their hands.

'Who're you?' the boy said in a high voice. He was about ten years old, with long dark hair and the red sheen to his gray skin that betrayed him for a Ma'aweshi.

'I'm Eskandar,' I said.

'You—you're not robbers,' the girl said, with a slight frown. She wore her white hair short and appeared the same age as the boy. 'You're not with those others.'

'Of course they're not,' the boy said impatiently. 'Else they wouldn't be killing them.'

'No, we're not with the robbers,' I said. 'We are the Pasandir Peaks Armed Forces.'

'There's no such thing,' the boy protested.

'There is,' I said. 'Now, can you two stand?'

Both scrambled to their feet.

'Of course we can,' the boy said.

'Excellent,' I said. I looked around at the Wastrels. 'Any survivors?'

Kellani snorted. 'None; those robbers die too easily. They're all footpads; there wasn't a true fighter among them.'

'What shall we do with the bodies?'

'Leave them,' the boy said, rubbing the rope marks on his wrists. 'The wolves will eat them. Two, three days and you won't find anything, my father says.'

'We've collected their gear and what they got in their pockets,' Sylas said. His broom looked like an armorer's stall loaded with swords, axes and even an expensive-looking pair of boots. 'They had very beautiful stuff.'

'Robbed from tombs in ancient ruins I'd say. Take everything to the office.' I grinned. 'Your first loot, Sylas. As I promised.' I looked at the two kids we'd freed. 'We better take you to our keep. We'll bring you home later.'

'What keep?' the boy demanded. 'There's us at High Morv, and the only other keep for miles around is the robbers' place.'

'I'll show you,' I said. 'Hop in front of me, boy. Naudin will take the girl.'

'How can you fly a broomstick?' the boy asked.

Instead of answering, I shot up and raced back over the trees. Against the wind, the boy screamed in glee, his long hair brushing my face.

'Wheeee!' he shouted as we dove from the heights down toward the keep. Then we landed on the grass.

'That's great!' he shouted. 'Can we do it again?'

I grinned. 'Not this time.' Then the others arrived around us. 'Let's get inside.'

When he saw the cave entrance, the boy seemed to realize where we were, for he gripped my arm. 'You can't go in there! The spooks have forbidden it.'

'Come,' I said. 'Welcome to Smalkand Keep, headquarters of the Pasandir Peaks Armed Forces.'

The boy opened his mouth but for once stayed silent as we entered the hallway.

Willow came hurrying up. 'Jornyll and Bamson returned with two other guys, strangers. They came from a robber keep, Jornyll said. They're waiting in the office.'

I stared at her. 'Guys from the robber keep,' I repeated. I took a deep breath. 'Naudin, you take those kids under your wing. Clean them, feed them, and put them to bed.'

'I'm not sleepy!' the boy said.

'You will be,' Naudin promised.

I smiled; those kids would sleep. Our Naudin wasn't a mindmage for nothing, after all. Then I grabbed Kellani's arm.

'Let's see what those two truants brought us.'

We hurried into the office. Jornyll and Bamson were sitting at the large meeting table, with two unknown boys finishing the last bits of a substantial meal.

One was a lean Ma'aweshi with bright red hair. The other, in spite of his shorter hair and beardless boy's face, looked so much like the robbers we'd just killed my still-heated blood began to boil again. But my brain caught no whiff of badness; only a massive anger mixed with distrust.

Jornyll jumped up as we entered. 'Did you win?'

'Without your mighty presence? Yes, we still managed to win,' Kellani said grimly.

'Good,' he said. 'I hate having missed it.' He glanced at Bamson, who sported a black eye and a swollen nose. 'We did have a little fight of our own instead.'

'Did you run into that raiding party?' the redheaded guy said, staring at both Kellani and me as if trying to see which of us was in charge. 'We were coming to warn you.'

There wasn't a falsehood in his thoughts, so I decided not to dig any deeper. 'Who are you?'

'He is Razoon,' Jornyll said quickly. 'The other is his brother Howy.'

'Brother? You're a Wastrel,' I said to the second boy and the last bits of my anger made it sound sharper than I intended.

His face flushed. 'Razoon and I have the same mother,' he said. 'Only the man who begat me was a robber. I don't know which one of them it is and mother refuses to tell me.'

I walked to the head of the table and sat down. 'We ran into this group of Wastrels by accident,' I said. 'They had two prisoners, children. We killed the Wastrels and freed the kids.' I pointed my hook at the two boys and let a little lightning crackle inside the curve. 'If you want our help, you're going to tell me all about yourself, why you came here, and why we should trust you.'

Razoon nodded. 'They kidnapped children?' He looked at Jornyll. 'I knew they were going nuts.' He pushed his plate away and put his fists on the table. 'Our keep is Pashwend. Top of the path to the ledge you go right; it's but a few miles.'

He stared at his hands as if collecting his thoughts. 'Them robbers have been with us all my life; they came when my mother was carrying me. We weren't a rich keep then, so we had only a few warriors, a walkover. When the mir fell, the remaining men surrendered.'

'Who was your mir?' I thought I knew, but I wanted to hear his answer.

'He was Razoon, like me; Mir of Pashwend.' Mir was the local word for lord—before the name for the keep lord, after the name for his sons and brothers.

'Does that mean you're related?' Kellani asked.

'Watch what you're telling them,' Howy said.

Razoon shrugged. 'We came here seeking help. What do we have to lose? He was my father; I'm Razoon Mir. The robbers don't know, else they would've killed me at birth. My mother pretended to be a servant, that kept me alive. The next year Howy was born.' He grinned at the other boy; it was clear the two were close.

'Yeah,' Howy said. 'Now I may look like those rotten dogs, but that only makes me hate them more.'

Razoon nodded, setting his long red hair swaying. 'For fifteen years them hounds have been lording it in our keep. Our village grows food for their table, whatever's left is barely enough to feed their own families.' He went on, a tale of woe that set my anger soaring.

When he was done, both boys sat back, watching me.

'I believe you,' I said, and they relaxed. 'Can you point out your keep on the map?'

Razoon walked to the map on the wall. 'Me mother taught me.' He trailed the lines with a dirty finger. 'We are here on the beach. The trail goes up there and then to the right,' he said. 'This little black dot is Pashwend.'

It was a few miles east of here, around twenty miles the other way from the spot we'd found the kids.

Kellani pointed a massive finger at the boys. 'Tell me all about your keep. How many Wastrels, how many others. Defenses, daily routine, the lot.'

That was her territory. I listened and filed every item away for later.

Suddenly I caught a word that set all of my mind's warning bells clamoring. 'Did you say ship?' I asked of Howy. 'What ship is this?'

The boy's brows furrowed. 'Dunno what ship. Every few months one comes into the bay. Then the robbers send a cart to the beach with all the loot they've gathered. They haggle with the sailors, get their bags of gold and return to the keep.'

Jornyll turned to Howy, his eyes narrowed. 'Any idea when the next ship would come?'

The two Pashwend boys looked at each other.

'No,' Razoon said slowly. 'They jest come.'

Jornyll grunted and looked at me. 'Should we fly a sea patrol?'

Kellani nodded. 'Good suggestion, mate. I'll arrange it with Amaj.'

'After we've settled with the Wastrels,' I said. 'Today we rest the troops and tomorrow we'll have a look-in on your keep.'

'You wanna take them on?' Howy said. 'All of them?'

'Wastrels killed my family and a lot of other good people beside yours,' I said bleakly. 'There's no place for them, not in the Peaks or anywhere else. We will take them on.'

Howy gripped his half brother's arm. 'It's gonna happen!' He turned to me. 'Gimme a blade, I want to fight too.'

'Have you ever used a weapon?' Kellani asked. 'Sword? Axe? Spear?'

'Axe,' Razoon said. 'Chopped stacks of wood high as the mountains, we did.'

'We've got battleaxes. First you need to wash. Jornyll, show them the warriors' dorm and the bathroom. Then ask Willow for suitable clothing.'

'Come to me when you're done,' Kellani added. 'I'll see to your axes.'

When they had left, I sat back and looked at Kellani. 'Jornyll earned his money today.'

'He's using his mind more than I thought he would.' Kellani put her fists on the table. 'Sea patrols. Darn, we need our ships here; we're getting shorthanded.'

CHAPTER 11 – HIGH MORV

After the evening meal, I went back to the office for some much-needed time to think and be alone, away from the world. With my feet on the desk, I closed my eyes. The brim of my straw hat, now more-or-less part of the Peaks uniform, rested on my nose as I let my thoughts run around until they would grow tired and settle down. Blessed silence enveloped me. No ceaseless voices, no questions, no decisions; just me and my thoughts.

The gods gave me perhaps half an hour, before Cenn came running into the office, tearing the silence to shreds with his feet and voice.

'Soldiers approaching,' he blurted. 'Aya said come.' His eyes were big. 'They're riding strange animals.'

'Soldiers?' I said, staring at him. 'Not Wastrels?'

The child shook his head. 'Aya said soldiers. They wear armor and carry long pointed sticks.'

Armored soldiers, would that be a search party for those children we freed? I put away all thoughts of solitude and stood up. I buckled on my broom and straightened my hat. 'Let's meet our visitors,' I said and put my good hand on Cenn's shoulder as we walked back to the world.

Inside the entrance hall, Amaj waited with his troop, while outside Aya spoke with seven ironclad men on tall, shaggy mounts. Strange beasts indeed, with haughty faces and two heavy humps on their backs.

The leader of the soldiers was a man with long dark hair and a green riding-cloak, smooth-shaven and fraught with anxiety.

'Good evening,' I said. 'Can I help you?'

'I'm looking for my children,' the leader said with barely contained rage. 'They went out this morning and disappeared. I will not rest before I see them returned.'

'And who might you be?' I asked. After all, he was the visitor, and supposed to introduce himself first.

The man straightened in the saddle. 'I'm Llothyr, lord of High Morv.'

I smiled. 'Welcome, I am Eskandar. We discovered a raider party of robbers today, up in the woods. We rode to do battle, as is our duty, and destroyed them. Your children are safe and well. They have been cleaned up and fed, and are asleep right now.'

'Bring them here,' the lord demanded, clasping his hand to his sword.

'If you'd care to come inside, I will have them woken up,' I said.

The lord stared beyond me at the cave as if only now realizing where he was. 'This place has been inaccessible for ages,' he said. 'The Old Ones' magical doors prevented all who tried from entering. How did you get in?'

'We knew the way,' I said. 'Welcome to Smalkand Keep, headquarters of the Pasandir Peaks Armed Forces.'

Like his son, Llothyr gave me an incredulous look. 'The *what*? There is no such thing, young man.'

I lifted my hook hand to the little earring I wore; Kambish's earring, which my parents had given me when I was a baby. As I touched it, lightning crackled, and several men muttered.

'I am Eskandar, son of Prahan, grandson of Kambish, Wyrmcaller of Kalbakar Keep and Wings of the Mountains,' I said. 'Bodrus the Sleeping God and the Kavid Jar have called on me to gather an army of youngsters to defend them from their enemies. These are the Pasandir Peak Armed Forces.'

As if to give himself time, the lord clacked his tongue and his mount sank through its legs till its body rested on the grass. Then he dismounted and turned to me.

'Forgive my surprise; I didn't know there still was a wyrmcaller left in the Peaks. And you claim the title of Wings?'

'I certainly do,' I said. 'The Kavid Jar chose me and Bodrus himself confirmed me.'

The lord shook his head as if to clear it. 'Again, forgive me. I find it difficult to accept.'

'Yet it is true.' Lothi-Mo winged down from the ridge over the entrance and hovered at my shoulder. Small as she was, she made an impressive sight with her taloned wings and sharp teeth, her multicolored skin sparkling in the setting sun. She appeared to dance in the air, craning her long neck as she looked at each of the men.

'I say he is the Defender of Bodrus, Wyrmcaller and friend,' she said. 'I am Lothi-Mo of the Royal Sept. I know.'

'A wyrmling? A royal wyrmling?' The lord lifted both hands to his chest, his face a mixture of wonder and shock. 'There hasn't been a wyrmling born for a long time and the old tales tell us there are no more wyrms to beget any.'

'Old tales! Old tales!' Lothi-Mo said testily. 'What are those but the fears of little men? I am here, and more will follow. Forget the tales, they teach only ignorance. You cannot doubt my presence, lord of High Morv.'

Darnation, I thought. How haughty she sounds! Of the Royal Sept, she said... I had never heard her use that term before.

The lord's face showed he believed her.

'Your pardon, Lady Lothi-Mo,' he said, bowing to her. "I do not doubt your words! Your coming brings hope and so does the Lord Wyrmcaller.' He made a curt gesture and his men dismounted.

'Let us step inside,' I said. 'We should talk, and your men could perhaps use some refreshments.' Their faces betrayed they wouldn't mind a drink or two.

Inside, the whole crew waited, ready to defend our new home.

'The lord of High Morv comes visiting to fetch his children,' I said. 'Carry on, all. Willow, would you have our young guests brought to him?' Then I introduced Kellani, Naudin, and Amaj, and led the way to the office.

The lord looked around as we walked. 'A most magnificent place,' he said. 'And not a ruin either.'

'Because it had been locked up for so long, everything inside was preserved until we came,' I said.

'Yet you are of our people, not of the old ones,' Lord Llothyr stated. He turned to his soldiers. 'You men wait in this hall while the first lance and I speak with the lord Eskandar.'

We went into the office, and Averson arrived with a tray of refreshments. I sat down and waited until all were served. Then one of our girls brought in the two children, still sleep-tousled and thick-eyed.

'Father!' the boy cried, and ran to the man. 'You have come for us?'

'My children,' the man said, catching them in his arms, pent-up anxiety clear in his face. 'Are you well?'

'We are,' the girl said with a remarkable display of composure. 'The boys and girls in this keep are very nice. We were ambushed by robbers, Father. Those beasts were taking us to their keep, but then the wyrmcaller and his people arrived and killed them all.'

'It was a great fight!' her brother shouted. 'Lots of blood. They can fly, Father. They fly on broomsticks. One of them had no legs, but he could fly as well. I want to fly, too.'

'They have a little wyrm,' the girl said. 'It can speak and it fought with them.'

'And a very great wyrm she is,' Llothyr said. 'A royal wyrmling the world hasn't seen for ages.'

Then he turned to me. 'One of my scouts charged with watching the robber keep saw you arrive in your flying boat. We had seen ships before, but never one that could sail the air and if he hadn't been a well-trusted, steady man, I wouldn't have believed him.'

He hesitated. 'I supposed you had come to meet with the robbers. They and we always ignored each other, so I was prepared to do the same now. When my children disappeared, my first idea was to search here, as you were the unknown factor. When we found the dead robbers beside the trail I didn't know what to believe anymore. Then I came here and saw only...' He stopped, looking embarrassed.

'Only children,' I said, and I couldn't help but grin. 'So we are. Yet we are a proven army, too. Let me tell you our story.'

I didn't go into too many details. I spoke of my wandering years, of madmen and pirates threatening the Kavid Jar, my inheritance as wyrmcaller and being named Wings of the Mountains by Bodrus himself. I spoke of Lothi-Mo, who lay in my lap with her head resting on the edge of the table. I only mentioned the prophecy of a children's army and told a little of our battle at Kalbakar. Then I explained the kidnapped orphans, our capturing the *Marigold* and the *Drakon* and finally of our intention to hunt the pirates around here and search for their base Angsthafn.

While I spoke I watched the faces of my audience. The boy listened raptly, no doubt filled with visions of glory. His father remembered the old tales and wondered what my presence would mean for High Morv. The girl's face had turned inward, as if she heard things that touched her personally.

'The girl is listening to our thoughts,' Kellani said. *'I just spoke to Jem, and I think she heard me.'*

I saw a dark blush creep into the girl's cheeks. *'You do hear, don't you?'* I said.

'No...' she whispered. *'I mustn't.'*

'Do you have anyone with magic at High Morv, Lord Llothyr?' I asked.

'No,' he said curtly. 'Magic is bad, it...' Then he stopped and stared at me. 'Your pardon,' he said, 'I didn't mean...'

I nodded. 'You have forgotten. Magic is necessary to survive. We are facing very powerful enemies. We need magic users as much as we need soldiers. Without them, your keep is defenseless as the least cottage. Then there is another thing; magic must never be suppressed. It needs out, it needs to be used, trained. To hide it results in madness and great danger for all. Lady Kellani is a broomrider. One of her duties is to discover just these wild talents and bring them in for training.'

The girl made a strangled noise.

'Don't be scared. Magic users have honorable positions in the world,' I said. *'Do your parents know?'*

'Father knows, but not the commander.'

I looked at the High Morv officer. 'First Lance, would you excuse us for a moment? I have something of a personal nature to discuss with your lord.'

The commander half rose. He looked at Llothyr, who nodded. 'Wait outside. I'm perfectly safe here.'

With ill-concealed reluctance, the officer left.

'Your turn, or do you want me to begin?' I said to the girl.

She rose. 'I can mindspeak.'

Her brother squeaked, but for once he kept his mouth shut.

Llothyr stiffened. 'I... know.'

'I don't want to go mad.'

'Don't say that!' Her father wrung his hands. 'I'm not sure...'

'Your daughter has magic,' Kellani stated calmly. 'She needs training to handle her talents.'

'There is great honor in magic,' I said. 'My family brought forth many wyrmcallers. Kellani is a broomrider, a battlemage who fights with elemental fire. Naudin is a mindmage, strong on illusions. His one father is the Lord Spellstor, Prince-warlock and ruler of Vanhaar.'

'Magic is a good thing,' Lothi-Mo said with unshakable conviction. 'Morv girl can hear with her mind. People must, to make the Peaks our home again. Wyrms *need* people who mindspeak. Girl must learn. Naudin can teach as he does other magelings; he is a good teacher. She must learn. I, Lothi-Mo, say so.'

'I second that,' I said as firmly as I could. Sometimes, my wyrmling showed an unsettling decisiveness.

'I want to learn, too,' the boy said. 'I want to ride brooms and fight like a mir.'

'You're too young,' Kellani said. 'Can you read and write?'

'Course not,' the boy said, wrinkling his nose. 'Warriors don't.'

'Warriors do. If you'd join us now, you would have to learn your letters and numbers first, and how big the world is and why it rains and all those things we know. And perhaps we'd also teach you how to ride a broom.'

'I must speak with my lady,' Llothyr said helplessly. 'There would be danger, wouldn't there?'

'Not necessarily,' Kellani said. 'When the rest of our forces arrive, there will be more youngsters their age. They will stay here and go to school. We can instruct your son into our way with weapons, in addition to what your own men teach him. Your daughter must learn to channel her magic. The defense of her house is a skill every lady should possess, be it with a sword or with magic. Simpering never was a good line of protection.'

'That's what grandmother would have said.' The girl bit her lip. 'She died last winter.'

'I'm sorry,' I said. 'You don't seem the simpering kind.'

'She isn't,' her father said. 'Already a fair hand with the bow and a thin layer of meekness painted on steel.' He sighed. 'I will discuss this with my wife.'

He hesitated. 'What are your plans for the Peaks?'

'I will exercise my duties as Wings,' I said. 'Let us not beat around the bush, Lord Llothyr. I will unite the keeps and villages under one banner, the wyrm flag. Bodrus and the Kavid Jar called on me to defend these lands and that I will do. There are no other wyrmcallers to assist me yet; in their absence, I expect the lords to aid me when I call them. The defeat of our enemies and the return of the wyrms are the tasks I'm sworn to. One thing must be clear, Lord Llothyr.

High Morv needs a wyrmcaller. Be it your daughter or someone else, you will have to restore the strength of your domain.'

'But, my lord, there are no wyrms,' Llothyr said.

'Wyrms will come.' Lothi-Mo spread her wings and stretched to her full length. 'I must grow some more and then...' She looked up at me and her eyes were steady. 'We will go and find Ancho-Dar.'

Her words came as a shock. Ancho-Dar, the lost Wyrm Queen. Teodar had said she was still alive, but where?

'We will,' I said. 'I promise you we will.'

'That's my wyrm boy,' she said. *'Lothi-Mo knew you would be good.'*

I sent a snort. *'Me so good.'* That set her chuckling.

'There still are wyrms,' I said aloud. 'Only something had happened to their minds and they became confused. We must find a way to reverse that; the safety of us all depends on it.'

Llothyr sighed. 'You speak of things we lost. Our wyrmcaller died when my father was my son's age. There was no one to succeed him, and my grandfather saw no need for a replacement, as there weren't any more wyrms. So they locked up the tower and forgot about it. Somehow, the art of reading died, too. Our wyrmcaller did all the writing; my father wasn't a reading man, and my mother never learned, so there was nobody to teach me.'

'And you tried to forget magic existed,' I said.

'My father had a sister who heard voices. She went mad.' Llothyr looked at his daughter and clenched his fists.

'I hear voices,' she said. 'I don't want to go mad.'

'Of course you hear voices,' I said. 'They are all around us. Every thought is a spoken word to those who have the power.'

'Then I must know more of this,' the girl said, lifting her chin.

Llothyr put his hands on the table. 'I will speak with your mother. Would they sleep at home, or...?

'It would be best if they stayed here most of the time,' I said. 'The contact with the other children is important. We can discuss this when the ships arrive.'

Llothyr rose. 'I must go back. Knowing my wife, she will want to see this place for herself.'

'Of course,' I said, as I walked with him to the door. 'We will be pleased to show your lady around.'

The boy talked all the way to the exit, but I don't think his father heard much of it.

'One of these days I'll find an excuse to visit them.' Naudin said as we walked back to the office. 'I want to check the castle population for magic.'

I nodded. 'And no-minds.'

'That, too. I don't suppose any jinn are involved, but we'd better make sure.'

'Now, about those Wastrels,' Kellani said.

CHAPTER 12 – WASTRELS

The next morning, a tall woman arrived, escorted by the first lance and six men. She rode easily, wearing riding-pants beneath her skirts and a stout leather bodice. With her hunting cap and slender sword, she looked as if she rode to war.

'I'm Lady Esyrra of High Morv,' she said, looking down on me from the saddle of her overlarge camel.

'Welcome to Smalkand Keep,' I said politely. 'Would you come inside?'

Of course she would. She was burning with curiosity, though she hid it well.

It was clear the High Morvs were more sophisticated than Amaj's folks had been. The Kalbakars lived as fugitives, but even without that they knew nothing of the world outside the Peaks. Here on the coast people lived far less isolated; they saw ships pass and understood there were other lands and peoples beyond their vision.

I introduced her to Naudin and Willow, whose highborn good manners and down-to-earth sensibility impressed her as much as the keep itself, and then I excused myself.

'I have a patrol planned,' I said. 'Lord Naudin and Boss Willow will be pleased to show you around.'

I caught Naudin's mental grumble as I hurried away and I sent him a picture of my eternal gratitude.

'You slinky bilge rat!' he said, chuckling.

With a sense of relief I met Kellani and Lothi-Mo outside for our daily patrol over the area. I'd been cooped up too long and needed to do something. Talking with anxious mothers wasn't part of that.

Kellani saw my expression. 'Is she very difficult?'

'Esyrra? Not at all. She's much like her daughter, reasonable, impressed with us and everything. It's me; I'm not in the mood for being polite, grownup, and all that mess.' I felt restless and uneasy, without knowing why.

Kellani patted my arm. 'Let's go; a bit of fresh air will do wonders.'

'Flying chases bad thoughts away,' Lothi-Mo agreed.

I didn't say anything but launched into the air and sped toward the escarpment. Both girls could have outflown me, had they wanted, but they let me be, for which I was grateful.

At the top of the path I went left, the way to the robber keep.

'By now they must've missed those guys we killed,' Kellani said.

'Probably.' I had no idea what the other Wastrels would do. Would they suppose High Morv had killed them? Or would they have seen us arrive?

'Danger,' Lothi-Mo said unexpectedly.

I sent out my mind and caught a mass of coarse thoughts.

We flew only a few yards above the path, and now I shot up to the clouds for a bird's view of the area.

'Darn, there's a whole bunch of them,' Kellani said, right behind me.

Below us, a long line of fighters came down the path.

'Wastrels!' I said, seeing the long robes and headcloths. 'Armed to the teeth.'

'Forty at least,' Kellani added. 'Let's get some action. *Naudin?'*

'Anything up?' the mindmage said, surprised.

'Wastrels coming,' the broomer said. *'I want* Pewbara *with Amaj and his troops here in fifteen minutes. Top of the path left, follow the trail. We'll meet them there.'*

Below us, the Wastrels ambled along, not as a troop of soldiers but like men out on a jaunt.

'Foolish bandits,' Lothi-Mo said disapprovingly. *'Bad thoughts, not looking up, walking like children in park.'*

'They're careless,' Kellani agreed. *'No jinn among them; that's something.'*

'I feel magic,' I said. *'Not very powerful; hedge mage level.'* Hedge mages were like witches, mostly doing

cantrips, tricks, and basic healing spells. Nothing that could endanger us.

'What are they planning?' Kellani said. *'If they were to attack High Morv...'* She called Naudin again.

'Tangrid is getting the ship out', her cousin said. *'I caught Averson smiling! She likes the idea of shooting them.'*

'Please ask that first lance how dangerous a forty-man robber band would be to their keep.'

A moment long it remained silent.

'The good man nearly panicked,' Naudin came back. *'Forty is twice his own strength and six of his men are here with him.'*

'So that won't do. Tell him to relax. If the airship's beams are any good, those guys won't get that far.'

'All right.' Naudin was back in a minute.

'Kellie? The lady wants to come, troops and all. She's quite determined.'

'No problem; let her come.' She glanced at me and smiled. *'We'll give her a demonstration.'*

By now the first of the Wastrels had reached the spot we'd killed their friends. We watched their reaction as we hovered hidden by the mountains' shadow.

The sight of the bodies caused a lot of noise, shouting and raucous laughter. Then it dawned on me those guys were mocking their dead mates!

'Rabid dogs,' Kellani said, her mind colored by disgust. *'Not even loyal to their own. Jackals, the lot of them.'*

'We're here,' Naudin said suddenly. *'Let's see what those beams can do.'*

'Lothi-Mo, to me!' I said sharply. She'd been flitting about, looking here and there, and I didn't want her hurt.

An enormous, dark shadow fell over the jeering mass and the Wastrels looked up in shocked silence.

Then the gun barrels in the ship's belly turned around and a blue beam splashed over the ruffians. Many died, shriveled like quick-frozen butterflies, while others stood in shock, and a few quicker ones ran back up the path.

A second beam followed, dark and ominous, and more Wastrels turned to dust. The running ones increased their speed, but the ship and the merciless beam followed them, and it was over.

'Done,' Kellani told Naudin. *'We got them all.'*

The beam died and I flew down to inspect what was left. The dust had mingled with the soil, the shriveled ones were still frozen and that was all.

'Breath of the Mountains,' I whispered, trying to keep my stomach in its place.

Kellani didn't answer, but her reddish-brown skin had turned dull and her eyes looked sick.

'Good,' Lothi-Mo said coolly. 'Would take a half-flight of wyrms for same effect. *Pewbara* mighty efficient.'

'To the ship,' I croaked. We turned away and rushed to the now open door of the airship.

Inside, we hurried to the bridge. Here, too, the beams' unexpected power had caused a shock.

'Dear gods,' Wylmer said as I entered. 'I had no idea!'

Averson sat in the co-pilot's place, staring at the control panel of the deadly beams.

'You all right?' I asked.

'I... killed them,' she said, without turning her head. 'It was so easy, like cutting rock.'

I studied her face. 'What did you feel when you were killing them?'

She shrugged. 'Disgust. Anger.' She looked at me. 'Before, I liked the idea of killing them. But no longer. It had to be done, but it is horrible. I never want to like doing that.'

'The moment I think you start liking mass-killing people, I'll give you another job,' I said.

She nodded. 'Please. Thanks, I'm fine now.'

'You sure?'

She nodded.

I took a deep breath to steady my own shaken nerves and looked around. Both pilots were grimfaced but steady; Byroon the ballast handler was looking at his dials, but his face betrayed his shock. The lady and her first lance were watching from the adjoining navigation room, with Naudin and Amaj.

'Now we know what the ship can do,' I said, trying to sound composed. 'Before we press on and have a look at that robber stronghold, we'd better return her ladyship to her keep.'

'Certainly not,' Lady Esyrra said. 'I want to see their place.' She for one didn't look like the slaughter had in any way unsettled her.

'My lady,' the first lance said.

'Admit you want to see it too,' she said.

'Yes, but your safety...'

'I can handle myself. Wyrmcaller, carry on, by all means.'

Kellani gave me a tight grin. 'I told you. The defense of her house is the prime duty of every lady.'

'Of course,' Esyrra said calmly. 'My daughter mentioned your words. That is why she will join you for mage training. My son...' she presented a slight smile. 'He sorely needs the company of his peers, which you will provide as well. You have a mother's gratitude, Lady Kellani.'

'Pilot, steer for the robber keep,' I said. Then I turned. 'Razoon!'

Both Pashwend boys came running, looking ill and excited at the same time.

'We saw it all,' Razoon said in a loud voice. 'It was...'

'I've been sick,' Howy declared. 'Couldn't help it. I wanted them dead, but what those beams did was awful.'

'We felt the same,' I said. 'There is no shame in your reaction.'

'It was horrible, not an honorable death,' Amaj said.

'They weren't honorable people, Amaj Mir,' Razoon said. 'Them robbers were butchers, and if I could beam them again, I'd do it.'

'Me too,' Howy said, and his eyes glittered. 'Even if it were awful to watch.'

'Next round will be in the old-fashioned way,' I said. 'You two stand behind the pilots and guide us to Pashwend. We're going to finish this.'

'We're goin' to free the keep? Now?' Razoon shouted. He shook his brother's shoulders. 'We're goin' to be free! You hear? Free.' Then he turned to me. 'Thank you.'

CHAPTER 13 – CAPTURING A KEEP

Silent and far more deadly than we'd thought, *Pewbara* followed the forest trail, flying low over the treetops, past ravines and a large waterfall, until we came to the pass.

The ship lost way and Wylmer whistled tunelessly.

I stared out and cursed. The path ran over a ledge, with a sheer mountain on one side and a deep chasm with a second mountain on the other. The whole thing looked just wide enough for two ducks flying side by side.

'I think it can be done,' Tangrid said. 'But we don't want to scrape against the rocks.'

Wylmer turned around in his chair. 'Could you make a shield?'

I closed my eyes and pictured the *Pewbara*'s size. It would be difficult. A shield was simply a hollow ball of energy, a perfect sphere with me inside. That wouldn't work here; it would be enormous and far too large for the passage. Could I make a shield by hand? I sat down on the deck and let the energy flow out of me. Instead of letting it form on its own, I willed the energy to make a small layer around the outside of the airship. It was slow work, and it gave me a terrible headache, but finally something pinged in my head as the shield came together.

'Done,' I said, opening my eyes. I saw Naudin and Kellani staring at me.

'That,' Naudin said with awe in his voice, 'was beautiful! I must try it. A form-fitting shield!'

Kellani nodded. 'I never heard it done before,' she said. 'This is one technique every magic user should know.'

I waved my hand. 'Tell the world,' I said loftily. 'Make them remember my name!'

'Let's get through the pass first,' Tangrid said. 'You never know; we might even make it.'

'Hush now,' Wylmer said without looking, as he turned the telegraph to Slow Ahead.

The big airship crawled forward. Gray walls passed so close I could distinguish the various mosses in the cracks. It went agonizingly slow. Wylmer appeared calm; even his hands on the controls were relaxed. In the co-pilot's chair, Tangrid watched his instruments, his eyes half closed, but his concentration was almost palpable. At the gasbag controls, Byroon sat unmoving and stared at his dials. Averson stood legs apart and hands to her back as she followed everything the pilots did, with Razoon and Howy on each side.

A bump shook the ship, but no sound of ripping cloth on the hull or anything else followed, and after a few seconds I breathed again.

'No damage,' Byroon reported, his voice shaking only a little.

Finally, Wylmer let out a sigh, and we were through.

I touched the pilot's suddenly rigid shoulder. 'Well done.'

'Thanks to your shield,' Wylmer said. 'You can take it down now.'

I dissolved the shield and sagged for a moment. It had been more tiring than I had thought.

Lady Esyrra touched my arm for a moment. 'You don't live a dull life, Lord Wyrmcaller.'

'Rarely,' I said, and managed to smile at her and the rigidly staring first lance. 'It does keep us on our toes.'

'Is that the place?' Wylmer asked.

I turned to the window and saw us approach a walled building on a ledge, separated from the road by a deep ravine. With the drawbridge raised and the gate closed, those left inside must have felt very secure.

Razoon made a sound between a sob and a grunt. 'That's it. Pashwend Keep.'

I sent out a thought, and counted the minds inside the stronghold. 'Thirty, no more. Jem?'

The princess joined me, walking in that convincing way she used when there were strangers present.

'You want me to do a ground check?' she asked.

'Please.'

'Sure.' With a slight smile, she sank through the floor of the airship.

I turned to Lady Esyrra. 'She's our spy,' I said. 'The spell she's under makes her insubstantial and invisible at will.'

'How remarkable,' Esyrra said. Then she laughed and shook her head. 'My world is shaking on its poor feet seeing you people at work. All what the old annals tell of wyrmcallers pales compared to the real thing.'

'Twelve armed men,' Jem said after a while. *'The others are women and children. Servants, or worse; they have that hopeless look grandfather's drudges had.'*

'No jinn?' Kellani asked.

'Every one of them has a mind,' Jem said. *'Simple minds, mostly, but still human.'*

'We're coming down.' Kellani looked at the first lance and his lady. 'Twelve enemy and twenty civilians.'

'We outnumber them,' Lady Esyrra said, clasping a hand to the blade at her side.

'My lady,' the first lance tried again, but Esyrra ignored him.

'Action, people,' Kellani shouted and there came some ragged cheers from the troops waiting in the navigation room.

'All present and ready,' Amaj called back.

'Is there room to land?' Esyrra asked.

I shook my head. 'We're too large for the courtyard; we'll do it the magic way. Let's join my boys.' I grinned at the High Morv soldiers. 'It's only a little hop, men. A lot better than jumping.' With a wave of my hook-hand, I ported all of us down into the courtyard.

The moment we touched ground, Kellani raised a shield around us. 'Wait!' she snapped. Several arrows bounced off the force field. 'You've seen the archers?'

'Sure,' Amaj said. 'Let's go.'

The shield dissolved. A Wastrel showed his face on the wall, bow at the ready. My blast of air hit him squarely on the chest and bowled him over the battlements into the ravine. Looking round, I saw an older ruffian gaping at Razoon, as he came silently at him with his ax. Only in the last second, he lifted his blade, but Razoon knocked him down before he could defend himself. Kellani's fireballs sent another man running for cover, followed by Howy yelling obscenities at the top of his voice. I downed the Wastrel with a handful of air and Howy jumped him. His ax flashed, and I didn't have to look at his victim to know the ruffian was very much out a goner.

The High Morv soldiers ran inside with their lady and our kids followed them. In the central hall, the remaining Wastrels put up a better fight than I'd expected. I saw Jornyll go down, and Aya running to stand over him and batter his assailant with her big sword.

I was about to join them, when Jornyll scrambled to his feet, shaking his head. He slapped Aya's shoulder and together they ran for another Wastrel.

As I stepped back, an arrow clattered against the wall behind me. I looked up and spied an archer half hidden in the shadows of the first floor gallery. I could just see enough of the spot for a port and without another thought, I went for him.

The archer screamed when I appeared before him, and again as I slashed my hook into his face. Moments later, Lothi-Mo's talons took him down.

'You were too fast,' she said, and she managed to sound chagrined. 'Porting not fair!'

I chuckled and wiped my face. Then Lothi-Mo hissed and dove at another Wastrel on the floor below. I saw a door open and close again at the end of the long wooden gallery and ran to intercept the villain I'd seen.

The door opened on a narrow staircase and I hurried down to a small room with several doors leading deeper into the keep. It was dark here, and silent; no torches to light the way and the keep's thick walls blotted out the sounds of the fighting. As I stood trying to concentrate, a tall shadow moved. 'Who are you?' a woman's voice whispered. 'You are no Wastrels. '

I relaxed my hook hand. 'No, we are the Pasandir Armed Forces. And you?'

'I'm one of the servants,' she said hurriedly, and she sounded very convincing. Alas for her mind was a proud pinnacle that refused to stoop to a menial level, and by that mind I knew her.

'I am Eskandar,' I said. 'We recently reopened the old caves at the bay. Yesterday, two boys came to our place and told us of the Wastrels. Now we come to liberate the keep.'

'Razoon and Howy?' the woman said, and for a second, her voice soared with motherly pride. With an effort she got her voice back under control. 'One Wastrel ran past; he'll go to the kitchens, where the women and children are. I fear he plans revenge.'

I sensed no deceit. 'Show me the way; I'll foil his plans.'

I hurried after her to some kind of storeroom. Through a half-opened door I heard a male voice shout and the sobbing of women and children.

'He's mad,' the woman said and there was rage in her voice. 'He will kill them all.'

I threw open the door and rushed inside. The kitchen was large and sparsely lighted by two torches. A Wastrel in a dirty green desert robe shouted at several women and children huddling in a corner. The man was waving a knife and whipping himself up into a frenzy.

'Hey, you!' I shouted.

The man wheeled around, his headcloth-wrapped face a mask of hatred. He snarled something and sprang at me.

I had hoped he would do that, and my blast of air hit him solidly in the guts. He bent double as the force of the wind slammed him back into a tall rack loaded with copper pans.

Amid a cascade of kitchenware, the Wastrel slid down to end up in a broken heap, with his head against the stone sink.

I turned to the woman who had brought me here. 'That made a mess of your kitchen, I'm afraid.' Then I took a deep breath. 'Is everyone all right?'

The proud woman looked at me. 'And you're so young,' she said in a voice of wonder. 'I hadn't seen before, but you are not much older than my boys.' She rubbed her eyes. 'Your pardon; I must remember my manners. I am Tahhya.' She gripped the edges of the table. 'Lady Tahhya. After ten years I can say it once more.' She glanced at the women and children, who stood watching her with big eyes. 'The Lord Eskandar comes to set us free, girls. We... we are all right now.'

'We wiped them out.' Kellani said. *'Where are you?'*

'In the kitchen,' I said. *'Any casualties?'*

'None here,' she said.

Moments later, Razoon and Howy came running in.

'We won! We won!' Razoon shouted. He vaulted over the table and embraced the woman. 'They're all dead, Ma! We got the keep back!' He turned to me. 'Thank you. I'm so glad we found you, Wyrmcaller.'

'Wyrmcaller?' the lady said. 'So it is true!'

'I am Eskandar, of the House of Kambish, wyrmcaller of Kalbakar Keep and Wings of the Mountains,' I said.

To my embarrassment, the lady bowed. 'Ancient titles I thought we had lost. Then I saw your wyrmling fighting our oppressors, and I got new hope. Have you come to defend us, like in the old days?'

'I have,' I said. 'The Kavid Jar chose me, and Bodrus himself confirmed me. I am gathering an army to fight the enemies of Bodrus and to unify the Peaks. This time, we had help from the Lady Esyrra of High Morv Keep and her men.'

Kellani came in, with Naudin and all the others, and for a moment things got a bit confused, with little children crying, and the keep women overwhelmed by the strangeness of it all.

Only Lady Tahhya stood upright and proud. I introduced Esyrra, and both ladies eyed each other. The High Morv lady smiled and offered her hand. 'We are neighbors. If there is anything we can do, let us know. In times of trouble the keeps must stand together.'

'Thank you,' Lady Tahhya said. Then she stiffened and her eyes grew dark with shock. 'High Morv! The Wastrel headman departed early today towards your keep with forty men!'

'We got them,' Razoon said triumphantly. 'They're all dead!'

'Blessed be the Spirit of Mountain,' his mother said and for a moment she stood silent.

'Are these here all the people? Aren't there any men?' Kellani asked, gesturing at the women.

Tahhya shook her head. 'The men are in the village. Only women and children were allowed inside the keep, to serve...' She pressed her lips together.

Kellani gave a swift nod. 'Are there Wastrels in the village?'

'None,' the lady said. She turned to a younger girl. 'Run to the village and tell them what happened. Everybody is to come to the keep right now.'

She looked at Razoon and Howy, and her stooped shoulders straightened. Somehow, as the truth of their liberation sank in, years slipped away from her and she embraced both of them. 'You did it! You two found help and came to save us all. I'm very proud of my two sons.'

'Rightfully so,' I said. 'And what about you? Can you manage the keep?'

The lady stood straight. 'We can take care of ourselves,' she said. 'There will be enough arms left behind for every man and woman. With those villains gone, food will no longer be a problem either.'

'Should you have a surplus, we'll want to trade with both keeps for provisions,' I said. 'We will need greenstuff, fruit, whatever you can spare.' I smiled. 'We can pay, in goods or coin.'

'Of course,' Lady Tahhya said. She hesitated. 'One request, if I may. My sons need to learn the way of the warrior. Neither I nor any of mine walk that road. Would you take them and teach them?'

'With pleasure,' I said.

Razoon looked sharply at his mother. 'Ma, I'm needed here.'

'Not yet you are,' Tahhya said. 'You need to learn the things your father would have taught you. I can manage the keep, but I cannot turn you two unruly layabouts into warriors.' She smiled. 'Remember this, Razoon; you may be mir, but until you're eighteen years old, I rule here.' She hugged both boys. 'I love you two. Now follow the Wings and make me even more proud to be your mother.'

She looked at me. 'Pardon me if I sound ungrateful. I am not; believe me. For fifteen years I have lived toward this moment. I knew it would come; Spirit of the Mountain would turn his face back to us again and all would be well. Now he did, you came, and we are free. We must get to work. Rebuild, recover ourselves, and find a new balance. We have no time to celebrate. That will come later, when we are Pashwend Keep again, instead of a pigsty. So excuse me for leaving you; I must get to work.'

'Ma'am, I admire your courage,' I said. 'We will leave you to your duty.'

She whirled around. 'Courage?' she whispered. 'Need! I cannot afford to falter; my people depend on me.'

I nodded. 'If you lack anything, send someone to Smalkand.'

She bowed again. 'I will. Thank you.' She kissed her two sons and went to receive the first villagers.

I gathered the High Morv people and my little army and ported back to the airship.

'Why didn't she want our help?' Razoon said, fighting against his tears. 'It's my duty too.'

'It's not,' Amaj said. 'The keep is her job. As long as you're underage, she's both lady and lord. That's why you're still Razoon Mir, and not Mir Razoon. Be glad she sent you to us and not kept you around to run her errands. You and I, we're here to learn how to fight. And learn you will; got that?'

Razoon sighed. 'Yeah.'

We returned home and took our leave of Lady Esyrra.

'We met two proud ladies today,' Kellani said as we walked inside. 'Esyrra and certainly Tahhya. That woman's duty is her life. I bet she made things difficult for those Wastrels.' She pulled a face. 'You realize all those kids are...'

'Half Wastrels?' I said. 'Does it matter?'

'I don't know,' Kellani said. 'Wastrels are strange. They're not like other peoples. Sunstruck, people call them. I caught a whiff of magic but I couldn't find whose.'

'Naudin will see to that,' I said. 'If there is any magic, he'll find it.' Suddenly I felt elated. 'Two more keeps behind our banner.' I skip-hopped a few steps and grinned at Kellani. 'Now how do we get those caravans running? We need them to spread the word, but I can't send out Shaw or Nathan. They are unfamiliar with the mountains and their quirks.'

'I think you should hire people,' Kellani said. 'Drivers, merchants, guards; that's a job for older folk. Why don't you invite Mazuun over, and Lord Llothyr and perhaps Lady Tahhya, and talk the whole thing over with them? After that we'll need to find a mage who can conjure spelldrakes, and we're set.'

'Spelldrakes?' I said. 'What is a spelldrake?'

Kellani looked at me. 'You don't know? They're conjured animals. Naudin and the reclaimers rode them when they went to search for us after our crash.'

'I never heard of them. Could they pull those wagons we found?'

'Easily,' Kellani said. 'The only reason most merchants use oxen for their carts is that else they'd have to hire a mage. Those drakes need to be respelled after a while, like our brooms, and mages are far more expensive than oxen.'

'Conjured beasts,' I said slowly. 'Do they need food or anything?'

Kellani shook her head. 'Nothing; no food, no water, no sleep. Ask Naudin about the spell.'

'Love of the Mountains!' I said. 'Here I was thinking of camels and stuff, and all that time we had a free alternative.'

'I should have mentioned it before,' Kellani said. 'I did wonder why you kept talking of camels, but I never realized you didn't know the spell.' She pinched my cheek. 'Curse it, even I sometimes think you're all-powerful.'

'I'm not!' I said. 'There must be hundreds of spells every Weal mage knows and I don't. Naudin must teach me that spell.' I rubbed my hands. 'Great; let's ask what Shaw thinks.'

'Be careful with that girl,' Kellani said. 'She wants to do everything on her own, but she can't. I understand her motives, but Aunt Darquine doesn't run the day-to-day business of the Company herself either. As proprietor she has whole armies of merchants operating MCTC businesses, from shipping lines to building contractors, grocery stores and the gods know what. Shaw must learn to delegate.'

'But how to convince her of that?' I said. 'This business means so much to her.'

'She's obsessing over it,' Kellani said. 'That's not good; not for her and not for the business. Don't you tell her; I'll ask Naudin to do it—obsessions are part of his training.'

I sighed. I knew Kellani was right; Shaw was overdoing it. To her, the business was a way of compensating for the loss of her parents. But however hard she worked, her old life was gone and she should come to terms with that.

I looked up at her. 'True, Naudin will do it much better than me.'

'Don't worry; you're doing fine, sonny,' Kellani said.

'Sonny!' I said as she walked away.

'Wyrm boy!' Lothi-Mo called from outside. *'Come and have a swim. Water is good and clears the mind.'*

'I'm coming,' I said, and hurried outside, to the beach.

CHAPTER 14 – WIND ON A SCHOONER

The next morning I woke up with Lothi-Mo's shrill cry in my ears.

'Ship! Ship! Enemy ship! Up, sluggards; enemy in the bay.'

I shrugged into my tunic and boots and ran to the entry hall. From the cave mouth, hidden in the shadows, I saw a tall schooner at anchor in the bay and a ship's boat rowing to the small beach.

'Pirates?' Kellani said as she joined me. 'Must be those fellows the Wastrels do business with.'

I nodded. 'Tell everyone to stay in the cafeteria and be silent.'

As Kellani ran back, I closed my eyes and concentrated on the pirate crew. No Brisans, these; they were Bokkaners. Still, they too were under the same compulsion as their southern brethren.

'Jinni aboard,' Naudin's voice whispered in my ear.

'Later,' I said without opening my eyes. 'Search for a navigator; they may have the Angsthafn location.'

If they had a navigator, he wasn't wearing a sign around his neck. That meant searching them mind for mind, all forty of them.

'Here,' Naudin said. 'Think I got him.' I followed his mind into the head of a tall, thin pirate with a goatee. Among his memories, there was an image of a mountain rising up from the sea. It must be a dead volcano, with a small fringe of tropical forest around its foot. In the distance were other islands, most grim and rocky. I saw an opening in the mountainside; a rent, as a skirt torn on a nail, with a ship sailing in. There was a confused impression of wooden walls and towers, bristling with cannons, and that was all. Each image was protected. The pirate could think of them, but not speak. The slightest hint of danger and his brain would overload most fatally. Luckily he wasn't a mage, so he wouldn't detect our reading his mind.

'We got it,' Naudin said, gripping my shoulder. 'That's Angsthafn.' There was awe in his voice. 'We got it, guy! The whole Weal has been searching for it for years and years, and we kids got it.'

I punched his chest softly for emphasis. '*You* got it. Now we only need to find those flippin' islands.' I clenched my one fist. 'First, we must take the ship.'

'What are they doing?' Amaj had joined us.

'Not much,' I said, peeping out. 'I think they're waiting.'

'The jinni is the second mate,' Naudin said. 'A mousy little fellow with a beard.'

'*Jem? Any idea what manner of jinni is aboard the schooner?*'

'*Nope, just that it's another lesser one. It won't be a flame jinni like in the slave market. Not aboard a wooden ship.*'

I sure hope so, I thought. But you never know with jinn.

Kellani came back. 'I've gathered all fighters in the cafeteria.'

'We're outnumbered four-to-one,' I said. 'We can't jump them as we did at Brisa. We can't get out the *Pewbara* in time, either. They have the ship's guns, we don't. Besides, we don't want her to sink in the middle of the bay.'

Naudin looked at me. 'That elemental you called in the Atnortod palace...'

'Gods,' I said. 'I was desperate then. Dare I try it again?' I looked around me at the faces of the kids. I could easily endanger all of them. 'Ulaataq?' I saw the engineer looking my way. 'You studied the keep's forcefields,' I said over the heads of the crowd. 'Is there one that closes off only the cave entrance?'

'There is a button for every separate shield,' he said. 'I haven't tried them, obviously, but they're there and I got them marked.'

I swallowed. 'I will port to the path to the ledge and call the wind elemental. Meanwhile, Ulaataq activates the first shield, so it can't get in if it should want to. If there's any danger, I port into the cafeteria. Any questions?'

'I'm coming with you,' Kellani said.

This time I put my foot down. 'You're not. There is no need and I can't risk being distracted. You and Lothi-Mo both stay inside.' They didn't like it, but I wasn't going to budge on this. 'Ulaataq, go flip your switches, mate.'

'I'll take you to the machine thingy,' Amaj said. 'Hop onto my broom.'

As they flew away, I turned to the others. 'Keep an eye on the door; I'll be knocking when I'm done.'

Kellani grunted. 'You be careful, you hear,' she said angrily.

'I will, I don't want to risk the prophecy,' I said with a grin as counterfeit as the lead coins churning in my stomach. Then I ported away.

I came out on the path and I walked a bit to find an unobstructed view of the ship and the men on the beach. I counted twenty pirates; half of the crew, walking around as men did who had been at sea for a long time.

I sent my mind to watch the keep and waited until suddenly it was as if a door slammed closed and I couldn't sense them again.

On impulse I took out the little roadside guy statue I carried everywhere, the image of Bodrus. *'Give me strength, god,'* I asked. I stretched out my hook arm and concentrated on the prosthetic's curve.

Wind gathered before me, stirring up the fallen leaves. It grew into a disturbance, the tiniest of whirls dancing on the circle of my hook hand. The disturbance grew into a puff, and now the shrubbery swayed. I couldn't move, and hoped those on the beach didn't notice anything. The puff broadened into a whirlwind, still touching my hook, but not with its full weight, or I'd have broken my arm. By now it was a six foot monster funnel of dark air, emitting sparks of

117

lightning and ice-cold rain. Still it grew, seven feet, eight, nine, and more... It roared, making it sound like a question.

'Those men on the beach and the men on the ship,' I said. 'They are bad men, who want to harm Bodrus and the Kavid Jar. Please go and kill them. But not the ship itself, Bodrus has a need of it. Now, mighty whirl—go forth and battle for Bodrus!'

I nearly fell backward as the whirl sprang from my hook hand. It raced down the path, collecting shrubs and branches, sand and dust. The men on the beach scattered, screaming, but to no avail. The whirl danced after them, and one by one they were taken up and slammed to the ground, never to rise again. When the last pirate had been thrown, the whirl crossed the water.

I had to see this, so I mounted up and flew toward the schooner. The whirl darted round the deck, smashing pirates around as if they were nothing.

Suddenly there was a wild roaring, and a creature appeared on deck, a monstrous being looking like a cross between an eagle and a toad. It was easily as big as the whirl, moving on powerful hind legs and beating strong wings. Its first jump topped the schooner's main mast. It kicked at the whirl and sent it dancing away over the deck. Again it roared, clawing at the whirl. 'None defy Wahazz and live!' it shouted in a mighty voice. 'Wahazz Jinni serves Hyloman the Undefeatable Prince!'

I lifted the roadside guy and called a beam of solid ice. It struck the jinni squarely in the back. The creature moved its shoulders, and the ice broke harmlessly off.

The jinni turned around to me. 'Who you are?' he shouted. 'Puny human thinks to hurt great Wahazz?' Then he jumped at me.

I ported back to the beach. The jinni roared its anger and spread its wings. They weren't made for flying, apparently, but powerful enough to let the jinni hop over the water on its wide toad feet.

With a wave of my hook, I sent another gush of wind at the oncoming monster. It staggered and sank to its knees into the sea. With a wild beating of wings it heaved itself up again. My great whirlwind was on its heels and the jinni had to fight him back before running at me. I waited until he was almost within reach and ported away. I stepped back and tripped over a piece of driftwood. I went sprawling, while the jinni ran at me, its wings giving him extra speed.

The whirl attacked again, and the jinni stopped. Flat on my back I pointed my hook in the direction of its feet. 'Freeze!' I cried. The jinni stumbled and fell. The whirl pounded away at the jinni's feathered chest, while I jumped to my feet. I gathered enough air to create a vacuum and threw the most powerful fist I could make at the beaked head. Blood ran from its maw and it tried to get up again. But the whirl hammered into him and the jinni went down again.

I ran forward. 'Rain!' I shouted, waving at its head. A deluge of water roared, running down the jinni's feathers. Its frog's leg shot out and kicked me flying. I landed hard on my chin and lay there for a moment, wrestling to stay conscious and desperate not to lose control over the whirlwind.

'Freeze!' I croaked, again pointing at the jinni. With a loud crack, the head froze. The body struggled for a moment longer before it stilled. I gripped a fistful of air and changed it into a glittering spear. Gripping it with both hands, I rammed the long shaft through the jinni's body, pinning it to the ground.

'Gotcha!' I cried, exulting. I turned to the whirl that seemed to pant as heavily as I did. 'Bodrus thanks you for your mighty work, great whirl,' I managed to utter. 'Go with his blessing. Begone!'

With a sigh, the whirl dissolved, and I stood alone on the beach with the jinni's body.

Utterly weary, I managed to mount my broom and fly to the entrance of the keep.

I saw Kellani and Naudin, and all other anxious faces, and I grinned. 'Come out,' I mouthed, giving them two thumbs-up.

After a moment, the screen disappeared and they crowded around me.

'What did you do?' Kellani cried, her face red with barely contained anger. 'You fought something. What the heck was that?'

'A jinni,' I said. 'A big one. Not Ozoezd, but nearly so.'

I led them back to the beach. 'My whirl friend did those,' I said, waving at the bodies. 'He killed all Bokkaners; only the jinni was too much for him alone, so I jumped in to help.'

Then Kellani saw the dead jinni, and she uttered a string of terrible curses. She whirled on me, grabbing my tunic.

'You fought that?' she shouted in my face. 'All alone? You idiot!'

'Greedy fellow he is,' Lothi-Mo chirped, winging overhead. *'Silly jinn-hoarder grudges his friends piece of battle. Fights alone, stingy boy.'*

'Not alone,' I protested. 'There was a twelve-foot tall whirl, too. And Bodrus was with me with his power.'

Kellani's hands clenched on my shoulders as if she wanted to shake me, but instead she embraced me. 'You idiot,' she repeated softly, holding me tight.

I started to shake as the reaction set in. Then I buried my face in her blue broomer uniform and let my tears run.

'To bed with you,' Kellani said. 'You lost a heap of energy, bud.' She scooped me up and raced back to the keep and my bedroom. The last thing I remembered was her hands unbuttoning my tunic and then fatigue swallowed me up.

CHAPTER 15 – TREASURE TROVE

I'm not obsessing! Shaw fumed. *I'm concentrating, you idiot!* She sat in the bow of the ship's boat rowing her to the new ship. Mentally, she gripped Naudin's throat and shook him. He had dared to tell her not to obsess! *Curse the guy! Is Eskandar obsessing with his pirates and his prophecy? No! He's building a country and fighting for Bodrus at the same time. And like him, I'm building. I'm building a trade empire.*

She wanted to scream at their lack of understanding. *You all got your magic. I don't, but I got this urge to trade, to become rich and successful. Darn it all! If Darquine can do it, I can too. I'll be Harwans of the PTC!* She grinned. The Pasandir Trading Company. She hadn't told anyone yet, but that was the name she'd use to rock the world.

Blow them all! They aren't going to stop me. Delegate! Of course I have to delegate, but to whom? Nate isn't here. Nate. She closed her eyes and saw him, so tall and strong and... *Stop that, idiot! He won't look at an ugly girl with a queer eye and knobby knees. Nate is a partner, no more.* That stupid eye. Na'a had given her a black patch to wear over her good eye, a pirate patch, from a real, dead pirate. And she would have to see a lensmaker for glasses. Great! Who'd pay for a pair of glasses? She didn't have a thousand gold to spare. So...

'Ah, Shaw?' Wylmer said, interrupting her maelstrom of thoughts. 'We're at the ship.'

She grunted and glared at him. Then she relaxed. 'Sorry, I was busy killing someone. Not you!' she added hastily.

He grinned. 'It's all right. Now please get aboard; the guys won't hold that rope ladder all day.'

Shaw colored darkly. 'No, of course not. Thanks,' she said to the boys. Then she climbed up the side of the schooner.

Ships didn't mean all that much to her. They had been the receivers of her father's supplies, no more. Then there had been *Marigold.* But this schooner was roomy, compared to

Marigold. Twice as big, too. She looked around, automatically checking for cargo. Nothing. She wandered round, back in her own world, and found a hatch. It wouldn't move, so she looked around.

'Can you open this?' she asked of a boy inspecting a gun.

He laughed. 'It's locked; try the next hatch,' he said. 'That's the way below.'

Again, she felt heat rise in her face. *Snap out of it, idiot!* She hurried to the other hatch, and climbed down into the semi-darkness of the hold. It stank of rotting water, poop, and other nasty things, but she wasn't squeamish and shrugged it off.

She walked round, letting her eyes getting used to the dark. 'Barrels of wine,' she said. 'Unknown vintage.' She produced pen and paper, and quickly wrote down the particulars. 'Next.'

Item for item, she checked everything and wrote it down.

With every new item, her heart raced faster and the drumming in her ears got louder. 'What a catch!' she muttered. All were exotics, never before seen in the Weal. Spices, boxes of tea and loads of brown beans called cawah, porcelain, and an enormous shipment of rare fabrics. Her brain whirled. This was money! No sharing among the crew; that would be idiotic. Give them a bonus and invest the rest. This was what she needed to build her empire!

'Shaw?' Wylmer's voice cut through her rich dreams. 'Shaw! We're going back; dinnertime. Tomorrow is another day.'

She wasn't done yet, and she wanted to protest, but a little voice whispered, *No. Don't obsess.*

She pocketed her notes and walked to the ladder. Back on deck, she stood blinking against the light of the setting sun. She looked at her grimy hands and clothes. 'Have I been below all day?'

'Yeah,' Wylmer said. 'You skipped the noon meal. I came to warn you, but you didn't listen. Is it a good haul?'

'It doesn't look bad,' she said offhandedly. 'It is all outlandish stuff, so I'm not sure of its worth.'

Nor was she, but she did know it would fetch quite a lot. She wouldn't tell them that yet, though.

CHAPTER 16 – COMING OF THE SHIPS

'Good morning, great and mighty lord Eskandar,' a familiar voice said in my mind. *'Sunup was beautiful. Not that you noticed it, I suppose, but we poor sailors did.'*

I crawled to a sitting position. *'Dear gods, is that you, Keena?'* Her voice chased away all after-the-fight fatigue. *'You sound cheerful, so you didn't sink, or lose the* Marigold *or anything.'*

'Not at all,' she said happily. *'Both ships are nearly at the gates, oh mighty lord, about to enter your grand hole-in-the-ground.'*

Hole-in-the-ground had me confused, but then I remembered I'd fibbed them with the idea we lived in a primitive cave here and I grinned. *'I'll warn the guards at the entrance we dug so they won't shoot you. Oh, and don't mind the schooner already inside. She's all ours.'*

I dressed in a hurry and went into the cafeteria. *'Lothi-Mo? You awake?'*

'Course I am. Gonna fly?' she said. *'Got another jinni to fight?'*

'No, dear. The ships are outside and we should be ready to greet their arrival. So I'd like you to chase the kids out of bed.' Lothi-Mo chuckled; that was something she loved.

'Wakey wakey,' she shouted as she flew past me to the dorms. *'Ships are coming. Up, up; lazybones!'*

I walked outside in the clear light of dawn. Not sunup, perhaps, but not all that much past, either. Then I stared. Gone were the bodies and there wasn't a trace of the fight left. The schooner's sails were neatly furled and a second anchor cast. Now, too, I read her name, *Killarn Ranni,* painted in some curly foreign script on her bow.

'You shouldn't be up yet,' Kellani said as she joined me, big and comfortable in broomer blue. She always managed to dress in the time another needed to wake up.

'With the ships coming, I can't stay in bed,' I said. 'I swear I'll take it easy today.' I waved around. 'Where are the bodies?'

'We dumped them in a nearby ravine,' Kellani said. 'That winged jinni in parts. It was frozen solid when Averson battered it to manageable bits. After that, Wylmer and Amaj's troop did the schooner. They furled the sails and threw out a second anchor; we left the search for another time.' She chuckled. 'Shaw was on board first of them, checking up on any cargo. I think she wasn't displeased.'

Shaw would, I thought, grinning. Suddenly I remembered her eye-trouble, and I wondered if she had already seen our wisewoman about it. *I must ask Na'a.*

Willow came out, trim and businesslike, with Naudin looking owlishly crumpled. Behind them, Amaj and his guys came running, buttoning up their uniforms.

'The ships?' Amaj shouted. 'Where?'

'About to come in. I thought to wake you all first.' I clapped his shoulder. 'You guys did a good job on the schooner yesterday.'

Amaj shrugged. 'No trouble. She's a nice ship, Wylmer says.'

'So we're short on officers again,' Kellani said. 'Back to the port captain?'

'We'll sail the ship to Port Naar,' I said. 'You never know.'

By now most kids had gathered outside. A cry from above was Sylas on his broomstick, pointing at the sea passage.

A moment later I saw the *Drakon* enter the bay, sails furled as she stately crept forward on her engine alone.

We all shouted and waved, and from the ship many hands waved back.

'They're looking nice,' Naudin said. 'Very smart.'

'Wyrm ships,' Lothi-Mo said. She slapped me with her tail. 'Need more wyrm flags for the keep.'

I grinned. 'I'll ask around for a needle-woman.' We watched the two ships sailing across the bay to anchor a cable apart behind the schooner.

Minutes later, several ship's boats raced for the beach. I saw Captain Abia sitting in the stern of her gig with Imooga the engineer and many other familiar faces. Close behind her, Miya of the *Marigold* and a white-haired guy I recognized as Myk, shouting at her crew to row faster. Both boats touched the beach at the same moment, and the kids tumbled out, shouting as if they'd returned from a two-year voyage.

'Welcome,' I said, but then a cry from above interrupted me. Sylas came swooping down to meet his sister, yelling a battlecry. As brother and sister embraced, the others cheered.

Kellani and I walked forward with Naudin close behind us, pausing to shake a hand or slap a shoulder. All kids were in high spirits; the Qoori among them seemed to have shed their earlier fears, and many even spoke a bit of Vulgar.

When we reached her, Abia hugged both of us.

'Thank you,' she said. 'It's great to see Sy so happy, so *active*.'

'I fought my first battle,' Sylas told her. 'It needs a lot of tuning still, but I can do it.'

'Welcome in Smalkand,' I said. 'Come and join us inside. Breakfast is ready.'

'Porridge?' Abia said.

'Just wait,' I said. 'Take it easy. You don't have to dig today; we'll start you all excavating tomorrow.'

Kellani looked at me, but she didn't say anything. Naudin and Sylas guffawed as we left.

'You're mean,' Kellani said. *'To make them think we live in a hole or something.'*

I grinned at her.

'You had a good journey?' I said, shaking hands with Miya.

'Perfect,' she said. 'Good journey, good crew, nice ship, and a great engineer. What more can a gal want?' She slapped Myk's shoulder. 'He did a good job on his own. That engine sang all the way.' She looked around the bay. 'Fine harbor you have here. That schooner?'

'She's ours,' I said. 'A pirate; sailed right in, so we took her.'

'*You* took her,' Kellani said.

'My whirlwind did most of the work,' I said hastily. 'Let's get inside. There are a few new faces, we'll tell you all about them. For now just relax.'

'Is it really bad?' a girl asked. 'I mean, they're caves.'

'Dark and full of creepy beasties,' I said in a lugubrious tone. 'You be careful where you put your hands for the bats and the scorpions.'

The kids were strangely quiet as they followed me. But when they saw the cafeteria and the bright lights, they yelled and laughed.

'Some caves,' Nate of the market gild said. 'You fooled us, master wyrmcaller. All week we thought we were going to the mines, or something.'

'Sorry, I couldn't resist,' I said, feeling vaguely ashamed. 'It's even better than the fort, actually.'

Then I saw Shaw coming, her good eye fixed on Nate. 'There you are,' she said. 'I need you. This business is big, Nate. Very, very big.' She grabbed his arm and dragged him off.

'One heck of a place, this,' a stout girl in a faded tabard said. 'We have our own guardhouse, but no soldiers?'

I remembered her as Hella, boss of the Harbangers, the castle quarter gild.

'Amaj is in command of the soldiery,' I said. 'We already fought a few battles. Would you want to join them?'

'Me?' she grinned, patting her stout hips. 'Nah, I'm not built for war. But if you need someone to care for the swords and spears, I'm game.' She hesitated. 'I suppose the gilds are done for?'

I nodded. 'That worked for Clam Street, but here we're in the adult world. Other rules, no bosses.'

'Only Willow,' she said. 'She got in at the top.'

'She is in charge of the keephold side, making everything run smoothly. That's not really the same as a boss.'

Hella shrugged. 'I'm not jealous,' she said. 'She's a good gal, and I was getting fed up with bossing anyhow. I'd rather care for the weaponry and things.'

'Speak with Amaj,' I said. Seeing more kids wanting to talk to me, I turned and faced them all.

'Guys, I know you're bursting with questions. We'll hold a meeting tonight, but for now relax, look the place over, and enjoy yourselves.'

After breakfast, I gathered the ship's officers, Shaw, Kellani, and Naudin in the office.

Shaw's whole attitude shouted "Just dare to ask!" and she wore a black pirate patch over her right eye. She noticed me looking. 'Must wear it regularly,' she said. 'And I must see a lensmaker.' She snorted derisively. 'As if I had the money for a guy like that.'

'If you need glasses, go get them,' I said coolly. 'We can stand the damage.'

She grunted and dropped down in her chair with thunder in her face.

Captain Abia came in and stared at the opulence.

'Of all things, I never expected this,' she said. 'This ain't a fort, it's a darned palace.'

I grinned. 'I can still barely believe it myself. And all powered by Qoori technology. Five centuries old...'

Xailin clenched her hands. 'We lost most of it.'

'How?' Naudin asked. 'That machine getting mana out of the multiverse. Those spell-machines. The lights. Those aren't things to forget.'

'Yet we did,' she said. 'After the wyrms left, the Troubled Times came. The emperor lost his trusted advisor, who with her smooth voice kept the peace between the proud *haintos*, the great nobles of the realm. Civil war followed, with the emperor only a puppet for whoever had the power for a while. It took us two hundred years until an imperial prince managed to defeat the warring *haintos* and take the throne back. By that time, much knowledge was dead.'

'Yet here it is alive,' Naudin said. 'It works.'

She shrugged. 'And nobody knows how. We can produce automatons, but the power that drives them comes from the small stock the High Academy has kept. We can't make those anymore.'

'Hush,' I said to Naudin. *'No need to tell her Ulaataq thinks he can build our own spell machine.'* It wasn't that I didn't trust Xailin; she had never done anything that could make me doubt her. But she was an imperial princess, and she had stated that her loyalty was to her House, not to us.

'A pity,' I said aloud. 'It's great stuff. Well, how was your journey?'

'Uneventful,' Abia said. 'Not even a storm to relieve the kids' boredom. No enemy sighted, no shot fired in anger, nobody to rescue from a wreck.'

'No booty,' Miya muttered.

'You want our reports, I suppose?' Abia said.

That had me grinning. 'In writing. I hate bureaucracy, so keep them short.'

'Promise,' she said. 'Now, about this place...'

Between us, Kellani, Naudin, and I told them all of our adventures, finishing with yesterday's intruder.

'Phew,' Abia said. 'You guys haven't been idle. Were you thinking to keep that schooner?'

'If I can find a crew for her, I will. We can use her for trading with Dvarghish and Port Naar.' I hesitated for a second before showing the images of the dead volcano and the surrounding islands. 'Does anybody recognize this?'

Nobody had.

'We know every salty mile of the Towne-Seatome-Port Naar route,' Perre said. 'But we've never been beyond that.'

I got that; while our young officers all knew how to sail a ship, their experience with the Wydemere as a whole was of necessity limited.

'What is that place?' Abia said. 'Is it important?'

I leaned forward. 'We think it is Angsthafn.'

Miya slammed the table. 'That volcano? And we have no coordinates?'

'We couldn't locate them,' I said. 'Naudin and I found the schooner's navigator. We went through his mind as carefully as we could without alerting him, but the images were all we could dig up.'

'So we'll have to search for it,' Vence said.

'For a handful of islands somewhere in the Wydemere?' Abia looked doubtful.

'If it is in the Wydemere,' I said. 'It could be way up north, for all we know. Let's ask around first. Tomorrow, I'd like to take the schooner north to Port Naar, if you can whip me up a crew. I want a word with the local authorities there and Purser Shaw is eager to set up a trade route. I'll ask the navy folks there about the volcano. If that's a bust, I will port to Seatome and see the commodore, and to Towne, to check with the merchant captains.'

'And if no one has seen it?' Miya said.

'Then we'll think again,' I said. 'Now, about that schooner.'

'The *Killarn Ranni*,' Wylmer said. 'Her papers named her a merchant from Tysare, wherever that may be, and they captured her last year somewhere north of here. She's carrying a load of stuff that made Shaw happy. If you want to sail tomorrow, we'll have to unload that first.'

'Boss.' Shaw leaned forward in her chair, fingers entwined and her earlier surliness turned into enthusiasm. 'I've been thinking. I was told I must delegate,' she closed her bad eye and glanced at Naudin, who looked back without expression on his round face. 'But I cannot delegate when it's only me and Nate. I want to start trading. That stuff Wylmer mentioned should fetch us enough. I want to take it to Seatome, hire some people and start making money.'

Her eagerness made me want to laugh, but I knew how much this meant to her, so I only nodded.

'You think you can sell whatever the *Killarn Ranni* carries?' I asked.

'Yes,' Shaw said. 'They're not common things, boss; we're talking about rarities.' She pulled a folded paper from her jacket. 'Eighty packages of silk, weighing twenty pounds each, bound together into bales of ten. Eleven chests of porcelain, packed in straw; twenty crates of fine wines, assorted spices in barrels, a very well-packed crate of sweets, and several other boxes I haven't had time to inspect yet.'

I fiddled with my hook hand as I thought. Shaw had shown herself a shrewd dealer and we needed that trade thing going. Every country needs income and I didn't think taxes were going to do it, with the state the Peaks were in.

'Let her go,' Lothi-Mo whispered unexpectedly. *'She is about to hatch, wyrm boy. A rare wyrm she'll be. Let her go!'*

No use asking her what she meant; I was sure she wouldn't tell me.

'All right,' I said. 'Go do it. You take Nate, I suppose?'

'Nate, and I'd like Keena too. We need a mindspeaker to keep in contact and she's agreeable.' Shaw smiled. 'I know; I asked her.'

'All right, but keep it small; don't bite off more than you can chew.' I grinned at the look on her face. 'Don't bite *me*; just be careful. I will transfer the goods to *Marigold*; the cutter can bring it to Seatome.'

'Yes!' she said, rubbing her hands. 'We'll have the gold come begging for our pockets.'

'Wouldn't that be nice?' I said. 'In what state is the schooner?'

Wylmer tapped his notes. 'I had a quick look at her insides. She looks a lot better than *Marigold* did, before the dockyard got at her. That mighty fight yesterday damaged a length of railing. I had it roped off, but we'll need a carpenter to repair it properly. That's it; no leaks, no nothing. She's sound.'

'Great,' I said. 'You take command of her, and Miya keeps *Marigold*. That way we only need to find more deck officers. As *Drakon* is our flagship, Abia will be flag captain.'

Wylmer pursed his lips. 'I need a first officer, a bos'n and ten sailors.'

'We'll reshuffle the available hands,' Abia said. 'Is there a place we can discuss things quietly?'

'We've a few smaller meeting rooms,' I said. 'But for now be my guest; I'll go and see Shaw's goodies transferred.'

'Yes!' Shaw said.

Kellani gripped my arm. 'You were going to take it easy today!'

'I will,' I said. 'Only a few short ports and then I'll put my feet up. And I'll have several days at sea to rest.'

'Well, I'm watching you!' she said threateningly. 'If you overdo it I'll tie you to your bed. I've not forgotten your fighting a big jinni alone yesterday, mister wyrmcaller.'

'I promise,' I said.

'*I watch with her,*' Lothi-Mo said. '*Me very good at tying up silly boys, jinni-hoarder.*'

CHAPTER 17 – PIRATE PRISONER

Three days after we left Smalkand, the *Killarn Ranni* passed the northern borders of the Peaks. The heat coming from the Nanstalgarod desert was as I remembered it, and I felt the familiar sweat drip down my back.

'Funny,' I said, standing on the quarterdeck, with my back to the railing. 'Here was where it all started. The Hellesands as a hazy kiln in the distance; me in this spot, Wylmer's unspeakable cousin pacing around—he never could remain in one spot. In Perre's place was the quartermaster, with the steersman at the wheel. Then Kellani came up and...'

'Ship to starboard!' Lothi-Mo's shrill voice called from the masthead.

I stiffened, feeling the blood drain from my face. 'That's what happened—we sighted a ship and went to investigate.'

'You want us to have a look?' Lieutenant Perre said, unaware of my shock.

I took a deep breath to steady my racing heart. 'Yes, why not?' I said, feigning nonchalance. 'It might be a pirate. Then it was *Ahaude*, a collier out of Dvarghish. And that flippin' sea monster trying to sink her.'

This time the other ship was a Navy cutter; a one-masted vessel even smaller than *Tipred* had been, whose three popguns bravely pointed at us.

'*Hove to and identify yourself,*' her string of signal-flags ordered. '*Destination?*'

'*Pasandir Navy schooner* Killarn Ranni, *bound for Port Naar,*' Perre answered.

'*Thank you,*' the cutter said. '*We are out pirate hunting.*'

It sounded so naïve, we all looked at each other. 'I hope they won't find any,' Naudin said. 'What kind of idiot sends a six-gun cutter after the Bokkaners?'

'*Silly boy playing captain,*' Lothi-Mo said disapprovingly from above. '*Shouldn't be out alone; comes to no good that will.*'

'Make, *Good luck*,' Lieutenant Perre answered.

The cutter dipped her flag in reply and sailed blithely on.

Seen from the sea, Port Naar looked like a poor fishing village painted on a desolate wasteland.

'All is gone,' Jem said. She stood at the railing, staring at the cheerless scene. 'This was a beautiful place of white palaces, palm trees, and fine ships. Now even the remains have all but disappeared.'

'They plundered the ruins to build the navy port,' Naudin said. 'Do you mind that?'

For a few heartbeats, Princess Jem didn't answer. 'No,' she said finally. 'You barbarians can't do worse than the way Grandfather murdered the land. Whatever honor we had was lost even before the sand came.' She waved a translucent hand at the bay. 'Carry it all away; use it for something decent for once.'

'Decent?' Naudin said. 'This?' He glanced at Perre, who stood beside Captain Wylmer, watching the approaching jetty. 'It may be welcome as a shelter in a storm, but for the poor souls who live here it is punishment.'

'I know it,' I said. '*Tipred*'s regular patrol ended here. There's an MCTC depot; a tavern, some fishermen, and a few desperate shopkeepers have set up a business, but that's all.'

'This is the place my dad wanted me to see?' Kellani said. 'Why? You must've goofed up good to be sent here.'

'And you hadn't?' Naudin said slyly and ducked to avoid her large hand.

I glanced at her. 'I know it's not much. If it weren't for the reclaimer dig sites in the desert, I think they would've abandoned it years ago.'

Naudin snorted. 'Be sure of that; my commodore dad loathes this place. It's costing him heaps of money and the reclaimers almost never use it. Fifteen years ago, when they first came here, they hoped it would stimulate trading with the lands to the north. But nobody is interested.'

'Everybody has been too busy rebuilding their own lands since the war ended,' Kellani said. 'It's only been twenty-five years, remember.'

The schooner berthed close to the palisade gates, watched by two scruffy kids and a dog loafing in the shade of a partly collapsed construction. I lifted my hand, and they waved back, but it was too hot to get them moving.

'Any shore leave?' Wylmer asked.

I couldn't suppress a grin. 'Sure, for what it's worth. Tell them to stay inside the palisade; it's crawling with scorpions outside. Meanwhile, we'll go visit the local commander.'

Naudin made an impolite noise. 'I met him on my way to Lyster's dig. That lieutenant is an unutterable cabbage who can't even spell the word "initiative". Any time spent on him is wasted.'

Our mage friend's opinion of the navy and his father's officers wasn't always to be trusted, but this time I could only agree with him. As the *Tipred*'s ship's boy, I'd met the port lieutenant several times as I ran errands for Captain Malkim or the first officer. He wasn't a bad guy, but commanding Port Naar was clearly beyond him and as a result he did nothing.

'Does anybody ever visit this port?' Kellani asked absently as her eyes scanned the primitive harbor.

'*Ahaude,* once a year, and a few other ships; that's all,' I said.

We entered Navy House, a grandiose name for a low stone building with unglazed windows and no cooling whatsoever. It was almost empty; the only one present was a young officer in a hammock, his white jacket unbuttoned and sweaty as he lay staring at the ceiling.

'Darn, visitors!' he said as we came in. His sudden move set the hammock swinging while he tried to sit and button his jacket at the same time.'

'I'm sorry to wake you up,' I said.

'It's the hour of sleep.' The lieutenant swung his legs to the ground. He was a thin Vanhaari, with rounded shoulders and a badly shaven chin. With a puzzled frown he peered at each of us. 'Did you arrive just now? You're not one of the regular visitors.' It was clear he didn't recognize me.

'We're your new neighbors,' I said, smiling. 'We came over to say hi.'

That went too fast for his heat-drugged brain. 'Neighbors?'

'We're from the Pasandir Peaks. We set up a trading base in a bay a few hundred miles south of here.'

'Oh,' he said, frowning as he thought that over. 'I do remember a directive from Navy H.Q. about how the Peaks were an independent country now. Some young fellow calling himself wyrmcaller is boss there, I believe.'

'So he is,' I said, on my most affable. 'That's me— Eskandar, Wyrmcaller of Kalbakar. My companions are broomrider the Lady Kellani of Kell-Spellstor and Lord Naudin, the commodore's son.'

The lieutenant's face flushed, and he moved his shoulders to look more martial.

'Your pardon,' he said awkwardly. 'I didn't mean... Darn, I shouldn't... I'm so *out* of it all here.'

I didn't dare glance at the others for fear of laughing. 'It's this dismal place. How much longer is your tour here?'

'Four years and I'm half-way,' he said, with something approaching desperation. 'Two more years in this hole where nothing ever happens.' He blinked at Naudin. 'I remember now. You arrived here a few months ago, to visit a nearby dig site. But you were a schoolboy.'

'A student of the Magic Institute,' Naudin said, looking down his nose. 'After that visit, I was seconded to the wyrmcaller's team as a mindmage.'

The lieutenant's face cleared. 'Of course I remember! Lady Kellani was the broomrider supposed to visit here, but you never arrived. Then you,' he stared at me with wrinkled brows. 'You're the one who was a ship's boy in *Tipred*, but that was all a sham or something.'

'Undercover,' I said with a straight face. 'It's very hush-hush, you see.'

'Sure,' he said, smiling now. 'It was you who saved *Ahaude*! Darn, you youngsters lead adventurous lives, while I'm commanding a post that's dead on its feet.'

'Do you have a ship?' I asked. 'Perhaps going to sea for a bit would break the monotony?'

The lieutenant waved a nervous hand. 'I have a cutter, but I'm not supposed to leave here. I sent her out looking for pirates with my mid in command.'

So that little six-gun was his, I thought. 'If she's the one we exchanged signals with, she's terribly outclassed. Most pirates around here have been building up their strength lately. I hope she can run?'

'Run?' The lieutenant laughed aloud. 'From what? Those pirates, Bokkaners, whatever they're called aren't dangerous. We sank one of their ships already and captured the crew.'

'You have pirate prisoners?' Kellani said sharply.

'I do,' the lieutenant said, beaming. 'My mid captured them someplace to the north of here. It was a felucca, almost a rowing boat with a sail. Four of the rascals on board, one of them a youngster shouting gobbledygook and waving his swords in defiance. My mid fired one shot and sank them. Then the fool fished them up and took them prisoner. I gave him an earful for saddling me up with those ruffians, believe me!'

Kellani and I exchanged glances. This didn't sound like any pirates we'd met.

'Have they talked?' she asked.

'Only the young rapscallion and he talked plenty.' The lieutenant shrugged. 'Of course no one here understands their lingo. I'm waiting for the next navy ship to take them off my hands. Let Seatome hang them; I lack the authority.'

Kellani looked at him, 'May we see these pirates?'

The lieutenant spread his hands. 'Well...' Then he gave in. 'I suppose it can't hurt. The talkative rogue is fourteen, fifteen years at most. The others are surly rascals, but we have them cowed.' He grabbed his saber from a hook. 'Follow me; I'll take you to our jail.'

I glanced at Kellani and saw her uneasiness. Three men and a boy in a felucca sounded unlike any pirate we'd seen.

We walked down a narrow corridor to the end of the building and a rough-walled room with an iron cage. Inside were three men dressed in simple smocks, and a boy who rose as we entered. He gripped the bars with both hands and spoke, his words commanding, but foreign.

'Pirates?' Lothi-Mi chirped. 'No, no, no. You caught problem, commander of Port Naar. You caught mighty big problem. Declaring-war problem.'

The lieutenant looked at her as if he only now noticed her presence. 'What's that?' he said. 'A speaking pet?'

Before I could say something, Naudin drew himself up to his full length.

'You will mind your manners,' he said. 'Lady Lothi-Mo is a wyrmling of royal descent, a friend of the Weal Council.'

The lieutenant stiffened. 'Your pardon, I... It was surprise; no disrespect meant.'

Lothi-Mo disregarded him. She spoke a few words to the boy who colored hotly and beat the bars with his fists. He had a strong face–lighter than Naudin's brown complexion, but not pale like a Garthan–with a hawkish nose, a stubborn chin, hot eyes and dark, wavy hair, shorn at the back and hanging low over his forehead.

'Of course I speak Vulgar,' the boy said in a heavy accent. 'But I didn't care to.'

'You be silly,' Lothi-Mo chirped. 'Why languish in jail?'

'They attacked me,' the boy said, rather inconsequential I thought. He drew his brows together in a scowl. 'My uncle will not react kindly to this.'

'Was a mistake,' Lothi-Mo said. 'Thought you were pirates, and you didn't say no. Bit not-clever-much, I'd think.'

'I take it you are not a pirate?' I asked.

'Certainly not,' the boy snapped. 'I'm Jazzaunt Hathwaari, Prince of Hizmyr.'

The port commander made a strangled sound in the back of his throat.

'I suggest you open this cage,' Kellani said to him. 'It seems someone made a grave mistake.'

The lieutenant squared his shoulders and took a key from a shelf on the wall. 'I don't understand. Now he can speak like a civilized being, instead of that funny gibberish.'

'Tell commander it is not gibberish,' Lothi-Mo said to me. 'Tell him it is the language of Hizmyr, a rich and powerful country not far away. Tell him lieutenants have been broken for less than putting foreign royal princes in jail.'

The lieutenant stiffened, his eyes wild. 'But how...'

I waved him down. 'Were you engaged in any illegal activities, prince?'

'I was not!' the boy said and his eyes flashed. 'I was out sailing my fine new yacht, when that stupid cutter came and sank us! They are the pirates, not me.' He pointed a finger at us. 'I demand compensation. This is going to cost you plenty! My beautiful ship, my birthday gift from the king!'

'I'm sure something can be worked out,' I said. 'Are you a sailor?'

'I wish I were,' the boy said, subsiding. 'My late father wanted me to become a general, like himself, but I'd far liefer go to sea.'

One of his men said something, and the prince snapped an answer. Then he turned back to me.

'What happens now?'

'I think we can turn this mess into something profitable,' I said. 'Given the choice, your royal uncle would rather trade than fight, I suppose?'

The boy sighed. 'Yes.' Then he narrowed his eyes at me. 'We're not talking ransom, are we?'

I grinned. 'No, honest trade.'

'And my compensation? I lost my ship.'

'We'll find something for that too.' I looked at the others. 'Of course the Weal should repair their mistake, but...'

'But that would mean giving them entrance to a new market,' Naudin said drily. 'So you're not going to tell m' father.'

I smiled. 'I'm not. And I am sure the lieutenant won't mind forgetting all about a felucca and things, won't you, lieutenant?'

'At least that way you will avoid a court-martial,' Kellani said.

'I will not tell my fathers either,' Naudin said. 'If we have a deal, that is.'

The lieutenant sagged. 'I think that will be best.'

'I'm going to ask for your trust, prince,' I said. 'I want you to come with us to our base, two days to the south of here. Then we'll change ships and sail you home in royal state.'

The boy frowned. 'You know, I do trust you,' he said, at a loss. 'And I don't even know you. Why?'

'Because you're a clever prince,' Lothi-Mi chirped and there was an undertone of laughter in her voice. 'You understand we're friends.'

The boy's face remained puzzled, but he nodded.

I glanced at Lothi-Mo, but she was innocently sniffing around, muttering 'Mice? Mice?'

'Let's pick up our purser and return to Smalkand,' I said. 'Prince, will your people miss you already?'

He lifted his hands. 'Dunno; I bet they'll think I'm overstaying my leave again.' He shot me a fleeting grin. 'I tend to do that, you know.'

'And your men?'

Jazzaunt glanced at the three men huddling behind him. 'Those? Fishermen my uncle hired to crew for me. They have no loyalty to me; their only wish is to go home.'

I got out my purse and handed the prince a few gold coins. 'Pay them. I'm sure they'll find a fishing boat willing to take them north.'

'You weren't afraid of pirates?' Kellani said. 'Sailing with only three men?'

'Pirates?' the boy said. 'My ship was much faster than those fellows.'

'Faster than a steamship?' I said.

'Pirates don't have any,' the boy protested.

'Lately they do,' I said. 'There's been a change of leadership among the Bokkaners and they're much stronger and more aggressive than before.' I turned to go. 'Coming, prince? If you want to try your hand at sailing a schooner, this is your chance.'

On the way back to Smalkand, the prince proved he knew quite a lot of small ship handling and navigation, and both Wylmer and Perre took turns instructing him in the bigger stuff. He hit it off with the troop, too, even when he did something stupid like trying to lord it over Jornyll and getting well trounced as a result.

The second day we came back to Smalkand Bay where we found only *Marigold* at anchor. The sun shone from a clear sky and the bay lay still and blue, reflecting the snow-topped mountains.

Prince Jazzaunt stared around in wonder. 'I've never been this far south. Those mountains are big, aren't they?'

'Welcome to the Peaks, home of Bodrus the Sleeping God.' I said. 'Yes, they're big, and farther inland they're even bigger.'

'I like it,' he decided. 'It's a good place.'

I grinned. 'Good. Let's call a boat and go ashore the old-fashioned way.'

CHAPTER 18 – STORIES TO TELL

Drakon's gig landed Kellani, Naudin, the prince and me at Smalkand beach.

'Now where is this keep?' Jazzaunt said, staring around.

'This way,' I said.

'Oh!' he said as we strode to the entrance. 'Caves?'

Willow, all a-glow with excitement, was the first to greet us.

'You're back at the right moment! Shaw did it, we're going to be rich, boss!' Then she saw the prince and smiled. 'Sorry, welcome to Smalkand Keep.'

'This is Prince Jazzaunt of Hizmyr,' I said. 'He'll be staying with us for a few days. He'll bed with Aya's crowd. Now what's this about Shaw?'

At that moment I saw Wylmer appear out of nowhere and now I noticed the machine in the corner of the entry hall, and some hastily chalked lines on the floor around his feet.

'Boss!' he exclaimed. 'We've got such stories to tell!'

I tapped my head with my hook hand. 'Wait. Is that a portal?'

'Yes,' he said, beaming. 'Imooga and her new pals just finished it. It only goes to Shaw's headquarters in Seatome yet, but it works great.'

'What new pals? And what headquarters? What have you guys been doing?'

Lothi-Mo raced in and with a flurry of leathery wings came to rest in the air beside me.

'It has happened,' she crowed. 'Shaw has hatched; ooh, and a fine wyrm girl she'll be.'

'What?' I said, thoroughly confused now. 'Shaw hatched?'

'Let's go to the office,' Kellani said firmly. 'Then I'm sure Wylmer can explain all.'

'Of course,' Wylmer said. 'I'll try to be cool about it, but I don't promise anything.'

Then Aya and her guys came in and I dumped Jazzaunt with them. 'Give him a tour, everything; I'm a bit busy all at once.'

Aya lifted an eyebrow. 'There is a smell of excitement in the air. Come on, guys, let's find out what it is about.'

I turned to Wylmer. 'The office,' I said urgently. I hurried across the cafeteria, answering greetings left and right, and when we were in the office, closed the door.

'Now tell me about Shaw,' I said, dropping down behind my desk.

'I only came in halfway,' Wylmer said. 'The rest you must ask her. I only know she dragged Nate and Keena to Seatome, got herself a grand warehouse in the harbor district, engaged a regiment of guys and is making money. She did it! In the time you were gone, she built a company, the Pasandir Trading Corporation. Now comes the best part.' For a moment Wylmer fell silent and his round face turned rapturous. 'Shaw had hired two clerks from Banker Pomfrith, who had died recently.'

'Pomfrith dead?' Naudin exclaimed. 'That's good news! He was a crook.'

'His heirs were worse,' Wylmer said. 'WyDir did business with him; he was the majority shareholder.' He looked around earnestly. 'What I'm going to tell is confidential. Some years ago, my father needed money to expand. In exchange for a loan he gave eighty percent of his stock to Pomfrith, who would be the sleeping partner. Well, he wasn't. He placed his own henchman beside my father, and a load of cronies in the board of directors. Together, they were sucking WyDir empty of money.

'I didn't tell Shaw all this, only about the stocks and that the heirs were going to resell them to their criminal relations.'

Wylmer smiled. 'Shaw and Keena burgled the Pomfrith house and got those blasted stocks back.'

I sat gaping at him. Shaw? Our shy, little Shaw? Burgling a house?

Then Lothi-Mo cackled, and Kellani laughed aloud. 'Good for her! So you're a rich man now?'

Wylmer shook his head. 'Never! Even the thought is a nightmare.' He folded his hands on the table, and I saw they trembled slightly.

'I signed them over to Shaw's company,' he said.

That came like a blow between the eyes. 'Just like that?' I said, reeling. WyDir was a mega big company, with thousands of employees.

'I never felt so relieved in my life,' Wylmer said softly. 'Whatever I did with my life, there always had been the fear that I'd have to inherit WyDir. Now that's gone, and I am free.' His face twitched. 'My father had a stroke. We went to his house, but he refused to see me. He... sent his own WyDir stock to Shaw.' Wylmer straightened. 'The Pasandir Peaks are now sole owner of the largest independent airship company in the Weal.'

'Well,' Naudin said. 'Well, well, well.'

'I must see this business,' I said, but Wylmer shook his head.

'Not you, not yet.' He smiled. 'Don't spoil it for her. She's told her PTC guys all about you and what you're doing for Bodrus. They all know you're the big man in the background. She'll want to have all neat and tidy, and then invite you formally.'

'Mountains' Breath,' I said. 'This is scary.'

'You can't do everything yourself,' Kellani said. 'Accept that other people can do things too.'

'Of course,' I said, surprised. 'I know she can, but still...'

'There's more,' Wylmer said. 'Shaw engaged a mover mage to start our first Peaks trading route. Callogan's a big, tough guy – for a Vanhaari – and born somewhere near the Peaks. Don't be surprised if there's a caravan rolling the next time you come back.'

Kellani put a heavy arm across my shoulders. 'Easy,' she said softly. 'These are all the things you want done but haven't got the time to do yourself. And what Naudin told Shaw goes for you as well. Delegate!'

I leaned my head against her side and nodded. 'I know, and I'm glad it's going to happen.' Then I grunted and sat up straight. 'All right. Anything else?'

Wylmer grinned. 'Before they moved in, Shaw's warehouse had been a clandestine pirate operation. The harbor guard had found them thanks to your actions at Clam Street; this guy Llynsing had been involved. For once they did something, and wiped out the pirates. Then Shaw bought the property. Apparently, the guard had overlooked some loot, for a pirate ship crept in at night and thought to steal it back.'

'And?' I said. Gods! Little Shaw and a bunch of pirates?

'She had been hiring people, and together they beat off the bandits. One turned out to be a jinni, so they killed him.'

'Shaw killed a jinni?' Kellani said. 'How?'

'They all attacked him, and it was touch-and-go, Nate said afterwards. Then this guy Callogan came in and ported the jinni out to sea. End of story.'

'Ha!' I said. 'Sounds familiar. She must've assembled quite a team.'

'She did,' Wylmer said. 'That jinni left a ship behind, a bomb ketch. Shaw got a Chorwaynie crew to sail her. She wants to start a merchant fleet. I don't think we'll get all those guys to become Peak citizens, so they'll not join the navy. I don't know what you and Abia say to that?'

'I'm fine with it, but I'll check what she thinks,' I said. 'Well, you gave me a lot to think of. Now I'd better go the rounds and say hello.'

'Meet Imooga's Thali engineers,' Wylmer said. 'One went to Seatome to set up a workshop. They're going to sell ice machines. We have four others, all working like happy beavers to discover Smalkand's secrets.'

I laughed; suddenly nothing could surprise me anymore. 'Was that all?'

Wylmer thought. 'Shaw wants WyDir to operate a line from here to Seatome and further,' he said. 'And she's told her guys to research the possibility of an airline along the length of the Peaks. I always thought it impossible, but I'm not sure of anything these days.'

I shook my head. 'Nor I.'

Lothi-Mo grinned. 'Leave it to the girls, wyrm boy.'

CHAPTER 19 – SINGER ANTICS

Jornyll crept on his stomach through the grass, his eyes on the little flag in the middle of the clearing. Bamson, Howy, and the prince were defending it, while he, Zaotinq, and Razoon Mir tried to steal the piece of red cloth and turn it in on the beach where Justym the singer waited to receive it. Amaj and Aya stood each on a side of the circle, hidden in the shrubbery and eying their every move, ready to cry foul.

He grinned as he saw Bamson nudge Howy and point to some movement on the other side of the circle. Howy and the prince now looked the same way. Then Jazzaunt roared and leaped at the creeping Zaotinq. Howy jumped his brother, and Bamson, instead of looking out for his third opponent, went to assist the prince.

Jornyll snatched the flag away and made off with it. He was the fastest runner of the troop, and with his two mates keeping the other party busy, he was certain of victory.

Joyously he ran, spurred on by the angry cries of the duped defenders. *That blockhead Bamson*, he thought. *It's like stealing cookies from a babe.* He sprinted down the path to the beach, leaping across obstacles. *Justym, where are you, buddy?* He looked around the beach. There was the circle, just as they had drawn it in the sand, but there was no Justym. He halted abruptly. Footprints, signs of a scuffle and a body dragged toward the water. Wildly, he looked out over the bay. There! A swift jollyboat disappeared behind the *Marigold*, running for the open sea.

Pirates? he thought with a shock. Then he wheeled around and ran back.

'What are you doing?' Razoon shouted as he came back, still clutching the red flag.

'Alarm!' Jornyll cried. 'Pirates!' He almost bumped into Amaj, who stepped from a bush right before him.

'What pirates?' the young lord said sharply.

'Justym's gone,' Jornyll said, gasping for breath. 'Saw a boat rowing away fast; not ours. Goin' for the sea.'

'Stealing Justym?' Amaj said. 'Darn! Get your arms and brooms, we're going after them.'

'What about me?' the prince demanded. 'I got no broom.'

'You're a guest,' Amaj said. 'You better go inside and warn the others.'

'No!' the boy said. 'If there's action, I want to be in. Give me a broom.'

'Come then, but don't cry on my shoulder when you're killed,' the young lord said.

'Ride with me,' Jornyll said, dressing fast.

Moments later they were in the air, speeding across the bay and through the narrow passage to the open sea.

The prince slapped Jornyll's knee and pointed. Below them was the boat, its six rowers working hard. Beside the steersman lay a blue-clad bundle.

They got him! Jornyll thought, and he waved to Amaj.

The leader nodded and gestured to fly on.

'What are we doing?' the prince shouted against the wind.

'Can't attack a small boat from the air,' Jornyll said in his ear. 'There ain't room, see.'

Past the narrow passage between the mountains was a sailing vessel, a beamy little ship with a tall mast and a large bowsprit. *Merchantman, six guns to a side,* Jornyll thought.

'That's where we're going,' he said to the prince.

Amaj waved, and the little troop swooped down to land on the ship's main deck.

'Don't resist!' Amaj shouted, sword in hand. 'Lay down your arms!' The sailors on deck lifted their hands, showing none carried a weapon.

They're not pirates! Jornyll thought. *What did we capture?*

'Who the heck are you?' a bony man in a dark brown suit said, waving his hands in agitation.

'Pasandir Armed Forces,' Amaj snapped. 'You're inside our waters. You will allow us to inspect your ship and papers or face the consequences.'

That skipper knows who we are, Jornyll thought. *He looks like a kid caught at... at stealing an apple.'*

Amaj pointed his blade at the man. 'Show me your books.'

At that moment, a tall man in a blue robe burst from the great cabin.

'You foolish children!' he shouted. 'You will not thwart me! I am Aera's hand and I won't be defied.'

Jornyll felt a shock of surprise, seeing the man. It was that same guy who had come to Fort Jamril, demanding Justym and who had threatened to kill Lothi-Mo.

'Singer Wador!' Amaj said. 'Still at your tricks?'

'You will be silent, blasphemous boy!' The singer lifted his hands and wriggled his fingers at the young lord. The surrounding air crackled as the magic built up.

Gods! Jornyll's muscles tautened, but then a square-built shape sprang at the singer and knocked him to the deck.

'Down,' Prince Jazzaunt snapped. 'You got your orders, dog!'

Amaj took a deep breath. 'You are all under arrest,' he said to the man in the brown suit. 'Bring rope and be quick about it.'

The man paled. 'What will you do?' he said. 'You're not going to hang the singer?'

'Of course not,' Amaj said. 'I leave that to my superiors.'

A sailor came hurrying with an end of rope. Jornyll took it and turned the singer onto his face. He then proceeded to bind him securely.

'There's the boat,' Amaj said softly. 'Not a word now.'

There were a few bangs as the jolly came alongside, and the sound of several men cursing.

'Careful there!' a voice said. 'Don't drop him into the water. Singer Wader wants him alive, fool.'

A man stepped on deck carrying an unconscious Justym.

Amaj moved. 'You will lay the boy down carefully,' he said in a harsh voice. 'Turn around slow and easy. You are all under arrest.'

A second man jumped past the first and attacked Amaj with a dagger in his outstretched fist.

No hesitation now. Jornyll sprang forward and the man fell, blood welling up through his tunic.

The first man gaped at the red stain spreading out over the deck and put Justym down before raising his hands.

'I'm good,' he said. 'No violence.'

'Tell your friends to come aboard and surrender,' Amaj said.

Minutes later, five men stood at the main mast, looking shocked and apprehensive.

'These are my hands,' the master said, with sweat on his face. 'All but the one you knocked down; he serves the singer. Wador hired our ship for a job, but we didn't count on anything criminal.'

'You can tell it all to the Wyrmcaller,' Amaj said.

'He's coming already,' Aya said, waving at the sky. Then she kneeled down beside Justym and checked his breathing. 'Lad's still with us.'

Jornyll looked up and saw a crowd of broomriders approaching fast. Amaj waved and there was cheering from above.

Eskandar, Naudin, and Kellani landed, while the others turned back.

'What's all this?' Eskandar said, looking at the wounded man, at Justym lying in a heap, and finally at the bound singer. 'Wador?'

'They thought to kidnap Justym,' Amaj said. 'So we went and told them no.'

Eskandar turned to the man in the brown suit. 'You're the master?'

The man nodded. 'I am. Singer Wador hired me and my *Liddel Maid* for a trip to the Chorwaynies, then to the Peaks and finally to their holy island. I had no idea he was planning something illegal! I mean, he's a singer of high rank...'

Eskandar nodded. 'I see. You will enter the bay, mister. You'll be our guests till we've got to the bottom of this business.'

Jornyll looked at the wyrmcaller. His face was bleak and drawn.

'What will you do?' Kellani said worriedly.

'I'd like to go to Cloudburgh right now and pull the high temple down around their stupid ears,' Eskandar said. 'But we must be calm. We must be responsible. Darn, we haven't got time for this tomfoolery. Naudin, please ask your Spellstor father to come here. I want him to handle this business, for if I must do it, things will get messy fast.'

'Don't do anything hasty,' Kellani said.

Eskandar turned a cold face to her. 'I'm not hasty. But I won't accept anyone coming into my lands and stealing away people under my protection.'

Jornyll had seen him angry before, but never this bitter rage, and knowing Eskandar's power, it made his blood run cold.

The broomer nodded; she, too, was clearly furious. 'Of course not. Those crazy singers! Do they *want* to cause another war?'

Jornyll gathered his courage in his hands. 'How did you know anything was amiss?'

Eskandar relaxed slightly. 'Lothi-Mo saw what happened from her nest on Wyrm Ledge and warned me. We came to assist you if necessary, but you guys had things in hand.' He nodded at Amaj. 'Well done, all.'

CHAPTER 20 – DIVINE ADOPTION

'I'm afraid you must,' Kellani said coolly.

'Darn and blast!' I shouted. Then I took a deep breath to steady my anger. She was right, and that idiot singer wasn't her fault either. Still, I wasn't pleased with our Weal allies, and the idea that I had to port to Spellstor and fetch Lord Basil myself tried my patience to the limit. Not that there was another option; if I wanted him here, I had to bring him. I couldn't very well send *Pewbara* all the way and they didn't have our portal coordinates.

I went to the hall, added Lord Basil's coordinates to our portal, and flashed away. It was just like any other port, short, cold, and bitterly airless, before I arrived in the portal room of Spellstor House. In the large white hall, Naudin's mother Siolde greeted me.

'Welcome,' she said, enveloping me with her arms and a few yards of shawls. 'You are all tensed up. Use your powers to relax; your body will be thankful for it.'

'I know,' I said. 'But my mind isn't responsive to calm right now.'

'Exercise,' she said with a smile. 'No matter, you will learn that trick. Come inside.'

In the salon, Basil greeted me with a warm handshake. Of course Queen Maud was there as well. Together, the two were the driving force behind the Weal Council.

Basil glanced at me. 'An unfortunate business,' he said.

'I am extremely angry,' I said candidly. 'I trust you and the queen will deal fairly with this matter.'

'We know Eghol,' Maud said. 'The man is a fool.'

'If you'd step closer, I will port us back.'

I wanted to give them a good look, so we arrived on the beach. The sun shone and a lone albatross screeched overhead.

'Welcome to Smalkand Keep,' I said.

'It's beautiful.' Lord Basil stared around at the mountains and the mirroring lake, and took a deep breath of clean air.

'A fine spot,' Maud agreed. She inspected *Drakon*, at anchor between *Marigold* and the schooner. 'That is one heck of a strange ship.'

'It's a Qoori design,' I said curtly. 'We captured her at Brisa.' *Darn it, do relax*, I told myself and tried a smile. 'Please follow me; I'll show you how we cavemen live.'

I led them inside and Basil stopped abruptly in the hall. 'Dear gods,' he said. 'The power of this place.' I saw his uncommonly pale face had turned splotchy and his eyes were great with an unfathomable emotion. He must sense the mana pump at the back of the keep, sucking power from the Intermedium.

'Mana is one thing we don't lack,' I said.

'It's incredible,' he said. 'Doesn't it make you giddy, all that power around you, ready to use?'

It hadn't. I never lacked mana for whatever I wanted to do. My body had its limits; my power didn't. I couldn't say that though, it would sound like boasting.

'There is one more thing you must know,' I said carefully. 'We have our own portal.'

Lord Basil stared at me. 'You do? How?'

'It was a matter of combining several technologies. Once we had them all worked out, our Thali engineers produced one in a matter of days.'

'You cannot sell them,' the Spellstor said.

I gave a curt laugh. 'I won't do that. It would bring the world down around us.'

'So it would,' he said. He walked over to the portal in the corner. 'That's it? Deceptively simple. Where do you get all that raw power?'

'Directly from the Intermedium,' I said. 'The keep's builders placed a pump at the rear end, to power our shields.'

'Who built this place?' Queen Maud said.

'Nanstalgarod, a long time ago. But I don't think the technology was all theirs. There are mysteries involved we haven't solved yet.'

I wasn't going to tell them about the Qoori and their technologies; a guy had to keep *some* secrets.

Luckily, the arrival of Kellani and Naudin spared me further questions. Kellani greeted her mother with a peck on the cheek and a smile, while Naudin and his father gripped each other's wrist for a second. Then we went to the office, where Amaj and Justym waited.

The young singer looked wan and sick; his abductor had walloped him hard and even Na'a hadn't been able to restore his full health in one go. He didn't lack anger, a bitter rage against Wador, Eghol, and every singer in the world.

'This is Justym of Marroth, Vystyn's great-grandson,' I introduced him.

'So that's you,' Lord Basil said, offering his hand. 'I'm glad to meet you. I always thought the singers overdid it in their distrust of Vystyn's kin. Apparently even I underrated their foolishness.'

'I agree,' Maud said. 'It's utterly unfair to blame you for what an ancestor did so long ago.'

Justym looked up, visibly surprised by their sympathy. 'I hate them for it,' he said. 'And don't say they're my brother singers, for they are not! I serve Aera with gladness, not those scheming rats!'

'Of course not,' the queen said. 'They treated you shamefully.'

I saw Kellani's startled glance as if her mother's reaction caught her by surprise.

'Would you mind very much if I read your mind?' Basil said as he sat down behind the long table. 'It's not that I doubt you, Justym; but the Council wants me to make sure.'

'I have nothing to hide,' Justym said, his chin up in defiance. 'Go ahead, lord; look all you want.'

'I will be very discreet,' Basil said. He folded his hands on the table and for a short while he sat motionless. I didn't peek; while I was curious to see his method, Teodar had taught me manners–the hard way.

'A nice, strong mind,' the Spellstor said after a while. 'Unformed, but that's not surprising, under the circumstances. I see traces of Naudin's influence; keep that up, my son knows what he is doing. You are good with the elements; that is a useful strength. And of course you're squeakily innocent of wrongdoing.' He grinned. 'I approve, young man. Eghol is an idiot.'

Justym blinked. 'Th-thank you.'

'Eghol is a double idiot if he thinks he can send his agents into my headquarters to abduct my friends and won't have me retaliate,' I said in a harsh tone.

'It was not a clever move,' Maud said calmly. 'What exactly happened?'

I had my witnesses waiting, so I turned to Amaj. 'Ask Jornyll to come in.'

Jornyll gave his part of the story, standing with legs apart, arms clasped to the back, no longer a street kid but a soldier.

'Well told,' Maud said when he was done. 'Well handled, too, warrior. One question, you went back to warn Amaj; why didn't you run to the keep and tell Eskandar?'

'Amaj is my commander,' Jornyll said. 'So I report to him, when we're on duty.'

The queen grinned. 'Sure thing. As I said, well done.'

'Amaj, your turn,' I said.

The lordling rose. 'I received Jornyll's report, then ordered my troop to arm and broom up.' He told everything, except for mentioning Prince Jazzaunt's identity, as I wanted to keep that part out of the story.

When Amaj had finished, he left the room to fetch the captain of the hired vessel.

The man in the brown suit bowed, hat in hand and visibly scared.

'I'm a trader, lords, Ma'am,' he said. 'Master and owner of the *Liddel Maid*. I ply between the ports of the Weal, buying and selling what's available. When Singer Wador wanted to hire me, I jumped at the chance. He offered good gold for what seemed an easy trip.' He wrung his hands. 'Had I known he was engaged in skullduggery, I would've refused. But he is a singer of high rank!'

'Yes,' I said. 'What was your first port of call in Wador's service?'

'The Chorwaynies,' the skipper said. 'That was strange, for we had to hove-to outside a bay and Singer Wador spent a long time sitting motionless with his eyes closed. Then he wanted to see my charts of the Kell-to-Hellesands coast and after a moment put his finger on a spot where he wanted to go to next.'

'And that spot was?'

'This location, lord,' the skipper said, bobbing nervously.

I nodded and sat back.

By turns, Basil and Maud questioned him further, and each answer depressed them more.

Finally, Basil nodded. 'We know enough.' He looked at me. 'Were you pressing charges against the ship's master?'

I had long before decided not to, so I shook my head. 'I am satisfied he acted in good faith.' I turned to the captain. 'You will give me your report in writing and then you are free to go.'

'Thankee, lord,' the ship's master said, bowing himself from the room.

When he had left, Lord Basil leaned back and sighed. 'A bad business.'

I nodded. 'Wador interferes with things he doesn't understand.' I tapped a sheet of paper under my hands. 'His hatchet man is dead, I'm afraid, but Naudin got what we wanted to know from the fellow before he died. That first stop was at Jamril Bay. Wador invaded our privacy and stole

Justym's whereabouts from the minds of our kids. That's how he knew where to find us.'

The queen made a gesture of disgust. 'That alone would be enough to condemn him.'

I looked at Amaj and Jornyll. 'We will not speak of this outside this room.' Then I turned back to Naudin's neatly written notes. 'Once they arrived at the entrance to Smalkand, Wador had sent his agent to the beach to spy out the situation and if possible to kidnap someone for information over the keep, its defenses and most especially about Justym's movements. When he arrived on the beach and found his quarry fast asleep on the beach, he thought it a sign from Aera. So he knocked the boy unconscious and returned to the ship.' I looked up and winked at Jornyll. 'Alas for him, one of us was wide awake and foiled his efforts.' I nodded to Amaj. 'Get Wador.'

The singer looked terrible. Wild eyed, his face twisted in a sneer, he was only a shadow of his former self.

'I demand you release me!' he cried as Amaj dragged him into the office. 'I...' Then he saw Basil and Maud, and he wilted.

'Singer Wador,' Basil said with a terrible calm. 'Our ally, the sovereign ruler of the Pasandir Peaks, accuses you of committing crimes on his territory. What have you to say for yourself?'

'I'm doing my duty to my goddess, lord,' Wador said. 'That Vystyn child is an abomination! He is planning the end of our world, of the Weal, of Aera and the other gods. He is a demon of tainted blood, traitor's blood! Surely you see how evil he is, lord!'

'So you thought to creep into a foreign ruler's domain and steal him away?' Basil said. 'Whose orders were that, Singer Wador? Who told you to come here?'

The man rose to his full length and lifted his arms to the ceiling. 'No one! I am a senior singer; I am a power, making mine own plans.'

'As did Vystyn. And like him you risked war between the Weal nations and the Peaks. The Weal didn't give you such power, singer. Nor, I deem, did High Singer Eghol. You will come with us to Spellstor and the justice of the Council.'

'You are fools!' Wador cried. 'Traitors, all of you! You are aiding that demon to bring us down.'

Suddenly Justym sprang up. 'You are the traitor, Wador!' he cried. 'You are denying Aera. When have you been to the temple last? When have you prayed last, Wador? You are an empty vessel, torn by false ambitions, and the goddess turns her back on you. You are godless, Wador! Apostate, like so many of you singers, those smooth-talking bureaucrats, filled with their own importance instead of Aera's glory!' There was an unmistakable aura of *something* surrounding the boy, a female shape, whose accusing hand enveloped Justym's smaller one. 'Begone!'

Wador gurgled and sagged to the ground like an empty robe.

Across from him, Justym stood shivering. 'Take care of the child, Wings,' an unmistakably female voice said. 'He *is* my chosen, you see. My share of the prophecy and my agent of change.'

I gripped the roadside guy statuette and bowed. 'Of course, Aera. We are of one purpose in this matter?'

'We are,' the goddess said. 'All that nonsense has taken too long. Tell him to hurry back, will you?'

Then she disappeared.

We stood all looking at each other. Amaj with his hands outstretched to Justym, Basil half-risen from his chair, Kellani, Naudin... The mindmage sprang over the table and kneeled beside Wador.

'He *is* gone,' Naudin said, and his voice shook. 'It's only his robe and boots left.'

Justym looked at me. 'I...' Then his eyes turned away, and he fainted into Amaj's arms.

'Gods,' Basil said, stupefied.

I nodded, taking him literally. 'They are very much active in this whole thing.'

'Why?'

I sat down. 'I don't know. There is a prophecy, perhaps that is the reason.'

'Can you tell us?' Maud asked.

I hesitated.

'Tell them!' Teodar's voice whispered in my head. *'After that visitation, they need to know.'*

'Where have you been all the time?' I asked.

'Hiding in my room. As I'll go on doing until you rid me of those pirates. So hurry, will ya?'

I cursed inaudibly. 'The prophecy. Long ago, the gods quarreled. They did so quite often, but this time one of them had enough of it, and he retired from the pantheon. He found a cozy spot for himself, created a monastery to keep his body, made wyrms to guard him, and slept. That is Bodrus.'

I grunted. 'It's not my place to criticize my god, but it wasn't a well thought-out move. For without him, the quarrel stayed alive. That caused the last war.'

I saw the look of anger on the rulers' faces. 'Imagine if someone had soothed Aera when Vystyn and his father stole those masks,' I said quietly. 'She wouldn't have turned her back on her people, and then there would've been no war.'

Basil closed his eyes for a moment. 'True.'

Maud said something unrepeatable. 'Go on.'

'Here comes the prophecy,' I said. 'The predecessor to the present Kavid-Jar, Bodrus' voice and my spiritual brother, got this vision of a young Wings of the Mountain gathering an army of children for a purpose none of us yet know. So the Kavid-Jar searched the lands and found me. He trained me and cozened me into this job. Now the gods keep shoving kids my way.' I paused and smiled at Kellani and Naudin. 'Some of these kids are a bit more than the others; they represent their gods. Like Justym does for Aera and Na'a for Gathea.'

Kellani grabbed my hook arm. 'You mean there's a purpose to that, too?'

I put my hand on hers. 'Remember when we first saw Wemawee, while your ma was accepting Aya?' I caught the queen's eye and grinned. 'Wemawee's first words were an echo of what Aera just said. *Tell him to come back; we need him.* Then she went on greeting me as if she hadn't spoken. I bet that first one wasn't the wisewoman, but Gathea. I bet Mother Gathea suggested that Wemawee send her own daughter as Nature's agent. Of course Na'a is a priestess, just as Justym is a priest, so their deities are closer to them to begin with. Yet I think Naudin and you represent gods too, only those are keeping mum about it.'

'Me?' Naudin said disgusted. 'What god?'

'Lumentis and perhaps Kallianura. And Kellani has Gorm and Otha. Ulaataq has his frosty Grandmother; Jem has that god who vanished when the sands came, and so on.'

'But why all this rigmarole? Why doesn't Bodrus simply wake up? He must know they want him to return,' Kellani said.

'Teodar mentioned there is a danger in him awaking right now,' I said and frowned at the thought. A danger threatening a god and I had no idea what it was. 'Perhaps I must first have my army complete, the wyrms back, and of course the monastery free of the lich.' I patted her hand on my arm. 'We'll get there, don't you worry.'

'Hmm,' Naudin said. 'Representing Lumentis ain't such a chore, but Kallianura is a warrior goddess.'

'Well, you're no slouch in a fight,' I said. 'So until they drop a stray Jentakan kid in our laps, you're it.'

'Yeah, all right,' he said.

His father grinned at him. 'You know Yarwan and I are proud of you, son. We always respected your mind, but that you prove brave and strong as well is a pleasant surprise.'

Naudin squirmed under the compliment, for once at a loss for words. Instead, he took off his glasses and began polishing them on his tunic.

Maud produced a little lioness-like growl in her throat. 'My husband thinks his daughter isn't doing too badly either. He has this trinket he wants you to have, girl, and left it to me to present you with it. So here it is. Catch!'

She threw a little box at Kellani, who plucked it out of the air as if they had rehearsed it. She opened it and stiffened.

'What is it?' I asked.

Maud gave a small smile. 'Broomrider First Officer. He skipped the lowest ranks as unsuitable for a top-level liaison.'

Kellani stared at the little box. I knew she was pleased with her unexpected promotion, and even more with her mother's approval.

I took the little golden brooms from the box and pinned them to the lapels of her uniform jacket. Then I kissed her soundly.

'There you are, and well earned,' I said, hugging her for a moment.

Then I sat back. 'I will leave Eghol to you councilors,' I said. 'Warn him the next time any one of his people tries anything, I will unleash the power of the mountains on him. Somehow I don't think Aera would mind if I did that.'

Lord Basil grimaced. 'We'd better call the Council together and have it out on the table.'

The queen gave a curt nod. 'If the Unwaari want to be part of the Weal, they must follow the rules. No funny doings.'

'What?' Justym sat up, grabbing his head. 'Ouch!' he said. 'What happened?'

'You fainted,' I said, mock-sternly. 'Na'a told you not to excite yourself, mate.'

He looked at me through his fingers. 'I remember Wador and then... Was it real? Really real? Aera was here?'

'She sure was,' I said. 'She named you her chosen one and made Wador disappear.'

'Me?' the boy said dazedly. 'She wanted *me*?'

'She was very clear she wanted you and she was very unhappy with the singers,' Lord Basil said. 'Maud and I will inform the high singer of this development.'

'I would suggest you stop wearing robes,' the queen said. 'If your goddess is displeased with the singers, you don't want to look like one.'

Amaj shook the boy's shoulders. 'Willow has several wardrobes full of nice pirate jackets and pants. You'll feel a different man in them.'

'Aera wanted me,' Justym said, and for the first time he smiled broadly.

'Good idea to take off that robe. Amaj and Jornyll, why don't you go with him and help him choose?' I looked at Basil and Maud. 'Perhaps you would be interested to see the whole keep?'

They were interested – of course they were, so Kellani, Naudin, and I walked them around, showing them everything but the machinery that made it all work. Basil asked a lot of questions, of which I answered most. I introduced them to Ulaataq, who had the word "secrecy" engraved on his tongue and talked a lot without giving away anything.

Maud was more interested in the defensibility of the keep. She offered us artillery – Kell makes the finest guns on the market – at the same price a Weal nation would pay, and I accepted.

'Are you open for recruits?' Lord Basil asked.

'Yes and no,' I said. 'We could use one or two young teachers for our school who could instruct in magic as well. Naudin does a lot of that now, but he's away too often. We need another healer and some capable officers for our schooner would be welcome.'

Basil smiled. 'I will pass the word,' he said. 'Mages and a healer shouldn't be a problem; Mage School will cough up a few souls in need of a traineeship.'

'That would be great,' I said, truthfully.

'I heard your people caught another jinni in Seatome, yesterday,' Basil said.

'Yes,' I said noncommittally. 'Luckily *our* defenses were strong enough.'

Basil snorted. 'I have set a shake-up in motion. We sacked that idiot colonel; after Clam Street we had him watched, and this affair was the limit. His replacement will put the city and harbor guards on a war footing. My Yarwan has ordered naval patrols guarding the seaside and I've confirmed your directors that they can arm their own guards as well. You have quite a nice place there.'

'Yes,' I said. 'We wanted to branch out.'

Basil grinned. 'You did in a big way. Labor Exchange was surprised with your custom.'

'You notice a lot,' I said, answering his smile.

'Everything that concerns pirates and jinn in the Weal has my attention,' Basil said. 'So when your people hired a former pirate trade house, my men went to have a look.' He rose. 'Don't worry; I will not be spying on you. You are allies, after all.' He pursed his lips. 'Your take-over of WyDir was unexpected.'

'It wasn't planned,' I said truthfully.

'I think old Wylmer's stroke made it impossible for him to continue running the company, so his stepping down is probably for the better,' the Spellstor said slowly. 'That his son signed over his shares to your people was surprising.'

'He didn't want to run WyDir,' I said. 'He didn't even want to profit from it. So this seemed the best solution.' That was a bit of fast-talking, for I really had no idea, but it worked.

'We do not want WyDir to fold, Eskandar,' Basil said. 'Should you run into any problems, be so kind to let me know.'

'Then we will return home,' Maud said. 'I'm glad to have seen this place.'

'It is full of wonders,' Basil said with a sideways glance. 'I can understand your not telling us everything.'

'I don't want to be unduly secretive,' I said. 'Some things we found here we don't understand ourselves yet, and others... well, as a young country we must think of our bargaining position.'

The two rulers laughed. 'I don't blame you,' Maud said. 'There are parts of our foundries we keep closed even for Basil, just as he wouldn't show me all of Casterglade Center. You keep your surprises, Eskandar; a nation needs its own strengths.'

Then we shook hands and Basil ported both of them away.

'Phew,' I said, turning to Kellani and Naudin. 'That went well, I think.' I touched the golden broom on her lapel. 'Quite well, actually.'

Then we walked to the cantina bar. 'Time for a lemonade, ice and ice cold,' I said.

We had just finished the evening meal when the lookout at the entranced came running.

'An airship,' he panted. 'A strange airship arrived over sea.'

I cursed as we raced for the exit.

'Not WyDir, it's a government Weal Transport vessel,' Kellani said, staring at the purple ship coming to a rest just past the beach. A bunch of exuberant youngsters jumped down and lined up on the grass, before marching toward us, followed by an older Kell woman in a severe uniform. She called to the youngsters and said something. The little troop halted and let her go first.

The woman limped stiffly over to Kellani and me, apparently unable to bend her left leg. Her posture, dress, and the half-salute with which she greeted us betrayed the veteran-turned-civilian.

'Good day,' she said. 'I'm from the M'Brannoe Foundry, to inspect the location and discuss placements and caliber of the artillery you will be needing.'

'Come with me,' Kellani said immediately. 'I'm not a gunnery buff, but we'll manage.'

I nodded and watched the youngsters, tall and muscled, but obviously no older than most of us. They were all impeccably uniformed and marched in the indomitable way typical of the Kell warrior.

One of them, with a tiny patch of black fur on his armor, gave a curt command, and they all halted as if on parade. The leader saluted.

'Acting First Tiger Cub Benwar,' he said. 'Are you the one in charge?'

I couldn't help but grin. 'I am Wyrmcaller Eskandar, sure. What can I do for you?'

'We're the volunteers, sir,' Benwar said snappily. 'You know.'

'Ah, I'm afraid I don't,' I said.

His face fell. 'Our commander said there were volunteers needed in the Borderlands, to assist our new allies there. Isn't that right?'

'We certainly can use assistance,' I said. 'If you are ready for battle against real enemies?'

The boy brightened. 'We sure are, sir. We eight are all tiger cubs, that means we've been trained as tigers, but we're underage for graduation.' He grinned. 'When commander detailed us volunteers, we were happy for the chance, sir.'

'Detailed you volunteers?'

'Of course, that's how volunteering works, doesn't it?'

'Not exactly, no, but then, I'm not a Kell.' I tried not to laugh. 'No matter; you are all most welcome.'

I looked back to the keep and saw Aya watching from the entrance, her arms crossed and her face unreadable. I wondered how she would take a bunch of Kell kids her own age. Then it dawned on me they were all boys, too. I'd understood most of the Kell armed forces were females.

'Follow me,' I said to Benwar.

Aya marched over to meet us. *Darn, where did she get that tough-marine-sergeant-look?* I thought.

'Lord Amaj is with First Broomrider Kellani and that lady from the cannon factory,' she said briskly.

'Queen Maud sent us some hands,' I said. 'First Benwar, Corporal Aya is second-in-command of our little troop. She will see to your accommodations. You didn't bring arms?'

The boy eyed Aya and swallowed. 'No sir,' he said stiffly. 'I was told we would be armed and kitted-out here.'

'No problem, we have arms aplenty,' Aya said in a no-nonsense tone. 'Follow me, First; I'll take you to our quartermaster.' She looked at me, her face perfectly straight. 'I can hear Jornyll's screams already; these guys are all bigger than him.' Then she turned and strode away, the boys following like a double row of ducklings.

I turned away and smiled. In a few words, Aya had shown them who was boss. I had no idea about the precise rank of an acting first tiger cub, but Kellani would surely be able to tell me.

'Acting first tiger cub?' Kellani said later that evening, when the airship and the foundry representative had left. 'That's a trainee rank. Tigers are infantry, just as leopards are archers, and cubs are trainees. These guys Mother sent us are all Sons of the Army, whose parents died or were otherwise absent from their lives.' She hesitated. 'They're more like our orphans than you'd think. They, too, had parents who were... stained. Insubordination, laziness, drunkenness, just like our kids. And just like our kids it hinders their prospects of advancement. Funny,' she added. 'I had never before thought of it, how unfair it is to judge them for their parents' failures.'

'It is,' I said grimly. 'They seemed eager enough, though.'

'Being away from their barracks must be a relief. Their instructors tend to be harsh. Acting rank or no, their leader must be good, to be in sole command; usually there's a more senior officer to keep an eye on them.'

'No girls among them?' I asked.

She shook her head. 'Trainee units are never mixed. I'll have a word with Aya about how to handle them.'

'I think she knows,' I said. 'She asserted her authority as second-in-command and young Benwar almost saluted her.'

'She's excellent officer-material, our Aya.'

'I'll keep it in mind,' I said. 'I do wonder if those boys are any good; they look awfully young somehow.'

'Kell boys mature slower,' Kellani said. 'But they must be up to it; Mother wouldn't give us untrained infants.'

I stretched and yawned. 'We'll see. At least we have a force to leave behind when we sail for Hizmyr tomorrow.'

'Who will go?' Kellani asked.

'You, Naudin, Justym, and Na'a. Amaj will be in charge here and in his stead, Aya can command our troop.'

'They can handle it,' Kellani said.

We were at our morning meal when Willow came with two unknown Vanhaari, a boy and a girl, looking like newborn owlets; round, downy and gray, with black eyes inspecting the world from behind round glasses.

'Lord Basil brought us visitors,' Willow said, trying not to laugh. 'He was like those awkward types dumping a baby on the orphanage doorstep, furtive and hurried.'

'We're not babies,' the boy said coldly. 'We came because you had a position for teachers of magic and basic knowledge. Is this correct?'

'I hope we're not wasting our time,' the girl said. 'I'm Martha, mage elementalist. My brother Tymon is a healer. We were looking for a traineeship, but there isn't much demand for teachers.'

'Not if you don't want to work for one of those so-called "quality institutes",' her brother added. 'We don't; we are heirs of the Revolution.'

'Oh gods,' Naudin said. 'Seatome revolutionaries?'

'We're the children of Noah and Rebecca,' Martha said. 'The leaders of the Seatome liberation.'

'That was my dad Yarwan,' Naudin said coolly.

Tymon sniffed. 'You must be Naudin? Ruth told us you were here. Indeed, Captain Yarwan was first.'

'And my parents,' Kellani said.

'Maud and Jurgis?' Martha crossed her arms. 'Are you all here?'

'It's a reunion,' I said. 'Even Vystyn's great-grandson is among us.' I pursed my lips. 'I hope that the history you plan to teach is less... biased?'

Tymon's face turned frosty. 'We use Izzabod's *History of the Liberation*,' he said. 'We will not brag about the important part our parents played in the liberation of Seatome.'

'That's great,' Naudin said. 'You know my sister?'

Martha nodded. 'Ruth was my mentor, the last year before she graduated. We always kept contact, even though our parents frown upon the Spellstor dominance.' Then she frowned. 'We don't teach that either. It's just our parents; *we* don't mind the Spellstors.'

I studied the two. I had heard of their parents; two minor local leaders of rival revolutionary groups, bickering and ineffective until Naudin's dad Yarwan arrived with his ship and kicked the enemy out of Seatome. I could understand their wish to paint their parents larger, but...

'Give them a chance,' Naudin said over our narrow private beam. *'Izzabod's book is sound enough; if they use that, it's fine by me.'*

'All right,' I said. 'You're in. Sylas will be here, so you can divide the work between the three of you. You can start tomorrow, for Naudin, Kellani, and I sail for Port Naar in the morning. Do you mindspeak?'

'Of course,' Tymon said. 'My sister is the loudest, but we both have long-range voices.'

'Great,' I said, and I meant it. 'With us away, you'll be contact officers, so try to meet as many of the *Drakon*'s crew as you can.'

Naudin jumped to his feet. 'Come,' he said. 'I'll show you around, introduce you to the others, and tell you a little of what we are doing.'

'When you see Cenn and Brat,' I said. 'Tell them they will go to school, starting tomorrow. I'm sure you can sell the idea to them so they'll think it something wonderful.'

'Me? School is wonderful?' Naudin's expression went from surprise to embarrassment. He had never been very complimentary about his own days at the Institute.

'Well, the teachers in *our* school aren't nincompoops, are they?' I said slyly.

'Of course not!' he said. 'Our teachers are the best.'

'Sell it to them,' I said. 'I want those kids literate.'

Kellani and I watched him walk away with our new mages. 'Heirs of the Revolution,' she said. 'Oh deary me.'

I gripped her hand. 'We'll see how they fit in. At least we'll have someone to warn us should anything go wrong.'

CHAPTER 21 – CUTTER IN DISTRESS

I stood on the *Drakon*'s quarterdeck, staring out over the smooth sea to the, for me at least, unknown northern coast of Nanstalgarod. Not that it differed much; the land appeared just as shimmering hot as the stretch south of Port Naar.

All of a sudden a mental scream shattered the drowsy quiet.

'Emergency! Pirate attack! Navy cutter Bluewing *under attack! Emergency all Weal ships!'*

'Got her coordinates,' Naudin said urgently.

'Give them to the steersman,' Captain Abia said.

I sent out my mind. 'Bluewing, *this is Pasandir navy ship* Drakon of Ilzhar. *We're on our way.'*

'Gods be blessed,' a voice shouted. *'Hurry! Before they kill us all!'*

'Bluewing, *can you give me an image, please?'* I asked, more to steady whoever was mindspeaking.

'Image? I never...' Then a blurred picture of a broken deck and across a bit of sea a sleek one-masted ship with a lateen sail barking flames.

'Nice image, Bluewing. *Who is that speaking?'*

'I'm the captain. No; Midshipman-in-Command. I... They tricked us! They... oh gods, I don't know what to do!'

'What are the pirates doing?'

'Circling us. They... they're jeering. Shooting muskets. I... My men ran below. They won't listen. What must I do?'

'Aya, get your troop ready; we're flying,' I shouted. *'Mid, keep calm. Show you're the captain. We'll be there very soon.'*

In minutes, we were in the air.

'Keep talking, Mid,' I said. *'We're homing in on you. Where did you learn to mindspeak? It's not a qualification the Weal navy wants for its officers.'*

'I know,' he said. *'I wasn't supposed to use it.'*

'A very handy trick,' I said. I saw Aya wave and point down. Then I saw the two little toy boats too.

'*Contact,* Bluewing. *We're almost overhead,*' I said and waited for Kellani to give the order. '

'*What?*' the midshipman said. '*Chottapan's Aid; broomriders?*'

'*Our ship comes on our heels, but we're faster.*'

'*Prepare to board the pirate,*' Kellani said and each of us lifted a hand in acknowledgement. Then we swooped down to the circling ship like a flight of eagles.

'*She's turning,*' I said, surprised. '*Trying to make a run of it?*'

'*She's turning away!*' the mid shouted. '*Oh dear gods, she's turning away!*'

'*Won't escape us,*' I said. '*I'm going out for a while; can't mindspeak and fight at the same time.*' I broke contact.

'*No jinn around,*' Naudin said. '*They're just a bunch of pirates.*'

'*Good,*' I said. '*Wait with landing,*' I shouted. '*Let me make some room first.*' It was a small ship, and the deck was crowded with men. I gathered a broad front of wind and saw them tumbling over each other. Several ended up in the sea, while the others landed in a squirming heap against the railing. Then I landed. Kellani appeared beside me, and Naudin, and a screaming bullet ran at the dazed pirates, slashing and hacking indiscriminatingly.

I blinked. Prince Jazzaunt's battle tactics left a lot to be wished for, but they were contagious. Razoon joined him, yelling curses at the top of his voice, with Howy right behind him. Jornyll followed, with Zaotinq and... A shot rang out and I felt a searing pain in my shoulder. I knew I was falling down, and then no more.

CHAPTER 22 – PORT NAAR

Kellani saw him fall.

'No!' she cried, running to his aid. 'Oh gods!' She saw the blood on Eskandar's face and spreading over his tunic, and her heart skipped a beat. He lived, her mind was strong enough to see that, but he looked in a bad way.

She swept him up and steered her broom into the air in one frantic move. Without a glance at the others, she raced back to the *Drakon*.

She landed on the main deck and ran to the great cabin. 'Na'a!' she shouted. 'To me, quick!'

The healer came running and followed her inside.

'Put him on the bed,' she said and Kellani lowered Eskandar on the quilted bedcover.

'He looks so bad!' she said with anguish in her voice.

'Not half as bad as he should,' Na'a said, ripping the shirt away. 'Look at that! Bullet went through the shoulder. Where's the bleeding? It can't have missed the arteries; he should have bled to death by now. Instead...'

Kellani saw disgust in her face. 'Instead what?'

'Those wounds are closing already. Curse it, Kellie; that guy doesn't *need* a healer. His body is repairing the damage even while he's unconscious.' She sighed. 'How does he do that?'

She straightened. 'I'll get water and clear the blood away. You go back to what you were doing, gal. No need to fret or waste your time here. He'll be fine.'

Kellani looked at Eskandar, so small and fragile. Then she chuckled. 'Darn, my instincts say to protect him. He's such a little guy and...' She shook her head. 'Stupid. He doesn't need my protection, he's the bleepin' wyrmcaller.'

Na'a cocked an eye at the broomer. 'You, ah, like him.'

Kellani swallowed. 'Yes.' She turned to the door. 'But he doesn't see it.' She walked outside and closed the door behind her.

'Kellie? We got the pirate. How is he?' Naudin's mind sounded anxious.

'Eskandar is healing himself,' she said, and marveled how calm she sounded. *'He'll be fine. Good work, coz. Take command for the moment; I'll go over to the cutter.'*

She mounted and flew over to the cutter. The only one on deck was a young fellow in a midshipman's uniform, sobbing his heart out with his ship adrift. The deck was a shambles. Someone had lowered the main sail by just dropping it and small caliber shot had plowed through planking and railing.

'Ho,' she said as she landed beside him. 'Don't despair; all is well.'

He jumped and showed a tear-splotched gray Vanhaari face framed by long, dark hair. 'What? Who...?' Then he saw her uniform and the bright golden brooms on her lapels. A broomer first was equal to a frigate captain, so she outranked him by a mile or more.

He jumped and saluted. 'Ma'am!' he said, relief clear on his face.

'We captured the pirate,' Kellani said. 'How is the situation here?'

'Bad,' the boy said, near to tears again. 'I failed. My men... Those cowardly dogs all fled below, and I... I didn't know what to do. I didn't want to surrender, I couldn't fight, it was horrible.'

'I can imagine,' Kellani said. 'It's not your fault, you shouldn't have been here. Pirate hunting is not a midshipman's task. How many men do you have?'

'Twelve, ma'am,' he said. 'Bos'n's mate, gunner's mate, ten sailors.'

Kellani nodded. 'You take the wheel and steer for the *Drakon.*'

'She's big,' the young midshipman said. 'What is she? I don't recognize her flag.'

'That is the wyrm flag of the Pasandir Peaks navy,' Kellani said. 'The Peaks are an independent country ruled by Wyrmcaller Eskandar,' she added, noting his puzzled face. '*Drakon* is his flagship. Now, get your ship under control while I fetch your crew on deck.'

The midshipman gaped at her. 'You, ma'am?'

Kellani rolled her shoulders. 'Why not?' She grinned at the boy's face and strode to the hold hatchway. Disregarding the ladder, she jumped down and walked toward the silent group of sailors huddling at the other side.

The sailors stiffened and stared at her like a clutch of sheep while she looked them over one by one, contempt clear on her face.

'Cowardice,' she said in a chill voice. 'Disobedience and insubordination. All three are court-martial offenses carrying the death penalty.'

'But... Who are you?' stammered a man in a petty officer's uniform.

'You're the bos'n's mate?' Kellani barked. 'I'm sure you recognize my uniform.'

'Yes, but...'

'Yes what?' Kellani said in a dangerous voice.

'Ma'am! Aye aye, ma'am,' the man said.

'You are a bunch of sniveling cowards,' she told them. 'Twelve trained sailors of the Weal Navy running below out of fear for a little pirate. I will leave your fate to the navy, but now you will all go on deck and make this ship ready to sail again. Then our vessel will escort you back to Port Naar. If one of you thinks to disobey even the smallest order, I will have him hanged. Am I clear?'

'Aye aye, ma'am,' the bos'n's mate said unhappily.

'Then do so.' Kellani watched the men shuffle to the ladder. *'Mid? You hear me?'*

'Yes, ma'am,' the boy said, surprised.

'Good. They're coming up now. Don't say anything; give them their orders and get under way as fast as you can.' Then she followed the last mutineer up into the sun.

The journey to Port Naar went slow. The pirate ship was undamaged and proved a fast sailor, but though the crew of the cutter obeyed every order with alacrity, the navy vessel had trouble keeping up.

'There's something wrong with her steering,' Naudin said as he watched the cutter's erratic progress. 'You can see her yawing to starboard.' He glanced at Kellani. 'I think I'll call my dad and report this whole shambles. I don't trust that port lieutenant an inch and I don't want him to cover it up.' He grimaced. 'Of course, that means the felucca business will come out, but I'll tell dad Eskandar will handle that bit.'

Kellani stared at the cutter. 'Mutiny. There's no way we can stay silent on that. Go ahead, call him.'

Naudin closed his eyes and sent out a thought.

'Meeting?' he said aloud. 'Call him out of it. I'm reporting an emergency. What? No, nothing private; this is the lord wyrmcaller's business. I'm ordering *you*, lieutenant. Call the commodore or suffer the consequences.'

Apparently his anger must have done the trick, for Kellani knew he and his dad were talking on a thin personal line. She couldn't hear, but watching Naudin's face, she guessed the commodore wasn't happy.

Finally, Naudin sighed. 'Done,' he said. 'Dad didn't like it one bit. Mutiny—darn, it felt as if I'd slapped him.'

'Don't you feel guilty for cleaning up his mess,' Kellani said.

'Stupid secretary wouldn't connect me,' Naudin said. 'I had to pull rank on her.' He snorted. 'What rank?'

Kellani raised an eyebrow. 'You're a top official in the Peaks,' she said. 'That ranks with my mother's highest generals or those bigwig warlocks at Spellstor Center. You're wrapped in gold braid, bud.'

'Mother would spank me if I tried that story,' Naudin said.

'Only if you did it frivolously or to be nasty.'

'I wouldn't!' he said indignantly.

'I know that. Don't worry, coz; you're first mage to the wyrmcaller of Kalbakar. That's rank a-plenty.'

The *Drakon* arrived at Port Naar with the pirate and the navy cutter and moored at the first free berth large enough.

'See that?' Kellani said, nudging her cousin. 'The result of your call, coz.'

They watched as a navy officer with a squad of marines strode to where the *Bluewing* made fast and disappeared on board.

'I'd better get over there, before they arrest that midshipman or something,' Naudin said.

Kellani looked at him. 'We'll both go; you handle it.'

Together, they flew over and landed on the little quarterdeck, where they found an older naval captain, and the midshipman close to breaking down.

Naudin muttered a curse and strode over. 'Good afternoon,' he said. 'I'm Lord Naudin, the wyrmcaller's first mage. The broomer is the Lady Kellani. Commodore sent you?'

The captain turned and saluted, his face sternly official.

'Lord Naudin, m'lady. You are the one who reported this sorry business?' he said. 'May I ask how the wyrmcaller became involved in this?'

'By accident,' Naudin said, willing a smile on his face. 'We were on our way north and picked up the midshipman's emergency call. Our marines secured the pirate vessel. Lady Kellani went on board the *Bluewing* and found her in a state of mutiny. She got the men back to work, whereupon the midshipman in command sailed the cutter back to Port Naar.'

'A nasty business,' the captain said. 'The midshipman should never have been in command, not when there was a risk of battle. I have relieved the port lieutenant of his post; the navy will employ him elsewhere, in a more suitable position.' He coughed. 'We do not want to spread this story, m'lord. It wouldn't do the navy's reputation any good.'

'So no courts-martial?' Naudin said.

The captain lifted his hands. 'Oh no, no. Navy House will quietly disrate those men and distribute them among the fleet. The midshipman will be discharged, his leadership qualities didn't meet the navy's requirements.'

'I don't think that would be fair,' Naudin said with a glance at the shaking boy. 'It is hardly his fault his commander sent him into a situation he wasn't trained to handle. Let me offer another option. The Weal Navy seconds him indefinitely to the Pasandir Armed Forces, where he will find employment suitable for his rank and a chance to acquire the experience he presently lacks.'

The captain smiled. 'I can agree to that, Lord Naudin. To be honest, we have too many midshipmen already. Parents think it an excellent way to educate their offspring without cost to themselves, but we can use only so many of them. That's why we retain only the best.' He gave a firm nod. 'You do realize the wyrmcaller will be paying his wages, do you?'

'Of course,' Naudin said. He looked at the mid, who stood staring at him and Kellani in total bewilderment. 'Get your things together and come back here,' he said. 'Then we'll take you to the *Drakon.*'

The boy nodded vaguely and hurried below.

The captain shook his head. 'We shouldn't take children as officers; that doesn't work at all.' Then he seemed to recall with whom he spoke, for his face flushed. 'I forgot... you all are... Harrumph.'

'We have a great deal of success with our young crews,' Kellani said. 'We are geared toward it; that makes a difference.'

'Yes, well...' The captain looked around.

'The ship is a mess,' Kellani said, wanting to change the subject. 'Those pirates were toying with her, trying to terrify the midshipman. That didn't work, but the cutter sustained damage.'

Then the midshipman came back, carrying a small bag and a fishing rod. 'I'm ready, lord,' he said, looking forlorn.

'Good,' Naudin said. 'You can ride in front of me.'

'Captain, we will sail again, our business is to the north,' Kellani said. 'We have no hands to spare to sail our prize vessel to Smakand; would there be some locals available?'

'You could ask the fishers, I suppose,' the captain said. 'I'm sure they would oblige you in exchange for some coins.' He smiled. 'I will arrange it, if you supply, say, five pieces of gold. My orders are to take command here as port captain. My frigate will arrive in a short while, to provide additional protection. With all those pirate activities, the commodore thought it better to strengthen the defenses.'

'That seems wise,' Kellani said. 'I will send someone over with the money.'

The captain beamed and with a polite exchange of salutes, they took to the air.

'You all right?' Naudin asked of the midshipman before him.

'I don't understand,' the boy said. He had taken off his hat and the wind blew back his long hair. *'I thought I was going to be dismissed the service.'*

Naudin chuckled. *'That captain wanted to kick you out. We can use you, so instead of dismissal, the Weal Navy has loaned you to us permanently. You'll be paid the same wages, but your rank and promotions are ours. Unless you'd rather be a civilian?'*

'No!' the boy said hastily, his mind tinged by revulsion at the thought. *'But I don't know you.'*

'We're the Pasandir Armed Forces. At least, most of us. I'm a mindmage of the Spellstor's family, serving with the wyrmcaller. The Pasandir Peaks are allies of the Weal. Now, what's your name?'

'Miran,' he said, suddenly diffident. *'Miran of New Winsproke.'*

'You're from Malgarth?' Naudin asked, surprised. *'My grandfather was prince-warlock of Winsproke but apart from my family, I rarely meet people who were actually born there.'*

The midshipman hesitated, as if weighting his words. *'It's not an exciting place. My father is a clerk for the warlock tower. It must be an important job, though I have no idea what he does in that place.'*

Naudin grinned. *'Better not ask. But I agree New Winsproke is dull. Below is our ship. I suppose you'll have many more pressing questions, so I'll get someone who can answer a lot of them. Ready for a new life?'*

'I suppose I am,' the boy said. Then he chuckled. *'Wrong answer. Yes, lord; I'm ready.'*

'Just call me Naudin; I use that lord thing only for business.'

Then they landed.

'Welcome on board the *Drakon of Ilzhar*,' Naudin said. 'Flagship of the Pasandir Navy. Captain Abia, this is Midshipman Miran, who will be joining us.'

Abia looked her surprise. 'We rescued him and then stole him as well? Perfect, I sure can use another watch-keeping officer.' She held out a hand. 'Good to meet you, I'm Abia. You're the only midshipman on board, so you'll have the cabin to yourself. You dine with us officers, but don't sweat; we're not the Weal Navy at all.'

Naudin grinned. 'Not at all. Come, there are your guides.' He gave a shout to Jornyll, who stood with Zaotinq at the starboard side, trailing a long fishing line.

'Here's another fisherman for you,' Naudin said when the boys came aft. 'Miran has joined us as a midshipman. Show him the mids' cabin and everything else. Eskandar will give the guy his little talk when he's up and about again, but don't let that stop you to overload the guy with information. And don't forget to take him to the purser's department for a change of uniform.' Then he poked Miran's shoulder. 'Don't look so lost. Go with them. The wyrmcaller will want to see you later, but for now these guys can answer any questions you might have.'

Miran looked at Jornyll, then blinked at Zaotinq with his unfamiliar green complexion and swallowed. 'I suppose I do have some,' he said.

When the boys were out of earshot, Kellani turned around and slapped the railing. 'The navy wanted to kick him out,' she said to Abia. 'A mindspeaking, trained midshipman. What the heck are Uncle Yarwan's people doing?'

CHAPTER 23 – A SHIP FOR THE PRINCE

When I came to, I lay on my back in *Drakon*'s great cabin. My right arm was stiff, my shoulder ached, and there was a heavy weight pinning my lower legs to the bed.

'Ouch!' I said, trying to focus my mind. 'What happened?'

'Nasty pirate shot you,' Lothi-Mo said. I heard her move and the weight on my legs disappeared as she wriggled her way to my side.

I turned my head to look at her. 'What?'

'One of those pirates pointed a pistol at you and the silly bullet found your shoulder.'

'Ah,' I said. 'It hurts.'

'These things do,' Lothi-Mo chirped brightly. 'You're lucky boy, though.'

'Am I?' I said, not very sure of that.

'Much, much. Your body good healer or you'd be dead boy now.' She gave a soft hiss. 'Sneaky Kellani stole you away when me was biting pirate. No necessary, your body closing all great veins stops you from bleeding to death. Could have told her that, hasty girl.' Then she chuckled. 'Likes you, she does.'

'What time is it?' I asked hastily.

'Hour before noon,' Lothi-Mo said. 'Slept long, long, long, you did.'

'Gods!' I said. 'I must get up.'

'Can,' she said. 'No need, but can.'

I swung my legs to the ground and stood. My shoulder protested, and I sent a trickle of healing to soothe the pain.

'Anyone else hurt?'

Lothi-Mo cackled. 'Little prince has an eye like peacock's head, but he no want it healed. Thinks to impress his royal sept, I suppose.'

For a moment I felt the deck heave, but then it steadied again and I reached the door without lurching like drunken Jack Tar. As I came on deck, several guys cheered.

'Kids are glad you're back to bully them,' Lothi-Mo said.

'Bully! As if I did.' Then my eye caught a ship leaving the port, a sleek ship with a lateen sail, and two dingy fishing boats in company.

'Hey,' I said. 'Isn't that the pirate we fought?'

'Su-ure,' Lothi-Mo said. 'That's *Raffix*. We took her from silly Bokkaners. Kellani-girl hired some fisher people to sail her home for us.'

'But why the fleet?' I asked.

Lothi-Mo flapped her wings. 'Fisher people wanna try the Smalkand fish. Use that empty place across the bay and build some shacks, we said. Don't need much, they do. Yummy fresh fish for us.'

I hadn't thought of that, but the bay was over a mile wide, with plenty of room for a fishing fleet. Us, and the people at Pashwend and High Morv would mean more customers than the whole of Port Naar.

'Good,' I said. 'Very good.' I turned to walk aft and saw Jornyll nudging Zaotinq, and holding out a demanding hand.

'I won,' he said.

Zaotinq sighed and gave him a copper penny.

'We had a little bet,' Jornyll said. 'I said you'd be up before the noon meal, and Zao said dinnertime.' Then he stepped aside and pushed another boy to the front.

'This is Miran,' Jornyll said. 'Our new midshipman.'

Automatically I checked his mind and then I started. *'You're the mid from the cutter,'* I said.

'I am,' the boy said. *'Naudin had me transferred.'*

I held out my good hand. 'I'm sure Naudin will explain all. Welcome; we have sore need of naval officers.'

'We're showing him around,' Jornyll said. 'He doesn't fully believe this ship, I think.'

'I believe!' the boy said hastily. 'But it's all so different. I thought I had mastered ship handling more or less, but here all is strange.'

'But logical,' I said. 'You'll get the hang of it soon enough. You showed you could command a ship; that's a big deal for a mid.'

'Until they mutinied,' the boy said bitterly. 'I failed to have them obey.'

'That was when the pirates attacked you?'

He nodded. 'They tricked me; said they were a trade vessel. I should've had my guns run out, but I didn't believe anyone would attack the navy.' He clenched his fists. 'They did. I ordered my men to prepare our guns, but they refused. My bos'n screamed at me to surrender and then they ran below. What should I've done?'

'Shoot one,' Jornyll said matter-of-factly.

'Shoot my men?' the boy said aghast.

'They were betraying you, weren't they?'

'Serving with us will give you action enough,' I said. 'That will show you how to lead under fire. It's most of all setting the right example.' I turned to Jornyll. 'Have you been to Ricco with him, to get his name down in the muster book?'

Ricco the ship's purser was one of Shaw's kids, a clever little guy who used to collect ox dung in Seatome's streets and sell it to the fuel vender for half a copper a piece.

'Not yet, but we were going to,' Jornyll said.

'Good. Tell him Miran shares in the capture. After all, without him we'd never have caught that pirate.'

'See?' Jornyll said. 'With us you'll be earning gold, mate.'

The remainder of that day I spent in a chair on the quarterdeck, letting the hot sun replenish my energies. I observed Miran standing his first watch and saw his initial nervousness evaporate through the comradeship between our kids.

The coastline north of Port Naar was rockier than the southern part, with ever-higher hills becoming mountains.

For a great part of the day, Princess Jem sat in the mainmast crow's nest with Lothi-Mo, watching dead Nanstalgarod glide by. Only when darkness fell did she drift down and seek Amaj's company.

The next day just past sunrise as I came on deck, Lieutenant Perre greeted me with a smile and a wave of his hand. 'Behold! There is life beyond the Hellesands!'

I turned and stared at the rolling hills covered in gray dawn and ancient woods. I saw the white beaches round shallow bays, with colonies of bluewings wheeling round and diving for fish in the surf.

'Did you think there wasn't?' I asked.

He laughed. 'Not after meeting our Qoori, but that's what many old sailors say; no life beyond the Hellesands.'

'And they never went to check,' I said.

He scratched his shorn white hair. 'True. We Vanhaari aren't adventurous. Dunno why, but we like our known sea routes and familiar ports. I never wanted to know either, content with running black coal to Towne. Until you hired us. Now I do, so it's good to be here.'

'Sail to the northwest!' the lookout cried from the masthead. 'Something small, could be a dhow.'

Perre turned. 'Shall we...?'

'Investigate? Yes, let's have a look.'

The lieutenant rang the telegraph to Full Speed Ahead, and the *Drakon* surged forward.

'That's something else a collier never does,' Perre said, rubbing his hands.

Moments later, Captain Abia appeared on deck. The change of speed must have woken her up, but she didn't say anything.

'Sighted a dhow,' Perre said.

Abia smiled. 'And now you boys hope it's a pirate.'

'Don't we all?' I said.

'Of course we do.' She killed a yawn. 'A dhow? That could be a long chase; those are said to be fast.'

As we watched, the sail grew and became a small ship with a striped roof of sailcloth over her stern.

'Time to call in the marines,' I said. 'Pass the word for Aya, someone.'

Like Kellani, Aya was always ready, and within minutes she was aft.

'There's a dhow,' I said. 'We'd like to say hi.'

'So you want us to stop them?' Aya said.

'Stop and search.'

'All right,' she said grimly. 'Time we had some action.'

Minutes later, six brooms flew away toward the strange sail.

'Darn,' I said suddenly, watching them speed away over the sea. 'They've taken the prince along!'

Both officers glanced up.

'Well, you did put him in with them, didn't you?' Abia said. 'So they must suppose it's all right.'

'He's a guest,' I said angrily. 'We can't have him hurt or anything.'

As they neared, a shot rang out over the water. Apparently nobody was hit, for I saw them all land on the narrow deck. There was a small scuffle, and three bodies thrown into the water. Then the little ship set course toward us and in minutes it was alongside.

I saw the prince at the wheel, waving at us, his face a big grin.

'That's a ship his size,' Kellani said thoughtfully.

'He can have it,' I said. 'Let Purser Ricco check for any valuables first.' I grinned. 'If it's loaded with chests of gold or pearls, I want them out first.'

I wanted to have a look at our catch, so I took Ricco over myself.

'Nice little ship,' I said nonchalantly, as I joined Aya at the ship's wheel.

'Manned by fools,' Aya said. 'Shooting at us! If they'd said they were simple traders, I'd have let them go.'

'Pirates aren't chosen for their intelligence,' I said. 'They're grunts, mostly.' I looked around. 'Let's search for papers or anything. This boat doesn't boast a cabin, I suppose.'

I avoided the prince's eyes and the silent entreaty in them, and jumped down into the hatch. Aft was a spot separated from the rest by a dark curtain. Behind it were an unmade bed, a mass of empty bottles, and a stout chest. It was locked, but I remembered something Jornyll had said once, and looked under the smelly pillows. There was a key, and it fit. Inside the chest were some charts, papers, and a little bag of gold coins. I pocketed the lot and walked out.

On the other side, Ricco's shadowy figure stood bowed over some bales.

'You'll damage your eyes,' I said, and called a mage light. 'Ask Ulaataq to whip up a lamp for you like those in the keep.'

He barely heard me, muttering as he went through a chest. 'Nah,' he said, 'we'll not sell that, not with a profit.' Then he looked up. 'Nothing much. I'm sorry, it would cost me more to transport this stuff anywhere than it would earn it. Don't think they're trading or pirating, boss.'

'Then what did they do?' I said.

Ricco shrugged. 'Messenger?'

'Could be,' I said. 'Perhaps their papers will tell more.'

Back on deck I stepped over to Prince Jazzaunt. 'Would this one do as replacement for your felucca?'

'Yes!' he said fiercely. 'She's beautiful.'

'The ship is yours then. I will leave Aya's troop on board to help sail her home.' Then I grinned. 'I'll send Justym over as communicator; in case you get lost, or anything.'

'I won't!' he said. Then his eyes strayed to the vessel's sails, and he forgot me.

CHAPTER 24 – SUNK AGAIN

'Fog!' Jornyll said disgustedly as he returned below. 'Couldn't see the sea as I pissed.'

'Yeah, that happens around here,' the prince said. He yawned and scratched vigorously. 'It'll lift when the sun rises.'

'Couldn't see the *Drakon* either,' Jornyll added.

They had paused for the night in a small bay, with the wyrmcaller's ship anchored outside, way to the south. A bit too far to Jornyll's mind, but the prince had laughed off his reservations. He'd used this spot before; it was perfectly safe.

'Whose turn for making breakfast?' Jornyll said.

'Yours.' Aya waved a big arm at him and grinned.

Jornyll muttered a curse. He should've kept his trap shut.

He grabbed his boots and hooked his sword to his belt. Perfectly safe spot or no, he wasn't taking any risks. He stepped over the railing into the lukewarm water and waded to the beach to rekindle the campfire they'd built the night before. He wasn't handy at these things; a city boy born and bred, he'd never been out of Seatome before joining Eskandar, and these techniques were still new to him. But after several attempts, he got the fire burning again.

'Yeah,' he said, as the first little flames bit into the dry kindlewood. 'C'mon, eat them up; there's plenty more.'

With the fire going, he splashed back to the ship to get the eats. As he walked forward, he felt the wind, and he saw the mist thinning.

He stiffened. Ships! Three big warships at anchor less 'n half a mile away!

He ran to the hatch. 'On deck, all! Strange ships!'

Aya cursed and bounded for the ladder. 'Take your shoes and arms,' she commanded, before running up.

One after another, the prince and the five others joined him.

'Hah, don't you worry, kids. They're the navy!' Jazzaunt said, grinning broadly. 'My uncle's navy, that is.'

'Your uncle's navy?' Aya said, frowning. 'Do they...'

Before she could finish what she was going to say, a heavy boom rolled over the water and a tall fountain of water drenched them all.

'They're shooting at me...' the prince said, stiff with astonishment.

'To the beach! Now!' Aya shouted.

'But...'

Jornyll grabbed the prince's arm and dragged him into the water. 'Hurry,' he said. 'The next one won't miss.'

They reached the beach and ran to the edge of the woods before turning to look back.

Another flame erupted in the side of the biggest warship, and seconds later their little vessel heaved violently as a heavy ball nearly cut her in two halves. Flames leaked out the rear end they'd just spent the night in.

'The oil lamp in the hold still burned,' Jornyll said, watching the fire spread.

'No!' the prince said, his face red with anger. 'Not again!'

A third shot crashed into the trees to the left of them.

'Away from here!' Aya said sharply. 'They're shooting at us now.'

'I'm the prince, idiots!' Jazzaunt cried, shaking his fist at the distant warships. 'My uncle will break you for this!'

'Shaddup,' Jornyll said. 'Move!'

'Justym?' Aya said. The young priest was dressed in a pirate's tunic and boots. With his tousled hair and smudgy face, no one would take him for Aera Skygoddess' chosen one.

'You call the boss,' she ordered. 'Tell him what happened.'

Justym gave her an anguished look. 'I'm trying,' he said. 'Nothing! It's like I'm suddenly deaf; I can't reach Eskandar, or even the keep.'

'Why not?' Aya asked sharply.

'I don't *know.*' The singer pointed an arm at a tree. Nothing happened, and he let go of a peppery sailors' curse. 'My spells won't work either.'

'Magic?' the prince said suddenly. 'You can't do that here.'

Justym stared at his still suffused face. 'Why not?'

The prince heaved his shoulders. 'We're in the Iron Reaches. They *say* it's because there is a lot of iron ore in the ground, whatever that has to do with it. We never had a mage at Kas-Bahaan; not even mindspeaking worked.'

'So that's it!' Justym said, relieved. 'Iron ore dampens magic! I thought it was me; that Aera had taken back my powers.'

Aya grunted. 'Idiot! Stop doubting yourself.' She stood deep in thought for a moment.

'The boss'll think we're all dead,' Bamson said gloomily. 'He will shrug us off and go back to Smalkand.'

'You're a fool,' Jornyll said sternly. 'Now shut your trap.'

'If we return to the beach, we'll be a target for those warships,' Aya said slowly. 'When Eskandar sees the burned wreck, he'll think we bought it. He'll probably go and yell at the guys who shot us.'

'And then he'll go home,' Bamson said stubbornly.

'Then he'll go on an' tell Jazz's uncle the whole thing, so he can hang that admiral or whoever gave the order to fire,' Jornyll said.

'Uncle will be very angry,' the prince said. 'I've been at his court most of my life, and he sees me as another son, he does.'

'He has sons of his own?' Razoon asked.

'Yeah, I'm only third in the line of succession. My cousins are both older than me; my father married late.' He sighed a little. 'I was born around here, at the royal castle of Kas-Bahaan. We could go there and send a pigeon to my uncle, ask him to send an airship and pick us up.'

'You know how to get there?' Aya said.

'The castle? Sure,' the prince said. 'It's further inland, on a river.'

'We'll go there,' Aya said. 'Razoon and Howy, take point. Follow the coast; that river should run to the sea somewhere.'

'Yeah,' Jornyll said. 'I remember Shaw explaining that rivers go from the land to the sea, not the other way round. Never thought I'd need knowing that.'

Aya cocked her head at him. 'You never know too much, mate. Now march.'

CHAPTER 25 – FOG 'N GUNFIRE

'Eskandar!'

I woke up from a bottomless sleep with Lothi-Mo slapping my face ungently with her tail.

'Kellani-girl wants you on deck!' she said. 'Wake up, big boy.'

'What's wrong?' I said, rubbing my eyes.

'Fog 'n gunfire,' she chirped. 'Trouble.'

I pulled on my shoes and went on deck. Fog? It was like running into a wall of snow. I couldn't see the ship's railing, it was that thick.

Then, muffled by the mist, I heard the sound of a heavy caliber gun. I hurried aft, to find Kellani and Naudin already there.

'I can't reach the boys,' Kellani said worriedly. 'Not even Justym. It's like... there's nobody there.'

I sent out my thoughts, searching for any of those kids, but I had no success either. 'Something is interfering with my mind.' I unclipped my broom. 'Let's see if we can escape the fog.'

'Straight up,' Kellani said. 'It won't extent that far.'

We rose and almost immediately were in a clear sky.

'Ships ahead!' I said.

'Warships,' she replied. *'Must be the Hizmyran navy.'*

I disregarded them for the moment and flew toward the spot where the evening before the prince's boat had been. The sleek little ship had been torn into halves, and those burned to the waterline. As a demonstration of the effect heavy caliber naval shot had on small ships, it was perfect. As a place where your friends had been in, it was terrifying.

'Gods!' Kellani nearly shouted. *'The boys?'*

'I can see no bodies,' I said, wrestling with my rage. *'This isn't shark water?'*

'Not as far as I know. They must've jumped ship. But where are they?'

'*Boat coming,*' Lothi-Mo said from above us.

I turned my head and spied a swift jollyboat speeding toward us. '*Cover me, girls.*' I sank to right over the waves and waited.

The boat, rowed by six uniformed men, came to a halt beside the wreck. At the tiller sat a young officer, who looked at us with disbelief written on his swarthy face.

'Flying brooms?' he said. 'What magic is that? Who are you?'

'Wyrmcaller Eskandar,' I said, not at all trying to conceal my anger. 'Who are you and what are you doing here?'

'Aspirant Hisain, Hizmyran Navy,' he said. 'I came to inspect our catch.'

'Your catch... Imbecile! That was Prince Jazzaunt's boat you shot up.'

Several sailors lost their disciplined pose, and the aspirant blanched. 'But they were pirates! We knew that ship and... The prince had a felucca.'

'Had, yes,' I snapped. 'Who is in command here?'

'Senior Captain Tazhan, he's on board the central ship.'

'I will seek him out. *Darn,*' I said to Kellani as we shot away to toward the little squadron. '*I never thought about that! I shouldn't have given the prince a pirate ship.*'

'*Those fine boys trigger-glad-happy,*' Lothi-Mo said. '*Shoot-without-looking is never good.*'

Without waiting for permission, we landed on the central ship's main deck. Sailors ducked out of the way as armed men in gleaming cuirasses came running, pointing long muskets with businesslike aggression as they formed a circle around us.

From the quarterdeck came a tall officer in a colorful uniform and a wrapped headdress. He had a long brown face and a spade beard, and displayed enough gold braid for a dozen admirals.

'Hold your fire,' I said loudly. 'I am the Wyrmcaller Eskandar. I need to see the one in command right now.'

'I am Senior Captain Tazhan,' the officer said in heavily accented Vulgar. 'What is the meaning of this intrusion on his majesty's fleet?'

'You are the Hizmyran navy?'

'Naturally, you find yourself inside our territorial waters.'

'Then I have to inform you, Captain Tazhan, that you just shot up Prince Jazzaunt.'

No, that wasn't tactful. It had effect, though. If I'd thrown a pail of dung in his face he couldn't have looked more horrified.

'The prince!' His face hardened and I heard the *click, click* of muskets being primed to fire. 'Explain yourself quickly!'

'Had you taken the trouble to inspect that little ship you blew up, you would have found Prince Jazzaunt on board – happy and healthy.'

'In pirate hands!' The captain clenched his hands. 'So you're pirates.'

'No, sir, we hunt them,' I said. 'Two days ago we captured that ship you destroyed so recklessly. I had given it as a present to Prince Jazzaunt, because he had lost his felucca through no fault of his own.'

The captain stiffened and stared at me for a long second. Then he waved his men away. 'Please join me in my cabin,' he said. 'This calls for some privacy.'

He led us to the most sumptuous captain's cabin I'd ever seen. A high-canopied bed covered with costly sheets; carpets that clutched at your ankles, and a golden cage full of singing birds.

Inside, he closed the door and wheeled to face us. 'The prince, is he dead?'

'They must have managed to escape,' I said. 'We found no bodies in the wreck, as the aspirant you sent over will confirm.'

Tazhan nodded, visibly relieved. 'My gunner said he'd seen small figures escaping across the beach. He fired a last round after them...'

'I will have a look,' Kellani said, and without another word she went outside.

The captain fixed his eyes on me. 'Who exactly are you, sir, and what is your part in this?'

'Meet the Exalted Wyrmcaller Eskandar, Ruler of the Pasandir Peaks,' Lothi-Mo said haughtily. 'I am Lothi-Mo of the Royal Sept.'

The captain started. Like others before him, he either hadn't noticed her or thought her a pet. 'Do the old tales come alive? A wyrmling?'

'A royal wyrmling, Captain,' she said severely. 'We are just as little a *tale* as the jinn. Only we're nicer. Much, much nicer.'

'Jinn,' Tazhan said. 'They are no tale, not at all. Welcome then, Lady Lothi-Mo, Lord Wyrmcaller. Where would we find the Pasandir Peaks?'

'We're on the other side of the Nanstalgarod desert,' I said. 'A mountainous country; the domain of Bodrus the Sleeping God, whose agent I am.'

'There are living lands beyond the desert?' the captain said. 'We never go there, thinking it all a ruin.'

'There are,' I said. 'We never traveled north either. Until now.'

'*Eskandar?*' Naudin's voice said in my head. '*You all right?*'

'*I am on board the Hizmyran command vessel. Tell Abia to bring the ship. Those fellows sank the prince's boat by accident; the kids have escaped inland.*'

'*Holy Lumentis! We're coming.*'

'We had found your prince after he had lost his first ship,' I said. 'On our way to return him home, we captured that little pirate vessel. I gave it to the prince as a mark of my esteem.'

'And we sank it. His Majesty will not be pleased.'

'Nor am I,' I said harshly. 'That ship had seven of my most trusted companions on board.'

The captain nodded. 'Search parties are already on their way. We must hurry. Of all the places to land, the Iron Reaches are worst.'

'Iron Reaches?' I said quickly as the name made me think of something.

'The whole province is extremely rich in iron deposits.'

I banged my hook in my hand in frustration. 'So that's what is keeping me from reaching their minds!'

'You use mindspeak?' Tazhan said. 'At sea it is fine, but once you go ashore, it won't work. Magic is nigh on impossible in the Reaches.'

'Raw iron ore does that,' I said. I sent out a thought to warn Kellani but couldn't reach her either.

'It's not the lack of communication that bothers me most,' the captain continued. 'What is worse, the area is rife with bandits. These use the iron as a cloak to hide from our searchers.'

Then Tazhan cursed softly. 'I just thought of another complication. There is a royal castle in the area, Kas-Bahaan. It served both as a hunting lodge and a naval outpost. The prince was born there, but after the death of his father, the prince's mother returned with her son to the king's court. His majesty ordered the keep closed down under a skeleton guard and the navy pulled back. If the prince went there for help, that would be disastrous.' He hesitated and lowered his voice.

'You see, last year, a bunch of pirates took Kas-Bahaan. The king knows, of course, and the high command, but I don't think his majesty told the prince.'

I thought of the boy's impetuousness. 'He would have badgered his uncle to go and take it back.'

The captain grimaced. 'Probably. The king is much attached to his nephew, but he hates being pushed.'

'...kandar?' Kellani's voice came. *'Darn nearly broke a leg. My broom quit as I reached the beach, and I lost contact with you and the ship.'*

'Captain Tazhan just informed me,' I said. 'I tried to reach you. The whole province is covered in raw iron. There's no magic possible, no flying, no mindspeak.'

'Of course,' she said bitterly. 'Those kids had to make it more difficult, hadn't they?'

'That's not all; the place is full of bandits.'

'I'm coming back; that idiot aspirant let his men trample all over the place, so any trace of our guys has been destroyed.'

CHAPTER 26 – GOING INLAND

A high scream somewhere close by froze them in midstep.

'Take cover!' Razoon and his brother came hurrying back.

'What was that?' Aya said softly.

'A Wastrel hunting cry,' Howy said, his eyes full of hatred.

'Wastrels? Here?' Jornyll said. *Of course,* he thought. *We're close to the desert border and those rich ruins.*

'There's only six of them,' Razoon said. 'They've stopped close by.'

Jornyll looked up. 'They got those funny Wastrel robes?'

'They're called kaftans,' Howy said. 'Yeah, why?'

'Just a hunch,' Jornyll said, looking at Aya.

'A disguise, you mean?' the girl said. 'Could be handy. Six Wastrels?' She drew her blade. 'Let's go *do* something for a change. Lead on, scouts.'

Razoon rubbed his hands. 'Gladly.' Then he and his brother moved away, and the others followed.

The Wastrels were sitting in a small clearing. One was busy lighting a fire while the others sat and mocked his clumsy attempt. They must think themselves safe here, for they hadn't even posted a lookout, and the attack caught them unprepared.

The prince didn't wait for the others, but jumped into the circle and swung his blade at the head of the crouching fire-maker. While the Wastrels gaped at the yelling boy, the one on his knees dropped without a sound. Aya engaged a bearded fellow in a green kaftan and a stained headcloth, who roared and parried her blow with his long, curved sword. Jornyll sprang at the next man, a gnarly type with only a few teeth. The man spat at him, but Jornyll wasn't about to be distracted, and slashed his saber at the wizened head. The Wastrel ducked, and with a knife in each hand went for Jornyll's groin.

'Raah!' Jornyll yelled as he jumped in the air, and brought his blade down on the man's neck. Something snapped audibly, and the Wastrel flopped down. 'Bungler!' Jornyll said. Then he saw Singer Justym, his young face grim, sneak up to Aya's opponent, and clobber him with a stout branch he'd picked up. 'One for the goddess,' Jornyll shouted, and the singer flashed him a smile.

'That's it, guys,' Aya said. 'We got them all.'

'Nice little fight.' Jornyll peered at Bamson. 'Don't say you got a black eye *again*? When they said to use your head when fighting, they didn't mean that literally, mate.'

Bamson grunted, but kept his mouth shut.

'Well done,' Aya said. 'Now take their kaftan-things and whatever we can use.'

'This,' Justym said, snatching up a small spiked club with a leather thong at the grip. 'Nasty and discreet.'

Jornyll slapped his shoulder. 'That's one very convincing argument, priest.' He stooped over the man he had downed, and removed his yellowish robe. 'Yech,' he said. 'Darned idiot bled all over it.'

'There's the river,' Aya said. 'Wash it out.'

Less than an hour later, dressed in wrung-out wet robes and colorful headcloths, they moved on, following the river farther inland.

CHAPTER 27 – THE COURT OF HIZMYR

The Hizmyran search parties returned and Naudin, Kellani, and I went over to their command ship.

The grim face of the senior lieutenant told me enough. It was scratched as if he'd been creeping through thorn bushes, but without success.

'We found footsteps leading from the wreck to the forest edge,' he reported. 'The other prints ruined the trail.'

'I noticed,' Kellani said. 'Your aspirant would've done better to stick to the wreck.'

The lieutenant glanced at her and gave a curt nod. 'We searched the whole area,' he said. 'Not a trace. The prince and your people must've been there, but it is unclear where they have gone.'

'I think only the king can do anything,' Tazhan said when the lieutenant had gone. 'He can send out the army—pacify that darned region once more—and send out airships to search from above. My men aren't trained for this sort of thing.'

I had to admit he was right. Without magic, we were even more helpless. We'd trusted too much on our mental powers, I thought. That left us severely undermanned on land.

'I shall station a ship here, in case the prince returns to the beach,' Tazhan said. 'I will return to Myrlia and report to the king. Perhaps it would be wise if you joined us.'

I looked at the others and saw the same sense of defeat in their eyes. To run away now, to leave those kids fending for themselves – it felt like betrayal.

'Not!' Lothi-Mo said. *'Not run away but regroup. Get more help. Then go back and search again.'*

She was right, of course. Still...

'We'll do that,' I said heavily.

The other two captains looked away, only Tazhan studied my face.

'It is not an easy decision, lord,' he said. 'But my king will spare no effort to get the prince and your friends back.'

'I am sure he will,' I said. 'I must return to my ship now. Perhaps you would escort us to the capital?'

'Unto the presence of the king himself, Lord Wyrmcaller,' the captain said. 'I will not leave you to wrangle with underlings and their endless questions.'

'Thank you.' I rose and the others with me. The captains all saluted as I walked out, but I felt like a terrible failure.

Myrlia was a major city of a size Seatome could only dream of. The harbor alone was as big as the Weal's capital, and the city beyond stretched out as far as the eye could see, covering a row of low hills before losing itself in the hazy distance.

Captain Tazhan arranged for *Drakon*'s berth in the navy port, and a large steamcart to drive us to the palace.

I took Kellani, Naudin, Lothi-Mo, and Captain Abia, and with Tazhan as the fourth passenger, the driver steered out of the walled port into the city.

A broad lane with room for six oxcarts riding shoulder-to-shoulder, well-paved and lined with trees, led us past shops and warehouses to an immense market square.

'We'll lose young Ricco in this place,' Naudin muttered. 'It's too big.'

I smiled. 'That's why I said no when he asked to go ashore. He'll need an escort for a place like this.'

'How do we go about shore leave?' I asked Tazhan.

The captain's thoughts had been far away, but at my question he stirred. 'Myrlia is a bees' hive full of sweetness and poisonous stings. You can hire guides and steamcarts in the navy port; I would strongly advise against any foreigner going alone and on foot.'

'Thank you,' I said. 'I will remember that.'

Then we turned into the tall wrought-iron gates surrounding the palace complex.

The royal palace wasn't one building, but rather a collection of pastel-colored dwellings, all crowned with shining cupola's, slender little towerlets, dovetailed banners, sparkling in the sun.

Tall guards in silver cuirasses and plumed headdresses saluted as we drove past.

Finally we came to the palace proper and a set of marble stairs at least fifty feet high.

Captain Tazhan beckoned a guard and said something. The man saluted and stepped back.

A mindspeaking soldier, I thought, catching a glimpse of mental activity.

'I took the liberty to inform the royal vazar of your arrival, lord. As a sovereign ruler, you are entitled to a different reception from even a senior captain,' Tazhan said.

I wasn't in the mood for ceremonial, on whatever level, but I was Bodrus' representative and I had to think of his honor. So I thanked the captain and lifted my chin, trying to look stern and regal in my fine dark red jacket.

Kellani's broomer blue matched me nicely, as did Naudin in his favorite white suit. Abia wore our uniform, tailor-made, with the shiny epaulets of flag captain. Lothi-Mo sparkled as only a royal wyrmling could, and needed no finery.

'Silly!' She slapped me with her tail. *'You don't see I be brushed! Chagan did with hard brushes. Wyrm girls need that to look their best.'*

'Chagan?' I said. I knew the young Qoori respected Lothi-Mo, but to brush her...

'He nice boy,' she said complacently.

At the golden doors, a magnificent official received us and led us through a carpeted corridor to a large room. It was round, with an immense cupola of colored glass that turned all into a cave of diamonds.

'His Reverence the Wyrmcaller Eskandar of Kalbakar, Defender of Bodrus and Sovereign Ruler of the Pasandir

Peaks,' the official shouted. As we walked down that endless carpet, past masses of bowing courtiers paying obeisance to a title they hadn't heard of before, I'd never felt more embarrassed in my life.

At the end, on a canopied chair of gold and blue, sat the Hizmyran king.

Rashaunt XI Hathwaari was a tall, elderly man, his brown face a crisscross of red veins and boasting an enormous white mustache.

He rose as I approached. 'Welcome,' he said. 'Apologies if I seem discourteous, but I cannot directly place you.'

I smiled at the honest answer. 'I am the Wyrmcaller Eskandar, ruler of the Pasandir Peaks, a country on the other side of the Nanstalgarod desert. With me are the Lady Kellani of Kell-Spellstor, daughter of the Queen of Kell, Lord Naudin of Maiwar, son to the Prince-Warlock of Vanhaar, and Flag Captain Abia of the Pasandir Navy.' Then I waved my arm. 'And the wyrmling Lothi-Mo, of the Royal Sept.'

Lothi-Mo always managed to remain unseen until I introduced her and I had no idea how she did it.

'A wyrmling!' the king said, with a mixture of awe and surprise on his face. The nearest courtiers gasped, and a murmur went through the throne room.

'We haven't seen a wyrmling at court for generations. Where did she come from?'

'I am the advisor to the Lord Eskandar,' Lothi-Mo said, sounding as queenly as Kellani's mother. 'Lord Eskandar is the Wings of the Mountains, disciple and martial arm of Bodrus, the Sleeping God.'

King Rashaunt pursed his lips. 'An unknown ruler of the barren south, with a royal company and a highborn wyrmling, accompanied by one of my most trusted captains. What have they in common?'

'Prince Jazzaunt,' I said.

The king jumped to his feet, and the blood drained from his face. 'Jazz? Where is he?'

'What we have to discuss are matters of high confidentiality that are better mentioned in private,' I said.

The king beckoned and a young man hurried over.

'My eldest son and heir Meshan,' the king said. 'You all come to my study.' Without looking back, he strode to a side door.

The royal office was a stately room in warm colors and wood. A desk the size of a small warship, a table and several chairs around it, bookcases, and the king walking up and down agitatedly.

'Sit,' he said. 'Close that darned door.' When his son had done so, the king snapped, 'Privacy. Now speak.'

'It is part of a longer story, so bear with me.' I fastened my eyes on the pacing king and told him how we found the prince in a Weal jail, and all the rest.

Halfway, the king sat down in a chair, scowling at me.

When I was finished, he pointed a finger at Tazhan. 'Why did you fire at my nephew?'

The captain swallowed. 'Not at the prince, I assure Your Majesty. It was that ship, Sire. She was a known pirate, thought to be a messenger. We had tried to capture her several times, but she was very fast and she slipped through our fingers every time. So when the fog lifted and we saw her at anchor, I told my gunner to sink her fast, before she could escape again.'

The king tugged his mustache. 'A most darnable coincidence.' He rose and went to a map on the wall. 'Exactly where did this happen?'

Both Abia and Tazhan joined him.

'Here, Your Majesty,' Abia said, tapping the map. 'The prince's ship lay anchored thus, close to the beach. My flagship lay here, about a mile south. Tazhan's squadron lay there, half a mile to the northeast of the prince. The fog cleared from the north downward, so his lookouts could see the prince's ship while we were still hidden.'

'And they did,' Tazhan said. 'My man reported sighting that cursed pirate, and I confirmed her identity myself. I ordered my gunner to sink her. As per regulation, our guns are loaded and run out at night, so he immediately fired our port bow chaser. The shot fell a few yards short.' He looked at his king. 'That at least gave them a warning; our second shot tore the ship in two halves. There must've been a lamp left alight, for in minutes the wreck was burning fiercely.' Tazhan licked his lips. 'My gunner saw the pirate crew escaping into the woods and he sent a third shot after them.'

Rashaunt cursed violently.

'He must have missed,' Kellani said. 'Both Tazhan's search parties and I checked the place the shot struck the trees, and we found nothing. Nor were there any bodies in the wreck. They must all have escaped.'

'All?' the king said. 'Who were with him? Those fishermen?'

'No,' I said and I let my own anger echo in my voice. 'The prince had seven of my most trusted companions with him; of his age, but well-trained and disciplined.'

'Prince Jazzaunt is a capable young man,' Kellani said. 'Together they should be able to handle any problems.'

'It is right inside the Iron Reaches,' Prince Meshan said. 'I don't think we told Jazz about Kas-Bahaan taken by pirates. Knowing him, the keep will be the first place he'll go to for help.'

'We must take it back,' the king said and slapped the armrests of his chair. 'Tazhan, you're excused, return to your duties. This is now a matter for the army.' Rashaunt turned to his son. 'Call out the *seshars*. As soon as they've boarded their airships, I want to hear. I'm going with them.'

The prince nodded and hurried from the room.

'The seshars are elite troops,' the king said. 'Four hundred of them should be ample to take back the keep and search the area.'

Then he sat down again and looked at me. 'Tell me more about yourself and your country, Divine... Darnation, what am I to call you?'

'I answer to my name,' I said. 'In official situations, Wyrmcaller would be sufficient; we are a rather informal bunch. Your nephew fitted right in with us.'

'I believe you,' the king said gruffly. 'He's the most easy-going lad imaginable. You have kept him out of any fighting, I hope?'

'Actually, we didn't.' I looked straight at the king. 'He is of the same age as my troops. Short of tying him to the mast, I couldn't keep him behind.'

King Rashaunt balled his fists. 'He's only a child.'

'He's fifteen, and warrior-trained. Would you have him lose face?'

'I want to keep him alive,' the king said harshly. 'He's my late brother's only son.'

'What is he supposed to become? A warrior, a bureaucrat, a courtier?'

'A warrior, of course, like his father. My brother was a most valiant man.'

I forced a smile. 'Then you will have to let him go. I know he would like to join us.'

'Join you?' Rashaunt glared at me. 'Send him away from my court with people I know nothing about? What exactly are you, Wyrmcaller? Not a king, obviously, but what then? A priest?'

'The wyrmcaller is the defender of Bodrus,' Lothi-Mo said. 'He is a holy warrior; the leader of the wyrms and wielder of godly power, temporal commander of the Pasandir Peaks Armed Forces and enemy of all who oppose the gods, be they man or jinn.'

I would never have been able to say that without sounding a complete, blathering idiot, but my wyrm girl brought it with the ringing voice of absolute truth. A swift glance told me my two best friends didn't laugh either. Kellani only nodded and Naudin looked so sure I had to suppress a shudder. Me, a holy warrior! I still felt like that little ship's boy of the *Tipred.*

The king sat staring at me, no doubt finding it just as difficult to reconcile my small stature and beardless face with the awesomeness of a divine's defender.

Therefore I smiled politely, settled down in my chair, and told him all, confident Teodar would stop me if I shouldn't.

When I was done, I knew I had convinced him.

'My priests knew there was something going on among the gods,' the king said slowly. 'But this full-scale quarrel is bad news. To make it worse, a lich working together with the jinn against your god?' He shook his head. 'I thought the jinn problem a thing of the past, but lately there have been rumors... And now a prophecy, and a bunch of children the age of young Jazz, to fight these powerful enemies? How could they hope to succeed?'

'We have had our victories,' I said calmly. 'We've killed at least eight jinn already, we brought the pirate activities in the south to a standstill, and we reopened a large base from which we can have a go at the piracy in the north.'

'And you want my nephew to be part of that?' the king said.

'Yes.'

'You're mad, Wyrmcaller.'

Before I could answer, Prince Meshan entered to report the seshar troops had boarded the airships.

'Follow me,' the king said quickly and led us through a maze of corridors to a large courtyard. Here, an airship waited, with two more hovering overhead. A rope ladder hung down, held taut by two burly warriors.

The king climbed up in the way of someone who had done this a hundred times before. After *Tipred*, rope ladders held no difficulty for me and my hook hand, and I went next.

'Message for the king!' someone called, running from a side entrance waving a paper. One of the men holding the ladder down accepted it.

As soon as I was at the airship's door I stepped inside, while below Kellani followed me surefooted. Only Naudin was slower; he could handle navigation, but he wouldn't ever make a topman. He finally reached the ship, panting but triumphant. After him, Abia walked up the swaying ladder as if it were a solid staircase. Then the two warriors followed. While one winched up the ladder, the other handed the message to the king.

'What's this?' Rashaunt said. 'I've no time for other matters now.' He glanced at the note and froze.

CHAPTER 28 – TO KILL A RED CAPTAIN

They'd been following the river, a broad expanse of water with rocky, well-forested land on both sides.

It was nearly dark when the prince suddenly stopped. 'We're close,' he said, barely able to contain his excitement. 'That dock upriver belongs to Kas-Bahaan. I remember a navy corvette was stationed here.'

'Ships can come this far?' Jornyll said, surprised.

'Sure, not the big ships, but anything smaller can sail right up to the castle walls. Further upriver are rapids, though.'

'Hush now,' Aya said. 'Let's see how things stand before we announce ourselves.'

The prince looked at her. 'But that's our keep...'

'Quiet!' Aya snapped.

They stood at the forest's edge. Before them Jornyll saw a walled building of gray stone, with high, thin towers and funny-looking battlements. The big double gates were closed, making the castle look cold and inhospitable.

Suddenly Razoon put a hand to his ear. 'Wait!' he whispered. He glanced at his brother and crouching low, they ran to a small copse of trees halfway between the wood and the keep.

Jornyll glanced at Aya, who crouched in the bushes watching the two scouts go.

In silence they waited, then the brothers came back.

'Wastrels inside!' Razoon said grimly. 'Heard them talk. Perhaps pirates too, dunno about that.'

'What!' the prince nearly shouted. 'This is a royal keep!'

'So?' Howy said. 'Wastrels don't care.'

'Be silent!' Aya said. She studied the castle with knotted brows, looking much like those big, tough warrioresses they'd seen in Queen Maud's palace, Jornyll thought.

Aya glanced at the two scouts. 'We need to know more.'

Razoon sighed. 'Sure. Howy, let's go say hi to the nice Wastrels.'

'How?' Jornyll asked. 'You can't get in.'

'Course we can,' Howy said. 'We'll be them.'

'If they're the same sort as the ones you knew,' Jornyll said.

'Wastrels are all the same,' Razoon said. 'Handshakes, calls, passwords, all groups use them. It's like a religion, y' know.' He nodded at Aya. 'Stay within reach,' he said. 'Either we come running out fast or we'll give an owl's call for you to join us.'

Then they walked boldly up to the keep.

Jornyll watched them go. Those two guys should get a bonus for bravery, he thought. He saw Howy bring his hands to his mouth and a high shout tore through the silence.

For a moment, nothing happened. Then the gates opened slightly, and the boys spoke a few words. Jornyll touched his sword, half-and-half expecting a fight.

An owl's mournful hunting call drifted towards them.

'Come,' Aya said, and they all walked briskly to the gate. Jornyll prayed their disguises were convincing enough from a distance, but there was no angry shout, no hail of arrows from the walls, and he breathed a soft sigh of relief.

'I get it; the headman is out with his men,' Howy said arrogantly as they neared. 'He left a skeleton guard. Now, do we get in or shall I speak to my *tathaim* about your lack of cooperation?'

'No,' a surly voice said. 'Let's leave the chiefs out of it. I've got my orders, but... Come in, quickly.'

They slipped inside and the old Wastrel bolted the gates behind them. 'The others are in the hall,' he said and turned to go.

Howy lashed out with his cudgel, and the man collapsed without a sound.

'One down,' Razoon said simply. 'Now to the hall.'

Jornyll looked at the Wastrel. 'Most definitely down,' he said.

Howy bared his teeth in a grin, but his eyes were dark. 'That was sorta the idea.'

As they hurried across the quiet courtyard, a bony boy came from a side door, carrying a pail of water. As he saw them, he froze, staring openmouthed.

Jornyll raised his sword, ready to kill any shouting, but the prince pushed him aside.

'Pashu!' he said, running to the boy.

The guy dropped his pail. 'It's you?' he whispered. 'I... I'm not goin' mad? Prince, what...?'

'We're going to take the castle back,' the prince said.

Aya, too, had drawn her sword. 'Who is that fellow?' she said in a deadly voice. 'Quickly now, before I kill him.'

The prince stared at her. 'He's Pashu,' he said, surprised. 'He and I, we grew up together.'

Aya's scowl deepened. 'That may be, but can we trust him?'

'Of course you can,' the prince said, aghast. 'Pashu...' He wheeled around to the strange boy. 'Are you loyal, Pashu?'

The boy dropped down on his knees. 'I am, Highness, as I always was. Those dastards killed everybody; the soldiers, my father... I hate them for what they did, for what they... do to me. If you come to kill them, let me help. I can wield an ax; I want to fight, Prince.'

Jazzaunt looked at Aya. 'Pashu is loyal,' he said, squaring his shoulders. 'He's a friend, Corporal Aya.'

Jornyll watched Aya, her natural caution warring with the prince's conviction.

'All right,' she said in a hard voice. 'I hold you responsible for him, Prince Jazzaunt. If he betrays us, I'll return you to your uncle in chains.'

The prince nodded. 'He'll not betray us. Where is your ax, Pashu?'

'In the stable,' the boy said. 'I use it for choppin' wood, you see.'

'Let's get it,' the prince said. 'A soldier needs arms.'

'Be quick about it,' Aya said grimly as the two ran off.

They were back in minutes. The boy had donned a rather long leather smith's apron and carried a well-kept ax.

Aya looked him over and grunted. 'You know the situation. How many villains are there now?'

'A Wastrel and eight pirates,' the boy said quickly. 'Their headman and the others are out hunting.' He hesitated. 'And below there are six captured kids,' he whispered.

'What captured kids?' Aya said softly.

Jornyll saw her face muscles tauten and her lips pull back in a snarl, and he remembered her rage when those pirates had caught her, Willow, and Keena.

'The Wastrels had been raiding someplace and captured them,' Pashu said. 'There were more, but the others have been taken away already. These six left in the dungeons are for another captain. He's out with the hunters, waiting for his ship to come back for the prisoners.'

'We must get them out,' Jornyll said.

'You can't go down below!' Pashu said. 'There's monsters guarding them.'

Aya looked up. 'What monsters?'

Pashu spread his hands. 'Three big dogs, very ugly dogs.'

'Dogs,' Jornyll said contemptuously. 'Who's afraid of *them*?'

'Me,' Pashu said. 'They're very mean dogs.'

Jornyll grinned. 'No sweat, just show us the way and we'll kill them.' He looked at Aya. 'All right?'

'Don't underestimate what you don't know,' Aya said. 'The boss ain't here to put you back together.' She tapped Pashu's thin shoulder. 'Take us to the dungeons.'

The boy gripped his ax with both hands and swallowed. 'This way,' he said, and ran across the courtyard to the tallest tower. He opened the door and Jornyll grabbed the prince's neck as he wanted to run inside first.

'You wait for your betters,' Jornyll said sternly, pushing Jazzaunt behind him.

'That's me,' Aya said, and with her sword in her hand walked into the dark opening. 'Watch it; stairs going down.'

Jornyll followed her, with Zaotinq on his heels. It was dark down here, and there was a heavy stink of rotting meat and dung in the air.

'Aera aid me,' Justym muttered.

'Us,' Jornyll said. 'Pray for us all, singer.'

'Sorry,' Justym said, and his voice sounded strangled. 'Aera, dear goddess, please aid all of us, for we are here on the gods' behalf.'

A terrible, mocking laughter filled the corridor.

'Hyenas!' Razoon said. 'They're not dogs. One of the Pashwend Wastrels brought a pup as a pet. After a year it slaughtered its master. Went for his throat, it did, and they had to kill it.'

'That's the awful smell,' Howy said. 'Those beasts like their meat long dead.'

Then they saw three pairs of eyes, glowing red in the dark.

'They can jump!' Razoon snapped. 'Watch...'

Again the beasts gave their taunting cry. Then something dark and hairy crashed into Jornyll, throwing him down like a doll. He yelled and rolled to a side. Zaotinq shouted a Qoori curse and an anguished yowl sounded where his blade had connected in the dark. Aya ran forward and more howling echoed against the walls. Frantically, Jornyll sought for his sword. His hand felt something wet and hairy that moved under his touch, and he screamed, slashing at it with his dagger. Then his foot found his sword and he snatched it up.

'Here!' a high-pitched voice shouted and an animal scream broke off abruptly. 'Die! Die!' the same hysterical voice shouted.

Then Aya's deeper voice came. 'You can stop now; it's dead. All three are dead. Anyone hurt?'

No one said anything.

'Good show, guys,' Aya said. 'Now where are those prisoners?'

A dead silence followed.

'Any kids here?' Aya shouted again. 'Holler, then we can get you out.'

'Here!' a voice cried. 'You... you come for *us*?'

'Sure,' Aya said.

They all hurried on and then Jornyll ran into an iron grating.

'Darn!' he said.

'Sorry,' a nearby girl's voice answered.

Then a small light appeared in the air. 'Yes!' Justym said triumphantly.

'Magic?' Jornyll said. 'How did you do that?'

'I don't know; it didn't work before,' the singer said. 'Perhaps being underground weakens the iron ore a little. It's only a small spell; I still can't mindspeak or anything that asks for more power.'

They looked around at two rusty cages, with kids inside.

Aya tried a grilled door, but it was locked. 'Where are the keys?'

'One of the Wastrels has them,' a hollow-eyed boy said. 'A fat one with a mean eye, who brings us food.'

Jornyll grunted. 'We'll have to take down those pirates first, then.'

'We'll do that,' Aya said. 'Chin up, guys; we'll be back with the keys.'

Halfway up the stairs, Justym's light died and they climbed the rest in the dark.

Back outside, the courtyard was still empty.

'Take us to the hall, Pashu,' Aya commanded.

They crossed the cobbled yard at a dead run. At the big doors they stopped.

'Careful now,' Aya said. 'I'll go first.'

The prince and Pashu pulled the big doors ajar, and she slipped through.

Jornyll followed her, motioning to the others to wait.

The hall was in darkness; two torches and the glow of the fire lighted the circle in front of the big fireplace.

Seven bandits lounged around, goblets in hand, trusting their lookout at the gate to warn them. Two others stood before a birdcage.

'Eat, you stupid beast,' one man said. 'It's meat, nice juicy meat; jest what you want.'

'Curse the filthy mongrel,' the other said in a vicious voice. 'We should hurt it a little, show who's master!'

'No!' the first man said. 'That critter's a present for Lord Nimmendal. We canna damage it.'

'Fine present,' the second man said, his voice dripping with derision. 'A starved little bat too stupid to eat.'

'It's not a bat!' the first man protested. 'Anyway the captain says it's a gift. Take yer complaints to him.'

From the cage came a high, shuddering wail.

Jornyll felt his heart grow cold. 'A wyrmling!' he whispered to Aya. 'Those darned villains got a wyrmling.'

She opened the door a little wider and gestured to the others. 'Attack!'

'Jazzaunt for the king!' the prince cried, and this time he evaded any hands that thought to hold him back. Slashing his sword in the air, he ran forward, and the others hurried after him.

'Idiot!' Jornyll growled and ran for the two at the cage. The first man, a bearded fellow in a dark jacket, went for his sword, but he was too late and caught Jornyll's sword in his chest. The boy cursed as his weight behind the stroke pushed the weapon all the way through his opponent's body. The man dropped into a heap at his feet and while he wrestled to retrieve his blade, the second bandit had drawn a long knife. Aya gripped the pirate's shoulders from behind, lifted the man off the floor, and slammed him down hard enough to break his spine.

Jornyll wrenched his sword from the body. Then he wheeled around and joined Zaotinq battling a fellow twice his size. The man broke away and ran to a door in the back of the hall.

'No you don't,' Aya yelled. She gripped a high-backed chair and threw it after the pirate. One of the chair's carved legs got him in the head and he crashed down.

Jornyll cheered 'True Kell power, Corporal!' An elbow rammed into his side and he gasped. As he turned around, he saw it was Bamson, clumsily beating a thin fellow with the flat of his sword. The man collapsed, and Bamson stepped back, panting heavily. Jornyll slapped his shoulder. 'You did him in, well done, mate.'

Bamson smiled hesitantly.

Finally, Razoon drew his arms around the last pirate, and Howy bludgeoned him out of the world. It was all over.

'We won!' the prince cried. 'Jazzaunt for the king! We won!'

Aya chuckled. 'For Bodrus and the Wyrmcaller, you mean.'

The prince didn't answer but ran over to Pashu. 'Where are the pigeons?' he said urgently.

The boy stared at him, the battle's horror still in his eyes. Then his face changed. 'Pigeons,' he said. 'There's one left, Prince. Those dastards ate them all, but I kept this one hidden away. It's one of the palace messengers.'

'Smart of you!' the prince said. 'Now get me pen and paper.'

'What are you going to do?' Aya said.

'Write a letter to my uncle. Pashu's dad was responsible for the messenger pigeons. The one that's left will bring my letter to the royal palace.'

'Clever,' Aya said. 'Carry on.'

The boy returned with a sheet of thin paper, pen and ink.

The prince chewed his thumb for a moment, frowning at the empty paper.

To my Most Dread Uncle and Sovereign Lord, Rashaunt XI, King of Hizmyr,

Beloved Uncle, I wish to report I just retook Kas-Bahaan from its foolish Wastrel occupiers.

I most respectfully request you send forces to relieve me here.

Signed at Kas-Bahaan, Jazzaunt.

PS: I beg you to remember who won the Aduur bet?

PSPS: I have friends from the south, who helped me. They're all well too.

'Nice you remembered us,' Aya said.

The prince flushed. 'I know, but I can't write it any other way. As prince, I must lead, y' see.'

Aya stared at him. 'Yeah? All right; we're not hurt.'

'What's that about a bet?' Jornyll said.

The prince looked away. 'That's just something to tell my uncle it's really me who wrote this.'

'Ah,' Jornyll said. 'Smart move. You're not dumb, even if you're a prince.'

Jazzaunt snorted. 'Go get the pigeon,' he commanded. Pashu ran off and returned with a scruffy gray bird in his hands.

'Here she is, Prince,' he said. 'Gimme the message; she's used to me handling her.' He swiftly rolled up the sheet and put it in a small tube on the pigeon's leg.

They all walked outside and Pashu lifted the bird over his head. 'To the king,' he said. 'Fly to the king, great messenger. Tell him we need help.'

The bird flew up and away to the north-west.

'Help me with the cage,' Justym called, and Jornyll hurried over to him. The cage was meant for tropical birds but instead it housed a little creature, huddling on the bottom. As Justym clutched the cage bars, the wyrmling lifted his head and wailed again.

'Gods!' Jornyll said reverently. 'It *is* a wyrmling.'

'Don't blather, open that cage,' the singer said.

Jornyll got his knife out and wrenched open the door.

'There y' are,' he said.

Justym stretched out his hand. 'Come, little one, let's get you out of there.'

The wyrmling looked up at him and didn't move.

'He doesn't trust us,' Aya said suddenly. 'Do like the boss and put him inside your tunic.'

Justym gripped the little body. 'It's all right,' he said, stroking the wyrmling as he'd seen Eskandar do. 'We come to save you.' Then he put him inside his tunic.

'You care for him,' Aya said. 'When we're back we'll let Lothi-Mo handle it. Now, who had the keys to the dungeon cells?'

'A fat guy,' Jornyll said, checking each of the fallen men. 'This one?' His quick hands searched through the dead Wastrel's clothes and found a rusty key ring. 'Got them!'

'Good,' Aya said. 'You and Justym go get the prisoners. All others check those bodies for the usual; valuables, weapons, documents, anything the boss would want.' She gripped Pashu's shoulder. 'You be gatekeeper,' she said gruffly. 'See they're locked, then go sit on the walls and warn us when anybody comes.'

The boy bit his lip and gave a quick nod, before running away.

Back at the cages, Jornyll waved the keys so they tinkled like rusty bells. 'Singer, could ya make another light?'

A small flame appeared. 'It's not much,' Justym said apologetically.

'It's great! You must have strong magic, mate.' Jornyll turned to the hollow-eyed boy in the first cage. 'We'll have you out in a jiff.'

He gripped the big padlock of the first cell and very carefully inserted a key in the hole. It refused to move, and after the third try he chose a second key. The fourth key did it, and the cage door opened with a nerve-shattering screech.

'There y'are,' he said. 'Careful now!'

The boy stumbled from the cage, followed by a girl and a second, smaller boy who was crying soundlessly.

'Next,' Jornyll said, moving to the opposite cage and repeated the process. Minutes later, three more kids came out, blinking against the light of the little flame.

'How did you get the keys?' a tall boy said.

'We killed the guys in the hall,' Jornyll answered. 'There were only nine of them.'

'Only nine?' the boy exclaimed. 'Where are the others?'

'Out hunting. We've locked the gates, so they'll not surprise us. Can you kids walk? Upstairs we've food and water.'

'For food? You bet we can walk,' a girl said. 'Come on, guys.'

And walk they did; some shakily and one had to be helped by his friends, but they reached the doors and the beckoning daylight.

Once they were out of the dungeon tower, Jornyll saw how ragged and dirty those six kids were. They stumbled through the doorway, blinking against the sunshine after their long stay in the dark and breathed in the fresh air.

'To the hall,' Jornyll said. 'Don't trip over the dead bodies; we haven't had time to tidy the place up for you.'

'As long as they're bandits, we won't mind,' the tall boy said. 'We've been imagining a thousand ways to kill them.'

Back in the great hall, the others had readied a table with loaves of bread, a pot of soup full of meat and greenstuffs, a large platter of cold cuts and a bucket of water to drink.

Aya waved to the freed prisoners. 'Go ahead, stuff yourselves. It's on the house.'

While they all ate, Jornyll watched the freed prisoners. They looked like tough kids at the end of their ropes. Worn out by maltreatment, hunger, and fear, but not broken. He exchanged a glance with Aya, who stood studying them with arms crossed and a grim face.

She gave a curt nod. 'Tell me about you lot while you eat,' she said to the tall boy. 'Who are you?'

The boy paused for a moment and touched an ugly welt in his neck. Seen up close, he had a heavy, freckled brown face and defiant eyes. *A rebel*, Jornyll thought. *Looks capable.*

'I'm Orin,' the boy said hoarsely. 'We're all that is left of the Zamidra Syndicate Institute. That is – was – a mining school. We were going to be craftsmen; smiths, engineers, like that.' He bit his lip, fighting to keep his face emotionless. 'There were fifteen more of us. Those cursed pirates dragged them out to a ship; I don't know where they went. We six were for another captain. He arrived yesterday but we haven't seen him yet.'

'So you're craftsmen?' Jornyll asked. As he spoke the wyrmling in his arms yawned.

'Yeah, more or less, that's what we are,' the tall boy said. He grimaced. 'A second chance, the instructors called it. It was a harsh chance.' He turned and pulled up his tunic to show a mass of welts. 'The instructors beat me for talking back.'

'Me, too,' another boy said. 'The Syndicate thought us cheap labor. They taught us, oh yes, they did. I can work a smithy as well as any city journeyman, but they never paid us, and they'd never let us go again.'

'We were nobody,' the tall boy said. 'We always been nobody.'

'You don't say you're street kids,' Jornyll said.

The tall boy's brows lowered. 'I didn't, but that's what we were, until the law caught us.'

Jornyll gave a curt laugh. 'So were we, but we bettered ourselves.' He glanced at Aya. 'I think we should tell them our story.'

Aya raised an eyebrow. 'Because?'

'Those guys are like us. We got our chance to join Eskandar, why not they? We need technical people.'

For a moment Aya stood thinking. 'We can tell them about our hunting pirates, but we better leave the details to the boss.'

Jornyll grinned. 'Eskandar? Why are we calling him boss now?'

Aya shrugged. 'Better for discipline. We're used to the word, and it's easier than wyrmcaller.'

All right, Jornyll thought as he turned back to the freed kids. *Boss it is, at least in public.* 'Guys, while you eat, let me tell you our story.'

'I must believe you,' Orin said when Jornyll was done. 'That tale of yours is too crazy for words, but so are you with your gray and green skins.' He stared at each of the troops. 'You tell us there is a castle in the south with only kids like you and we?'

'Yep, and most of us lived on the street before, or like Zaotinq in a kind of slavery that sounds much like yours.' Jornyll smiled. 'My togs lie in the wreck of that boat, but look at our Corporal Aya. She's wearing the uniform of the Pasandir Armed Forces. Justym, the one with the magic, is a priest of Aera Skygoddess. That talkative guy over there is your very own Prince Jazzaunt. Don't highness the chap; he's here as one of us. The only one with a title is the corporal.'

Orin grunted. 'That's the kid prince? I seen him ride with the soldiers, all grand in his glitters. This is just another guy.'

Jornyll laughed. 'Mate, they're all just guys without their trappings.'

'Yeah,' Orin said. 'I suppose so. Still, he's the law, and we're not very fond of the law right now.'

The prince looked over his shoulder. 'I don't know you,' he said. 'To me you're just a bunch of guys we freed from the dungeons.'

'Sure, and that's very good of you,' Orin said heavily. 'But where can we go? To the law, we're escaped prisoners.'

'I could ask my uncle to pardon you,' the prince said hesitantly. 'No, that would mean going against the guild; I'm not sure he would do that.'

'You can join us,' Jornyll said. 'We can use technical guys.' He saw Orin's doubtful face. 'Think it over. We expect the king to send help. We will tell his people you are with us; all right?' He looked at Aya, who nodded slowly.

Then she slapped her hands together. 'We will not betray you,' she said briskly. 'You just act like you are soldiers of the Pasandir Peaks. Wounded soldiers.'

'You'd do that?' Orin said. 'You would lie for us?'

'If you'd join us, it wouldn't be a lie,' Jornyll said, grinning. 'If not, we'd still help you out of this place.'

He fell silent as Pashu came running in from his post at the gate, his face working.

'They're back!' the boy panted. 'Them bandits are back!'

'Darnation!' Aya ran from the hall, with Jornyll close behind. Outside, they climbed the ladder to the wall walk and crouched. Peering past the merlins, Jornyll saw a motley group men waiting; four of them in Wastrel robes and the other seventeen looked like they were Bokkaners.

One of them called out in a strange language.

'He's calling the guy watching the gate,' Howy whispered. He lay flat on his back, his upper body on Jornyll's legs. 'Using a lot of swear words, too.'

Jornyll thought of something. He wriggled back to the ladder and beckoned to Pashu, watching them anxiously.

'Do we have bows an' arrows?' Jornyll asked softly. 'Swords?

'Yeah, old stuff,' Pashu said. 'Come and see.'

Jornyll looked at Orin. 'Anyone of you can fight?'

'Me,' Orin said, jutting out his chin. 'The others are too weak.'

'Tell them to wait in the hall, then come with me for arms.'

Five of the kids reluctantly went inside, while Jornyll with Orin and Zaotinq hurried off after Pashu. In a side room to the hall they found a rack of swords, axes, and several hunting bows, with strings and arrows, their feathers brittle with age.

'Pick a weapon for yourself. We'll share the bows and stuff among the troops,' Jornyll said.

In the courtyard, the bandits were banging the gates and shouting curses.

'We got bows, guys,' Jornyll said, with a quick glance at Aya. 'Show those villains Amaj didn't teach you for nothing. Careful when you string them, it's all old stuff.'

Aya nodded at him. 'Quick thinking. Guys, when you're ready, mount the wall but don't show yourself. When I say so, you stand and shoot to kill. When you've loosed your shaft, duck and nock another one. Then wait for my signal. Got that? You too, prince? Keep a grip on your enthusiasm, bud.'

The prince snorted, but nodded.

When they were all in position, Aya shouted in a voice loud enough to command a battlefield. 'You out there, this castle has been taken for the king by the Pasandir Armed Forces. You get the heck away from here or die.'

For a few heartbeats it was silent out there. 'What's that?' a voice said in heavily accented Vulgar. 'You're kidding, ain't you? That's our keep.'

Zaotinq looked over his shoulder at Jornyll. His greenish face had turned streaky gray and his eyes were big. 'Luzon!' he said in a strangled voice. 'Voice is Captain Luzon!'

Darn! Jornyll thought. *That thug who had captured the* Drakon *and her crew. But he'd escaped in Brisa...*

'Guys, rise and shoot,' Aya said in the courtyard. 'Then duck.'

Jornyll came up and aimed past the battlements at a fat Wastrel with a trio of dead rabbits on his back. The man was clearly visible in the moonlight as he stood staring at the gates, and never noticed what slew him. As the Wastrel fell, Jornyll took a second to look around the area. Then he saw the small Qoori in the red uniform, waving his arms and yelling. Jornyll ducked and nodded to Zaotinq. 'Saw him. Warn the corporal.'

'Bows!' Luzon's voice cried. 'Get your bows out!'

'Guys, rise and shoot,' Aya said again.

Jornyll saw the men below had backed away a bit, and were frantically readying their bows. He shot, but missed. Then, in one swift move, he drew another arrow and this time his man tumbled backward in the grass. Jornyll grunted and ducked again.

Moments later, there was the sound of an axe chopping wood.

'They're at the door,' Aya said.

Jornyll lifted his head and peered at the bandits. Then two arrows clattered against the wall, too close for comfort, and he dropped onto his stomach.

'They got us covered now,' he said.

Aya beckoned him over. 'What's that about Luzon?' she said softly.

'It's him,' Jornyll said. 'I saw the villain.'

Aya scratched her chin. 'So he came north after Brisa.' She looked at Jornyll and Zaotinq. 'We've got no use for his sort.'

There were more axes at work outside now, and the big gate doors shook under their blows.

'Quickly,' Aya said. 'Guys, hide in the shadows, bows ready. When they enter, shoot. Then take your sword and go for it.'

Jornyll shook her shoulders and grinned. 'We'll show them, Corporal.'

She ruffled his hair for a moment. 'You've grown, Vanhaari. You're not that small anymore.'

Then the gate crashed open. Eight bows sang out and several bandits dropped amid the wreckage.

Only half of them left, Jornyll thought. *And Luzon, of course; the little creep.*

'Enough!' the Qoori pirate said. He motioned his remaining men aside. 'I'll do this.' He walked forward; his face flushed darker green and his eyes shining with some inner amusement. Then he halted, spread his arms as if to embrace them all, and changed.

Gods! Jornyll thought, while raw panic tugged at his innards. *He's a jinni!*

'You puny kids thought to stop me,' the formless blob said. He was enormous, far bigger than the one who had kidnapped them. A mass of fat, covered with hairy skin and with long, tendril-like limbs. His mouth was a bloody red horror of pointed teeth and only his eyes were unchanged, still glinting with unholy glee.

'At him!' Aya yelled.

As one, her troop ran forward, screaming at the top of their voices, and hacked at the big body. The jinni curled one arm like a rope round Razoon's body and drew him toward the open mouth. The boy yelled and slashed at the jinni with his blade. Quickly, his brother and the prince sprang to assist him and with a few powerful chops, Howy cut off the arm. Freed, Razoon jumped back as the severed limb shuddered and withered to dust. The jinni laughed and a new limb sprouted from the body, grasping for another prey.

Jornyll retired to the shadows, readying his bow. He'd proven a fair shot during their training. Not excellent, but not hopeless either. And that flipping mass of lard wasn't hard to miss... So he shot shaft after shaft, but most simply disappeared inside the monstrous body. Then he hit a spot near the mouth, and green stuff welled up from the hole. The jinni screeched like a slaughtered pig.

'Aim for the mouth!' Jornyll shouted and the kids doubled their efforts. He saw Orin and the prince stabbing at the mouth, calling forth more green blood.

The jinni screamed in anger. His upper limbs lashed out, bowling kids over, but every time they came back, aiming at that one tender region. Then Bamson came too close and the jinni slapped him across the face with an arm. The boy crashed to the ground, his head a mass of blood, and someone dragged him out of the way. Jornyll cursed terribly and loosed another arrow.

The jinni grew frantic now. 'Aid me!' he shouted to his men, but the remaining pirates had melted away into the forest.

'You're alone, beast!' Jornyll shouted. He put down his bow and drew his sword. 'You're done for!'

Then all looked up as a dark shadow slipped between them in the courtyard and the sun.

'Concentrate on the jinni!' Aya commanded. For a moment, the jinni stood alone, bleeding green ooze and pulsating madly as he glared at the kids.

Then Zaotinq came forth, all alone. He gripped his sword with both hands, and stood poised for a long heartbeat. All at once he screamed something in Qoori, sprang and rammed his blade to the hilt into the spot beside the jinni's mouth. With a loud whoosh, the jinni imploded.

'We won!' Aya screamed. 'We killed a jinni!'

Jornyll dragged Zaotinq to his feet. 'Well done!' he said urgently, feeling the boy tremble. 'You avenged your shipmates!'

Aya wheeled toward them. 'So you did! The mortal blow was yours, Zaotinq.'

CHAPTER 29 – VICTORS

'Impossible!' the king said and he sounded utterly astounded. 'He... that rascal... Impossible!' He handed me the letter. 'Read this.'

'Prince Jazzaunt?' I said, trying to decipher the scrawled lines. 'He retook Kas-Bahaan from the Wastrels? Friends from the south helped him? All well?'

My voice must have echoed the king's stupefaction, for Kellani snatched the letter from my hand.

'That's my boys!' she said proudly, and passed the paper to Naudin. 'Aya and the others, I knew they could do it. Those kids are equal to anything!' She glanced at the king. 'The prince must feel at home in their company; those guys are tough.'

'Jazz wrote the letter, no doubt about it.' Naudin studied the paper over the rim of his glasses. 'That large-sized spirit of his almost leaps from the paper.' He pursed his lips, looking for a moment like those strange creature heads on some temples. 'A bet?'

The king coughed. 'That is something only he and I know. A moment of childishness on my part when he was little. It's not important.'

'But it's clever of the prince to use it as proof that he wrote the letter and of his own free will,' Naudin said.

The king stared out the window. 'He retook Kas-Bahaan? Alone, with a bunch of children?' It was clear the thought shook him.

Lothi-Mo cackled. 'Bunch of young heroes,' she said. 'Wyrmcaller told they are very, very good kids.'

'How soon will we be there?' I asked, trying to curb my growing impatience.

'It's an hour by air,' the king said absently and lapsed into silence.

I wasn't in the mood for talking either, so to soothe my thoughts I called up a small ball of water and kept it in the air until the spell died.

'We've reached the iron ore.' I closed my eyes and inspected my lower brain, where my magic is seated. It looked strangely asleep, but there were sparks of light here and there as a sign the iron ore didn't block everything.

I checked my spells. I couldn't call a wind to throw at my enemies. Everything based on my own power was down. My healing was alive; I'd always suspected I got that from Bodrus. Would that mean the god's magic wasn't affected? With great daring, I followed the healing force to its origin outside my mind and far away. It sprang from a bright light, still and unbearably clear, that hovered somewhere to the east. To the east? I knew where; it came from the monastery, from Teodar's place, where Bodrus slept. It was a source of unimaginable power. On impulse, I stole the tiniest bit of it and called the little ball of water. When I opened my eyes, I saw it reappear on my hand, dancing gleefully.

'Well done!' a humorous voice said. *'You really are my disciple.'*

'You don't mind I use your power?' I felt like a pickpocket caught in the act.

'Not at all, my brave defender,' the voice said. *'You will need it, and there is far more power than two humans can handle.'*

I almost said "two?", but then I understood where Teodar got his strength.

'Thank you, god,' I said. I hesitated. *'Am I doing all right?'*

'Rest assured I will tell you if you aren't,' the voice said with a chuckle. *'Be well, my Wings.'* With those words he was gone, and the airship was an empty cavern without his presence.

I stared at the little ball, now pirouetting like a dancing maid at a party.

'How?' Naudin said, watching the ball's antics. 'I couldn't call up a sneeze, let alone that!'

I turned my head. 'It's my god's power.' I heard the awe in my own voice. 'Bodrus permitted me to use it.'

'Why?' The young mage sounded anguished. 'Lumentis doesn't lend me his.'

'You're not a disciple,' I said dreamily and went back to studying my dancing ball.

Kellani's hard grip on my shoulder blade broke the spell.

'Ouch!' I said. 'What's that for?'

'Pay attention!' she snapped. 'The king was speaking to you.'

'Beg your pardon,' I said, blushing. 'I was testing a new theory.'

Rashaunt stared at my now empty hand. 'We're almost there.'

I hurried to the window and looked down. Below I saw the contours of a tall building; high walls, a courtyard... 'They're fighting!' I cried. 'Darnation! That's a jinni!'

Soldiers opened the side door and threw down a large net.

'I'll go first,' I said, and climbed down faster than ever before. Just as I sprang the last feet to the ground, a loud implosion tugged at the air around me and I stumbled back into Kellani, who had come down behind me. I heard Aya cry out and kids shouting as I ran up to them. I stopped, struck dumb by the sight of the courtyard, the fallen bandits, and all the youngsters staring at a whitish stain on the cobblestones where moments before the big jinni had been.

'Mountain's Breath,' I said softly. 'You guys killed it?'

Jornyll turned and his face lighted up. 'It's the boss!' he cried joyously.

At a loss for words, I embraced him, and Aya, Zaotinq, and the other idiot maniac warrior kids and we all shed tears. Last, someone pushed Bamson into my arms. The former Basher was covered in blood, his face battered as if someone had worked him over with a hammer.

I felt him shake, and the agony of his wounds tugged at me. Before I started the healing spell, I drew on Bodrus' power. Shielded by my god's strength, I dissolved his hurt, repaired bones and tissues, and replenished his strength.

When Bamson's body was whole again, I hugged him tight. 'You're tough, guy!' I said. 'Those wounds should've killed you, but your body refused to give up. You're alright. You did great, and now you're all right.'

He began to cry and I let Jornyll take him. 'He'll be fine.'

'Boss,' Jornyll whispered over Bamson's shoulder. 'Don't be surprised. We got six local kids. They were prisoners here. Keep it quiet. Act as if they're part of the troop and take them to the *Drakon*. I'll explain later.'

He was very much in earnest, and behind him, Aya gave an emphatic nod. I glanced at Kellani and Naudin, who seemed as puzzled as I was.

'All right,' I said. 'Keep the troops together.'

Justym came hurrying up to me. 'Where is Lothi-Mo? I need her help.' His face was anxious, and he pressed one hand to his heart.

I gave him a quick look-over, but I couldn't find anything wrong with him. 'She's flitting around somewhere.' I lifted my arm and called her. Moments later, she came winging down.

Suddenly I heard her squawk. She somersaulted in mid-air, uttered a long, piercing cry and jumped Justym, talking rapidly in her own tongue and beating the boy with her wings and tail.

As I gaped in surprise at her agitation, I saw something move inside the young priest's tunic, and a little wyrm head peered out, twittering anxiously. The wyrmling who crawled from Justym's tunic was smaller than Lothi-Mo, and instead of her many-colored skin he was of a dull bronze-green, with anxious yellow eyes. He spread his wings, and Lothi-Mo hummed at him, a cooing song.

'Tiu-Ti weak; no fly,' he said in a reedy voice. 'Hunger; much, much hunger.' He sagged back against Justym's chest and panted.

'Food,' Lothi-Mo commanded. 'Someone go catch a mouse! Ten mouse, bucket of mouse! Hurry!'

Justym looked around and waved to a ragged boy in a leather apron. 'Pashu, get a platter of meats and some water, please.' The boy rushed off.

Justym and a wyrmling boy, I thought. 'Where did you find him?'

'The pirates kept him in a cage,' the singer said curtly. 'We'll tell you everything later, if that's all right.'

The boy came back with his meat and Justym nearly snatched the plate from his hands. 'No mice, I'm afraid,' he said as he held the meat under the wyrmling's nose. 'But this should fill your belly well enough.'

Six, no, seven strange kids and a wyrmling... I was near to bursting with questions, but the boys had made it clear this wasn't the time for it.

'You did well,' I said merely. 'Feed him until he's had enough; don't be afraid he will overeat, he won't.'

I turned to the king, who had descended last and stood looking at his nephew. The prince was with the troop, flushed with the magic of victory, and had no eyes for anyone else.

'They defeated a jinni,' I said. 'It will take them some time to come down to earth again.'

'Yes,' the king said. 'I know the euphoria, though it was long ago. I... must accept he is no longer a child. My brother's son is a warrior.' He sighed a little. 'Strange; I never felt this way with my own sons.' He straightened. 'I suppose you want to return to your ship?'

'If you can spare transport, yes. Those lads are up in the clouds now, but when they do come down, they'll need rest and medical attention.'

The king nodded and called an order to the airship officer at the net. The man hurried up to me and saluted.

'Have your men board, Wyrmcaller,' he said. 'We will return you and His Majesty to the palace.'

'Thank you,' I said, suddenly bone-weary with emotion.

'Corporal Aya,' I called. 'Let's go home.'

'Sir!' she said, saluting. 'Come, lads; the boss brought an airship for us. Back to the *Drakon* the easy way.'

Without a word of command, the king's seshars lined up in two facing rows, leaving a path to the airship.

When our kids moved stiffly through the two lines of soldiers toward the scrambling net, the seshars began a doleful cry, slamming their hilts to their shields.

The prince nudged Aya, grinning hugely. 'Up your blades, Corporal, that's a great compliment to all of us!'

Aya's mouth curled into a smile. 'Is it now? Troop, raise your swords. Show those warriors the power of the Pasandir.'

With raised blades, the troop reached the scrambling net, sheathed their arms, and climbed up. Some of the strange kids needed help, and I noticed Jornyll and a tall boy almost carrying another guy into the airship.

The king followed last and once he was inside, airmen pulled up the net and the dirigible turned away from the keep.

Only now the prince greeted his uncle. 'Kas-Bahaan is ours again, my king,' he said, bowing like a true courtier.

His uncle looked down at him. 'We thank you, prince. Your bravery fills our heart with gladness.'

Jazzaunt inhaled sharply and they embraced.

After a moment, the king gripped the boy's shoulders. 'Nephew, the lord wyrmcaller suggested you could aid him in his battle for the gods. How say you join his forces for a while?'

'Yes!' the prince said jubilantly. Recovering himself, he took a breath. 'Ah, that would please me, my king.'

'Done, then,' the king said, and they grinned at each other.

Jazzaunt stepped back and bowed. 'Thank you, my king.' He turned to me and bowed again, drawing his blade. 'Lord Wyrmcaller, would you accept my sword in your service?'

'Gladly, Prince,' I said.

'Touch his sword,' Lothi-Mo said. *'Old ceremonial important to royals.'*

I felt a terrible giggle in my throat and I swallowed it down with some effort as I laid my hand on the hilt of the offered sword. All this was very strange and roundabout for one unused to kingly ways. The only royal court I knew a little was Queen Maud's and the Kell weren't interested in bowing and scraping.

The prince marched over to Aya, who stood watching everything with a skeptical eye and crossed arms. 'Reporting for duty, Corporal,' he said. Then he called out. 'Pashu, come! You want to report, too.'

The ragged boy came to stand beside him, one hand fingering an old woodcutter's ax. He looked at Aya and then at the prince. 'Would they wanna have me?'

'You showed you can do it,' Aya said gravely. 'You're in if you want to. Join the others; you've earned some rest, soldiers.'

'Good, good,' Lothi-Mo said, as we watched both boys go back to their new friends. *'Now the ship. Tiu-Ti needs food and sleep.'*

'He's so small; he must be very young?' I asked. I found I could mindspeak by using Bodrus' power. That left the question how Lothi-Mo did it. How strong was she?

My wyrmling cackled, but whether it was over my question or my thought she didn't say. *'Not so young, Tiu-Ti warrior boy; these smaller than girls, much smaller than royal sept girls. Had bad time, too; is scared and needs food, rest. Lothi-Mo will return his courage.'*

'So Tiu-Ti is warrior-class. That means he fights?'

'Fire-breathing warrior he is when grown.'

'And what does a royal sept girl do?' I asked.

I sensed another wave of amusement coming from Lothi-Mo. *'Diplomat, peace-keeper, advisor, and more...'* For a moment she hung still in the air beside me. *'Must find Ancho-Dar; she knows.'*

'No inherited memories?' I asked.

'Not the ones I need to know,' Lothi-Mo said, and for a moment she sounded very adult. *'Those memories are handed over in another way.'* She slapped me with her tail. *'Asking too much questions, wyrm boy.'* With a chuckle she rejoined Tiu-Ti.

CHAPTER 30 – BOSS

'My seshars will clean up the whole of the Iron Reaches,' the king said as we walked through the palace. 'I should have done that a year ago, but somehow it got postponed several times. No longer. I'll send a full garrison to Kas-Bahaan, with enough warships upriver to deter any pirate.'

He glanced at me. 'Your seven young warriors did a great job there. I don't want to hear about those six others. If you were thinking of taking them, do so. I would prefer it you don't let them go loose inside my borders.'

'I don't know who they are,' I answered truthfully. 'My guys freed them from the keep's dungeons; that's all.'

'They can only be one thing, guild convicts,' the king said with a vague smile. 'I heard, unofficially, there had been a Wastrel raid on a guild prison camp for street youth some time ago. The guild polices its own establishments, so I wasn't inclined to act. Let us say the guild and I don't always see eye to eye about things and leave it at that, shall we?'

Escaped convicts? A prison camp? I gritted my teeth. 'What would they be guilty of?'

'The usual,' the king said with a wave of his hand. 'Pilfering, breach of contract, all kinds of minor misdoings that fall within the guild jurisdiction. Major crimes are a matter for the Judges' Courts.'

Prison camps for pilferers! I felt my stomach contract.

Then we reached the main doors where a row of steamcarts bearing the royal coat-of-arms waited to bring us back to the navy port. I took my leave of the king and walked down the steep stairs to the last vehicle. The strange kids seemed apprehensive, looking around with fearful glances, but a tall, square-faced boy spoke with them and they hurried down to the cars.

The royal drivers weren't shy, enforcing right of way with a complete fanfare of blaring claxons and a complete disregard of lesser road users. At the dockyard gates the guards jumped to attention as the whole motorcade roared past and only when we reached the *Drakon*, the drivers slowed down to a gentle stop.

We alighted and walked the last bit to the gangboard. The strange kids froze and stared up at *Drakon*'s tall green-and-gold hull towering over the nearby warships, at the animal carvings along her gangboard and the armed guards at the entry port. Both Jornyll and the tall boy spoke to them and led them into the ship.

Once we were all on the main deck, I walked over to them. 'Welcome. I don't know who you all are, but here you are safe. I think you would like a wash and a change of clothes. The others will show you. Aya, Jornyll, and Justym, I need a report from you. Who will speak for those others?'

The tall boy I'd noticed earlier nodded.

'Good,' I said. 'After you've cleaned yourself up, you four come to see me. *Lothi-Mo?*'

'*Coming,*' she said. '*Tiu-Ti needs to talk before sleep.*'

'*We're agog to hear his story, dear heart. Does he want more food?*'

'*Not now, he needs to talk. He's very worried.*'

'*We'll go to the meeting-room,*' I said. '*Where are you?*'

'*Masthead,*' Lothi-Mo said. '*My nest. Tiu-Ti cannot fly much yet; so he stays with me for a bit.*'

'*No need to come down, we can hear you perfectly,*' I said. '*Tiu-Ti can mindspeak?*'

'*Tiu-Ti can,*' he said. '*Only is boy, not speak beautiful like princess.*'

'*No matter, we can understand you,*' I said.

The *Drakon*'s meeting-room was a low-beamed space with a long table and benches.

'*Must talk,*' Tiu-Ti said. '*Talk, then sleep. So tired much days and days.*'

I understood. Lothi-Mo had appropriated the main mast crow's nest for her use—for as long as she still fit inside it.

'Where does Tiu-Ti come from? I asked. *Are there wyrms in Hizmyr?'*

'North,' Tiu-Ti piped. *'Far, far north. Bad land, jinn land. Jinn hating wyrms; killing, killing. Sept mother dead, leaving me five littles alone. Cold, hungry, learning to hunt. Eating again. Learning to fly; happy. Me fly, fly, then SNAP. Cannot move. Scared, fall. Jinni trap. Cage, me afraid, know not what to do. Long travel, long, then tower. Bad mans talking, bad laughter, wanting to hurt. Tiu-Ti scared to sleep, scared to eat. Then kids come; fight, open cage. Tiu-Ti don't know what will happen. Then Justym hides me, warm, safe.*

'Other enemies come; many shouting many angry. Then flying ship brings the princess! Beautiful princess! So happy now! Only fear for sept. Must go north, find sept. Tell them of princess. Bring them to her, safe.'

'We must go north,' Lothi-Mo said decisively. *'Must get his sept kin. We need wyrms.'*

I leaned my chin on my hands as I thought. *'Do you know where in the north?'*

Both wyrmlings conferred.

'North,' Tiu-Ti said hesitantly. *'Will find it.'*

'Can you show us where you lived?' Kellani asked.

Slowly, a hazy picture of trees formed in our minds. Then something tall and solid looking.

'Ruins,' Naudin said. 'And a river.'

'That's it?' I said.

'Tiu-Ti is tired,' Lothi-Mo said. *'He is only a warrior boy, not used to thinking much. He will remember more once we go north.'*

'Let him sleep,' I said. *'We will make a plan, but we need more information first. If there are jinn in his lands, we must be prepared.'*

'Prepare, but hurry,' Lothi-Mo said. *'We must find those other wyrmlings. Now I will care for Tiu-Ti.'*

'It is not much to go on,' I said. 'A ruin beside a river, somewhere to the north.'

There was a knock on the door, and then Aya came in, with Jornyll, Justym, and the tall local guy.

I checked the strange boy's mind and found a mass of anger, confusion, and hurt. 'You're wounded?' I said. 'That weal in your neck...'

'They've beaten him,' Jornyll said. 'Show the boss your back, mate.'

Without a word, the boy pulled up his tunic and turned.

Beside me, Kellani cursed as she saw the mass of ugly red welts.

'Why?' she said angrily. 'Who did this? The pirates?'

'The guild bullies,' he said. 'They didn't like me talking back.'

'Give me your hand and relax,' I said. Then I sent him a wave of healing. 'There.' I grinned. 'Compared to others I've done, this was minor, but it must have hurt plenty.'

The boy sighed. 'The pain is gone,' he said. 'Can you do that for the others too?'

'Our healer Na'a will help them,' I said. 'They'll be dancing on the deck soon.' I sat down again. 'Your reports. Aya, tell me all from the beginning.'

I leaned back and listened to her calm voice. Now and then Jornyll added a detail, showing the two were working well together.

When she was finished, Kellani gave a curt nod. 'Well done, Lieutenant Aya.'

Jornyll sat up. 'Lieutenant?'

'Good jobs are appreciated, Sergeant Jornyll,' I said.

'Darn,' he said, collapsing back in his chair. 'Me?'

Aya poked him. 'You *were* doing a sergeant's job,' she said.

I grinned. 'Guys, you did great. More than great.'

'You acted like professional soldiers,' Kellani added. 'Killing a jinni is no small feat at all.'

'We were lucky his remaining men fled,' Aya said slowly. 'But why did they run away screaming?'

Naudin leaned forward. 'When did they flee?'

'As soon as the jinni showed his real shape,' Aya said. 'I thought they couldn't see that? Those fellows in the Brisan slave market didn't react either.'

'It must've been the iron ore,' Naudin said. He looked at me. 'That jinni couldn't bespell his men and without a compulsion blinding their senses, they saw he wasn't Luzon.'

'So they ran,' I said. 'That's handy knowledge. Would that mean his shapeshifting isn't dependent on magic?' I filed the thought away and turned my attention to the new guy.

'Your turn,' I said. 'What's your name and how did you end up in those dungeons?'

The boy's mouth twisted. 'I'm Orin, from the back alleys of Myrlia's poor quarter. Me and my friends, we were street kids. Most of us got into trouble with the law and the city watch handed us over to the Zamidra Syndicate.' He paused as if to collect his thoughts.

'The syndicate is owned by the all-powerful guild in Myrlia,' he continued. 'They operated a school—a prison school—near one of the biggest iron mines in the Reaches. It was a harsh place where kids got schooled in a craft as much as in blind obedience. At sixteen, we'd be transferred to the mines and work our butts off for no money and bad food.'

'I thought it sounded like Zaotinq's tales,' Jornyll said. 'Never supposed I'd be grateful to the Clam, but we at least were free.'

I could only agree. At the Clam Street orphanage you could get into a fight, but no one would take a cane to your backside.

'Go on,' I said. 'What happened?'

'Robbers,' Orin said. 'The goons weren't prepared for that, and when the bandits dragged us away, the school wasn't there anymore.' He looked at me. 'I'll be honest; if those pirates had treated us half decently, we'd have joined them, just because they liberated us. But they didn't. We were as... as cattle. They took us to that castle and locked us up, awaiting transport to someplace else. They took away the first group and had us waiting for another ship. Then your guys came and everything changed.'

'For the better,' I said. 'We can use schooled hands at our trading base to the south. You'll be housed, fed, clothed, and paid wages. Or if you'd rather go your own way, we'll give you some silver coins and you're free to go. Don't decide now; just eat, sleep, and talk with our kids. We'll be here for a few days; you can decide before we sail.'

The boy sat staring at me. 'You let us decide?' he said. 'No force?'

'We don't use force in the Pasandir Army,' Jornyll said. 'That is, only to our enemies, of course. But we sure could use you guys.'

'I'll speak with the others,' Orin said. 'See what they think. Some of them will need convincing; they're scared. Life gave them no reason to trust people.'

'That's familiar,' I said. 'I was a street kid too. Then the navy roped me in and I spent nine years as a ship's boy, until all this began.' I tapped the table with my hook. 'Anyone knows the wages for a senior apprentice?'

'Three pence a day,' Orin said.

'Sixpence in Seatome,' Jornyll said. 'That's artisans; merchant apprentices earn less, but get a share in the sales.'

'Sixpence it is,' I said. 'We use Weal rates for the navy, so we do the same for our skilled work force.'

'That's... a lot of money,' Orin said. 'Do we need to buy our own tools and things?'

'Nope, it's all there. Wait, I'll show you.' I closed my eyes and gave him a quick view of Smalkand. The artisans had their workshops in a giant cave behind the stables. All had been left ready for use as if the occupants had been confident they'd return to rekindle the fires and take up their unfinished tasks. I showed him the cafeteria and the dorms, the lake and the mountains, and when I was done, Orin whistled slowly.

'That's some place,' he said. 'Would we be our own masters there?'

I grinned. 'Well, you'll be in the company's service, and help running the business. That's why we pay for everything. But you'll be free to do your job as you see fit. Nobody is walking around with a whip to make you work faster. If you're slacking, we'll start paying less, and if you prove useless, we'll sack you.'

'Fair enough,' he said. 'What exactly is it you're doing there?'

'Apart from fighting pirates? Originally the keep was a trading house, running camel caravans across the mountains. That's what we're going to be doing.'

'Camels,' he said, looking up. 'How many have you got?'

'We'll be using other beasts,' I said. 'Magic beasts.'

'You're a wondrous lot,' Orin said, yawning.

'You don't know half,' I said. 'Now you go and rest. Whatever you decide, I'm glad we got you out of there.'

'I think they'll stay,' Naudin said as the three left.

'Sure,' I said. I thought the same, but my mind was on something else. 'I don't get it. Pirates who kidnap Clammer orphans to ruin the prophecy are one thing. But why steal them here? What were they going to do with those guys?'

'We thought it was to man their ships?' Kellani said.

'We did,' I said. 'But I'm starting to wonder. Those guys in the dungeons weren't exactly treated like prospective recruits.'

'Perhaps they've a prophecy of their own,' Naudin said sourly. 'Wouldn't that be nice?'

I stared at him. 'You're kidding.'

'Am I?' Naudin said. 'I'm not sure I am.'

'He's right,' Teodar whispered. *'They do. I wasn't aware of it either, but the moment that young genius opened his mouth, I realized it was the truth. Only not the pirates—it must be*

the jinn. They are running the show in you-know-whose name.'

'*Wrachazd,'* I said.

'*Quiet!'* Teodar said. '*I don't know much about jinn. I do know you need those wyrmlings.'*

'*Tiu-Ti's siblings?'* I asked.

'*Who else?'* Teodar snapped. '*They're in the next kingdom somewhere. Go find those wyrmlings, then seek the jinn prophecy.'*

'*And the pirates?'*

Teodar sighed. '*I fear the jinn are the greater danger.'*

'*Why? Jinn and pirates both serve the lich.'*

'*Call it a hunch.'*

I sighed. He's keeping secrets again. All right, Master Kavid-Jar; I'll find out. '*You never said, but have we gained anything, apart from some more kids?'*

He snorted. '*Am I supposed to pat your little head? You foiled another jinn plan, you got some more kids, and a valuable ally in King Rashaunt; you found a wyrmling – and boy, you don't know half how important* that *is! You have your fine base, your money wizard Shaw is earning you gold by the bucketful, and you know where to go next. Yes, kid; you gained something.'*

'*Shaw?'* I said. '*You don't say you're following her?'*

He coughed; Teodar wasn't into girls at all. '*Yeah,'* he said curtly. '*I sort of have to. She's part of it. By the way, Bodrus is pleased with you, my fine brother. That you brazenly stole from his power tickled him to no end.'*

Diversion much, old chap? I thought. All right. '*What's so special about my using his power? That's what you did before me.'*

'*No,'* Teodar said softly. '*I never thought of that. He gave it to me.'* He chuckled. '*You're the big hero, kid; not I.'*

His mind left me and I groaned softly. 'Teodar wants us to go north again.'

'Further north,' Kellani said. 'What lands are those?'

'Young Jazz should know,' Naudin said. 'He must have had some education beyond waving a sword.'

I liked Jazzaunt, but I had no illusions about the kid's scholarship. 'Let's start with Captain Tazhan. He hasn't sailed yet, so we could go over and ask him for info. And maps, if he has any.'

'We'll send Perre,' Kellani said firmly. 'That's a job for a junior lieutenant, not for the boss of the Peaks.'

'Boss!' I said a bit overloud. 'Why has everybody started calling me boss?'

'Because you're not just one of the guys,' Kellani said coolly. 'You're a ruler now. Be glad they settled for boss—which is rather informal—instead of Lord Eskandar, or worse.'

A chill gripped my heart. 'That's nonsense,' I said. 'Darn, I'm only seventeen; I...'

'Ask my mother. She felt the same when she became Clanfirst at eighteen. That was the old queen's doing. She wanted Mother to fix all Kell's problems and gave her the highest-but-one title in the country to do so. Suddenly everyone started calling her Ma'am, and she hated it.'

'You won't do it,' I begged. 'Please not you two.'

'Of course not,' Naudin said magnanimously. 'To me you're still that ragged little snot who couldn't write his own name.'

Kellani gripped my arm. 'I won't either, don't you worry. Nor will Amaj and Jem, but for the newer kids it is more comfortable. They do look up to you, and boss is a jovial title.'

I must have looked as miserable as I felt, for she pulled me half over the table.

'Stop being sorry for yourself,' she said, holding me. 'You can't become a ruler, a big-time magic user, and a god's disciple, and expect your world to stay the same. It doesn't. Well, you're a big boy; handle it.' Then she kissed me on both cheeks. 'There! Now man up, kid.'

She let go of my shoulders and I sank back into my chair, feeling my face glow.

'I'm going to take a stroll on deck,' she said. 'When I see Abia I'll ask her to send Perre to get the maps and the info you wanted.' She patted my good hand and strode from the cabin.

Naudin couldn't hide a grin. 'Me cousin ain't nothin' but direct,' he said. Then he rose and smoothed the sleeves of his jacket. 'I'll check up on those new guys. Don't go an' try for a crown yet, bud; the kids aren't *that* impressed.' Then he hurried out before I could throw something at his silly head.

'Boss guy,' Lothi-Mo said lazily from her nest in the main mast. *'You're getting big wyrm, boy.'*

'Go north now?' Tiu-Ti asked anxiously.

'Soon,' I promised. Then I put up my feet and closed my eyes. *'Now is think time.'*

'Nice nap,' Lothi-Mo said.

LIST OF NAMES

Abia, Captain of the *Drakon*; sister to Sylas
Amaj Mir, a Kalbakar lordling; Eskandar's friend and troop commander
Ancho-Dar, the Wyrm Queen
Averson, pilot-trainee, a miner girl
Aya of the Weevils, warrior under Amaj
Bamson, boss of the Bashers
Basil, Lord Spellstor, Prince-warlock of Vanhaar; Naudin's father
Benwar, first tiger cub
Brat (Bratolomeus) of the Weevils, the boy with the kitten (Cat)
Byroon, *Pewbara* ballast handler
Callogan, a mover mage in Seatome
Cenn of Brisa, Garthan ship's boy
Chagan, Qoori apprentice mate *Drakon*, later 2nd officer *Marigold*
Dadine of the Weevils; she leads the gild in Willow's absence
Darquine of Piright, High Merchant Proprietor of the MCTC
Eghol of Unwaar, ruler, High Singer of Aera
Eskandar, Wyrmcaller of Kalbakar
Esyrra, Lady of High Morv
Gotan, Qoori bos'n's mate *Drakon*
Hella, boss of the Harbangers
Howy, half-brother to Razoon
Hyloman (see Nimmendal)
Imooga of the White Shore Clan, Thali engineer, cousin of Ulaataq;
Izzour, a sathee jinni
Jazzaunt Hathwaari, Prince of Hizmyr
Jem, Princess of Nanstalgarod
Jornyll of the Bashers
Jurgis of Kell-Spellstor, Lord; First Broom, Kellani's father
Justym of Marroth, Unwaari skysinger; Vystyn's great grandson
Kambish (D), the Wyrmcaller of Kalbakar, Eskandar's grandfather
Kavid-Jar, the, Spirit of Mountain; Bodrus' avatar
Keena of the Weevils, mage
Kellani of Kell-Spellstor, broomrider
Llothyr, Lord of High Morv
Llynsing, a pawnbroker in Seatome
Lothi-Mo, a royal wyrmling
Martha, mage instructor, twin to Tymon
Maud of the Kell, Queen, mother of Kellani
Mazuun, Lord of Kalbakar, Amaj's half-brother
Meshan Hathwaari, crown prince of Hizmyr
Miran of New Winsproke, Midshipman *Drakon*
Miya of Brisa, 1st officer *Marigold*

Myk of the Weevils, engine room assistant
Na'a of the Arrangh, Kell wisewoman, healer of Gathea
Nate, boss of the Nightowls
Naudin of Maiwar, mindmage
Nimmendal, the First Chair of the Five Tradeports (jinni prince Hyloman)
Ozoezd (D), a jinn prince
Pashu, a boy from Kas-Bahaan, Hizmyr
Perre of Longash, 2nd officer of *Drakon*, brother to Vence
Prahan (D), father of Eskandar
Quaylay, cook's assistant
Rashaunt XI Hathwaari, King of Hizmyr
Razoon Mir, of Pashwend Keep.
Saul of Spellstor, Lord, Warden of Spellstor; Chief Reclaimer
Shaw (Ashawta) Harwans of the Nightowls, purser
Siolde of Seedgraft, Witch, mother of Naudin
Sylas, Abia's brother, teacher
Tahhya, lady of Pashwend; mother to Razoon and Howy
Tangrid IV Tangridi, pilot *Pewbara*
Tazhan, Senior Captain, Hizmyran fleet
Teodar, the Kavid Jar
Tiu-Ti, a wyrmling boy
Tymon, healer teacher, twin to Martha
Ulaataq of the White Shore Clan, Thali engineer
Vence of Longash, 1st officer *Drakon*, brother to Perre
Wador, a singer
Wahaz, a jinni
Wallanck of Piright, Overcaptain of the Chorwaynie Archipelago
Wargall of the Arrangh, Broomrider Commander, father of Na'a
Wemawee, senior Wisewoman of the Kell, mother of Na'a
Willow, gild boss Weevils; later boss of the keephold at Smalkand
Wrachazd, the lich king of Nanstalgarod
Wylmer, Githeon; captain *Marigold*; chief pilot *Pewbara*
Xailin, Qoori third officer *Drakon*, Imperial Princess of Qoor
Yarwan, Commodore Weal Navy; Naudin's father
Yathub (D), a sathee jinni
Zaotinq, a Qoori warrior under Amaj

Aera, Sky Goddess

Chottapan, Sea God
Gathea, Nature, the Mother
Gorm & Otha, the Siblings of Battle
Kallianura, Defender of the Home
Lumentis, God of Knowledge
Tenaaz, God of Trade
Thi-a-Yuuk, the Great-Grandmother of the Ice
Zenyunthalata, God of the Lands

www.ingramcontent.com/pod-product-compliance
Lightning Source LLC
Chambersburg PA
CBHW060132130626
46556CB00006B/2323